SOMETHING IN
THE WATER

Other Books by Phyllis R. Dixon

Forty Acres

Down Home Blues

Intermission

A Taste for More

SOMETHING IN THE WATER

Phyllis R. Dixon

kensingtonbooks.com

Content warnings: addiction, drug abuse

DAFINA BOOKS are published by

Kensington Publishing Corp.
900 Third Avenue
New York, NY 10022

All Kensington titles, imprints, and distributed lines are available at special quantity discounts for bulk purchases for sales promotion, premiums, fund-raising, and educational or institutional use. Special book excerpts or customized printings can also be created to fit specific needs. For details, write or phone the office of the Kensington Sales Manager: Kensington Publishing Corp., 900 Third Avenue, New York, NY 10022. Attn. Sales Department. Phone: 1-800-221-2647.

DAFINA and the Dafina logo Reg US Pat. & TM Off.

ISBN: 978-1-4967-5419-6
First Trade Paperback Printing: August 2025

ISBN: 978-1-4967-5420-2 (e-book)

10 9 8 7 6 5 4 3 2 1

Printed in the United States of America

The authorized representative in the EU for product safety and compliance is eucomply OU, Parnu mnt 139b-14, Apt 123 Tallinn, Berlin 11317, hello@eucompliancepartner.com

For my parents, who taught me to love words and books.

Acknowledgments

They say it takes a village to raise a child. It also takes a village to get a book published. As always, my village starts with my mother, Maggie Jackson-Hale, my biggest cheerleader. The backbone of my village includes Michael Stewart and my children, Trey, Candace and Lee. I probably don't say it enough, but I thank all of you for your love and support.

Special thanks to my agent, Marlene Stringer, for seeing the vision. Thanks to the Kensington team, especially Michelle Addo-Chajet and Leticia Gomez for everything from editing to designing beautiful covers. Others in my village include Nicole Baskin, Tanya Beckley, Tujuana Britton, Sheryl Dean, Hariett Halmon, Arlender Jones, Janis Kearney, Crystal Maddox, Jackie Miller, Patricia Montgomery, Suzetta Perkins, Joan Prince, Angela Ray, Michael Ross, Juel Richardson, Betty Washington, Ruth P. Watson, and Sharon Williams. Thank you for your advice, energy, and commitment. Other supporters include the Elite Literary Club, members of Delta Sigma Theta Sorority Inc., Memphis Alumnae Chapter in particular, and my St. Andrew A.M.E. Church family. I also appreciate the booksellers, librarians, and book clubs who have helped champion my work.

And of course I thank you the reader, for spending time with my characters. Of the millions of books published annually, I'm honored that you selected this one. I hope you find it time well spent.

Not everything that is faced can be changed, but nothing can be changed until it is faced.
—James Baldwin

SECTION I

Troubled Waters

Chapter I

"This is BJ your DJ and that's it for another fun day on KBLK, the local station you love and the station that loves you back. This has been another edition of *Relationship Radio*. Stay tuned for the afternoon drive show and remember to keep listening for your chance to win Golden State Warriors tickets."

Billie Jordan had just spent the last three hours hosting a relationship call-in show. She had been a fixture of Oakland, California, radio for twenty years, starting as an intern at the small, family-owned station, and now headlining the weekday morning drive show, serving as News Director—jobs she loved in a city she loved. She had interviewed everyone from Kevin Durant to Zendaya and even former Vice President Kamala Harris when she was San Francisco District Attorney. Her show had been integral to galvanizing support for Black Lives Matter protests and hosting local election candidate forums. Her show *Let's Talk About It*, had run a series titled, *Get the Lead Out*, which publicized findings of lead in the water of several area schools and had earned the station a Braddy Award nomination for broadcast radio in the large urban news category market.

Last year, she was asked, more like told, to take over the

Relationship Radio show, when the long-time host retired. Rather than replace him, station management divided his assignments, giving her the relationship show and cancelling her news and issues show. Billie offered to do both, but the station manager said the relationship show brought in more commercial revenue, and the news show didn't break even. She was not a sympathetic host and never understood baby mama drama, or why people stayed in bad relationships. Her no-nonsense approach was a hit with listeners and the show's ratings doubled. Today's dilemma had been a young woman who was cheating on her husband with his sister—a long way from the hard-hitting news she thought she'd be reporting when she majored in journalism at the University of California, Berkeley.

After hearing the trials of so many of her listeners, she knew she shouldn't complain. Her bills were paid, and her family was healthy. Her daughter, Kendra, was a Navy petty officer, stationed in Virginia. Her son, Dylan, was a high school junior and already had multiple college scholarship offers, both academic and for the swim team. Billie and her husband Cole would soon be empty nesters, and she was collecting ideas from her favorite HGTV shows to update their three-bedroom house to reflect the next stage of their life. Cole, a college professor, had recently completed his Ph.D. and was being considered for tenure. Their twenty-year marriage wasn't perfect, but he still had his sexy Texas drawl and was as good-looking and attentive as he had been when they met in college. She had been looking forward to their date this afternoon, but two hours into her shift, she'd received a text from Cole that they needed to go to Bradford to meet with their son's counselor.

Nothing today had gone as planned. Billie rose early and packed sandwiches, apple slices, cookies, and their favorite merlot wine, for the date she and her husband planned to have at Alameda Beach. But on her drive in, she heard the beach was closed due to a red tide alert. Then, the machine at Starbucks wasn't working, and she couldn't get her daily oat milk vanilla espresso. And when she got to the station, she learned the traffic announcer had called in sick, and Billie would have to do traffic and her regular duties. The raggedy phone system kept dropping calls during her show, and, she had gotten her second period this month, something that was happening more often now that she was forty.

Since they couldn't go to the beach, she and Cole planned to meet at Ricky's, a pizza restaurant they'd been going to since college. They met when she was a junior and Cole was a graduate student. Cole came to California to pursue a master's degree in economics and play baseball, using his last year of eligibility after graduating from Calder State College, an HBCU in his hometown of Calderville, Texas. He was the teaching assistant for her public finance course. She got a 'B' in the class, and even better, she got Cole. He was amazed that they could go get pizza at three in the morning and he loved the beach. She thought his naiveté and wonder at living in a large city were cute. "This campus has more people than my whole hometown," he'd said. He was intrigued by her outgoing personality and what he called worldliness. He called her his city girl. Her mother thought it was endearing when he called her ma'am, and her sister Maya liked him because she said he had cute fraternity brothers.

They dated, then lived together, and eventually married at Cole's insistence when she became pregnant with their daughter. They had endured many ups and down since then, but remained committed to each other.

Dylan had gotten in some trouble a few months earlier. Billie attributed the trouble to the injury he sustained, which prevented him from going to swimming practice and left him with too much time on his hands. Now that his rotator cuff had healed, he could rejoin his team. Billie was looking forward to a favorable report from the Bradford counselor on her son's progress, and that he could return to his regular school.

She removed her headphones, fluffed her locs, then headed out the door. If she'd known she was going to Bradford, she would've worn something other than leggings and a "Say Her Name Sandra Bland" sweatshirt. An accident caused traffic to crawl, but she viewed it as an opportunity to revel in the cornflower blue sky and budding magnolias. Spring was her favorite season, and spring in Oakland was breathtaking. She had been born and raised here. Even with the outrageous cost of living, relentless wildfires and stinky red tide, there was no place she'd rather be. Most outsiders revered Oakland's larger, more glamorous neighbor to the west, San Francisco. But locals were proud of Oakland's underdog spirit and soul which had birthed everything from the Black Panthers to Raider Nation. Her position at KBLK kept her on the pulse of the city.

Cole was in the counselor's office when she arrived. "So sorry I'm late," Billie said as she entered. "Traffic on the interstate was backed up—even more than usual."

"I appreciate you coming on such short notice. This is something we need to address right away. Your husband and I were discussing your son's test results," the counselor said, as she handed Billie two sheets of paper.

Billie scanned them, then slowly said, "I don't understand. This report says Dylan is—"

"Pregnant," Cole said, shaking his head.

"This doesn't make sense," Billie said.

"Obviously, this isn't your son's urine."

"Looks like someone on your staff mixed up the specimens," Billie said, as she handed the paper back to the counselor.

"Mrs. Jordan, we have a rigorous testing process. This isn't a staff error."

"So what happened?" Billie asked.

"He got someone to do it for him," Cole said, while drumming his fingers on the table.

"Your rigorous testing process doesn't seem to be working very well," Billie said. "I thought Bradford was one of the best drug treatment centers in the state."

"This isn't jail," the counselor said. "If someone is determined, they can find a way around any rule. I'm sorry Dylan didn't put this much effort into our program."

"When can we see him? My husband and I will get to the bottom of this."

"Dylan is packing. This is your son's third infraction, and—"

"You're kicking him out? What sense does that make?" Billie asked. "He needs your help, not punishment."

"We reviewed the rules with you both and your son when he was admitted. We can only help people who are ready to be helped. Dylan isn't ready to end his addiction."

"We registered Dylan for forty-five days," Cole said. "It hasn't even been a month."

"It may be time for a longer, more immersive program. There are several programs more appropriate for your son, that work with your insurance company. I discussed those options with him. Pathways in Vermont and Oasis outside Boulder, Colorado are highly recommended. Dylan pretended to ignore me, but he showed interest when I told him several NBA players had gone to these facilities."

"If they're so good, why were we even wasting our time here. Plus, we've already paid you," Cole said.

"The contract requires your son to adhere to the rules and specifies that there are no guarantees. We are willing to accept Dylan at a reduced rate when he decides to pursue his sobriety. And we are still available for counseling for you and your wife. Addiction affects the whole family and—"

Billie didn't hear anything else the counselor said. She was well informed about addiction, and knew people from all walks of life were susceptible. So many people were impacted, addiction stories could be featured every week on her radio show, if she wanted. Her uncle had been on crack for decades. The first guy her mother dated after leaving her dad turned out to be a functioning alcoholic. The station owner's youngest daughter had died from a heroin overdose, while at their Palm Springs condo. Billie had even experimented while in college, but thankfully, she didn't like the way weed made her clothes smell and cocaine made her jittery.

Since she knew all this, she had been intentional about knowing what was going on with her children. They stayed involved in extra-curricular activities. Billie was frequently team mom, and couldn't count the games, recitals, and swim meets she and Cole had attended. She met their friends' parents, monitored their classwork, and had their phone and computer passwords. She had even endured Girl Scouts, charm school, and make-up classes—girlie stuff she didn't care for, but Kendra loved. Occasionally they tested their boundaries, but overall her children had never given her a moment's concern.

Cole coached Dylan's peewee baseball team, and worked out with him so he could play on his middle school team. Swimming had come about by accident. Dylan had been born seven weeks premature with underdeveloped lungs. Billie had read that swimming increased lung capacity, so she got her younger sister, Maya, to teach her to swim, then enrolled Dylan in tadpole swimming classes when he was eight months old. San Solano High School had an Olympic size pool, and all students were required to take swimming. It was the only 'C' that Kendra got—she didn't want to get her hair wet. However, when the coach observed Dylan racing his friends, he invited him to try out for the swim team, and Dylan made the team.

Swimming conflicted with baseball, so he dropped it

altogether. Cole never said so, but Billie knew he missed that time with his son. As first place medals and ribbons accumulated and scholarship offers began pouring in, Cole accepted his role in the stands with Billie. Dylan was the only Black kid on the team and shattering school records brought him attention, which he loved. With his good looks and fun-loving personality, he was popular at school. He didn't make the grades Kendra had made, but he managed to stay within striking distance of a 'B' average.

His carefree demeanor changed when he tore his rotator cuff during a swim meet. After Dylan's swimming injury, he was in such pain, all Billie cared about was making him feel better. Tylenol and Advil weren't working and when the doctor prescribed Exalgo, she was grateful they found something that worked. His pain was alleviated, but his shoulder wasn't healing, and physical therapy didn't seem to be working. Surgery was the next alternative.

Her mother, Zuri Russell, a nurse, raised the alarm when visiting her grandson after surgery. Dylan was groggy and had fallen back asleep, so Billie and her mother went to the cafeteria for coffee.

"Dylan's pain medication will need to be monitored. Those medicines have fancy names, but they're all opioids and there are a lot of side-affects. Get them to try something that doesn't have him so out of it."

"Mom, he just had surgery. You expect him to be laughing and cracking jokes?"

"I'm not dismissing his pain. Males are babies anyway. But they barely let you stay in the hospital twenty-four hours after having a baby, and all they give you is Tylenol. Shoulder surgery can't be any worse."

"I'm sure they know what they're doing and don't need advice from Dr. Zuri."

It was advice she wished they had taken. But regret wouldn't help Dylan now. She remembered the words of the counselor who was a frequent guest on her shows about addiction, "You didn't cause it, you can't control it, you can't cure it." She knew that, but had hoped Bradford could cure it.

"I know I screwed up, so can we skip the lecture?" Dylan asked as his parents entered his room.

"No, we can't," Cole replied. "I can tolerate a lot of things, but not stupidity. This stunt you pulled is costing us thousands of dollars."

"He needs help, not a lecture," Billie said.

"And how is coddling him and ignoring reality helping him? We tried it your way and we see how that has turned out."

"So, all this is my fault?" Billie asked.

"I didn't say that, but we are where we are. Obviously, what we've been doing hasn't worked and we need to try something else."

"That's what the counselor was saying. It's not up to us. It's up to him."

"But he's not the one paying the bills," Cole said.

"Feel free to continue your conversation," Dylan said, as he grabbed his backpack and walked toward the door. "My Uber is here."

"Boy, if you walk out of here—" Cole said.

"What?" Dylan asked with his hand on the doorknob.

"If you walk out of here, you're on your own. That's what."

"Let's go home, relax and talk later when we've all calmed down," Billie interrupted, as their son walked out the door. "Dylan, wait," she said, rushing after him.

"Mom, go home. I'll be fine," Dylan said as he got in the backseat.

"You can't leave. Where are you going?" Billie cried running behind the car until it reached the end of the circular driveway and turned onto the street.

"Let's go, honey," Cole said, while putting his arm around her.

"Don't touch me," she said, jerking away from him. "How could you let him leave? You practically sent him off. That tough love crap sounds good on TV, when it's someone else's child. He's not street smart. If something happens to my son, I will never forgive you."

"He's my son too. Don't you think I'm heartbroken to see him hurting and you too? But we can't lock him up and we can't want his sobriety more than he does."

"I'll send Narcan home with you," the counselor stated, handing them each a small box and a brochure.

"Isn't that the spray used to counteract an overdose?" Billie asked.

"Yes. It's available over the counter, and I suggest you get several. Keep the spray in different parts of the house, in the car and in your purse. You never know. Time is your enemy when someone overdoses."

"You're talking like Dylan is a hardcore addict, nodding off with a needle in his arm."

"We know Dylan has a problem, but I think you're overreacting," Cole said. "It's only pills, not heroin or meth."

"Most opioid abusers eventually move from pills to smoking or needles. There are now more drug deaths from smoking opioids than injecting. Fentanyl is often the next step for opioid abusers who start with prescription meds. It's fifty times stronger than heroin and one hundred times more potent than morphine. You should also remove any alcohol in the house."

"We occasionally have a glass of good wine, but we don't have hard liquor at home," Billie said.

"It doesn't matter. People with substance abuse issues often substitute one drug for another. You need to be prepared. I also suggest you both attend Nar-Anon meetings.

These meetings are helpful for families impacted by addiction."

"This is the treatment plan we paid for—a lecture, a brochure, and an overdose antidote?" Cole asked. "I thought the objective was to keep him from overdosing, not treat the overdose. Let's go."

They walked across a courtyard to the parking lot, and passed a few groups huddled around picnic tables and patio chairs. If you didn't know this was a drug rehab center, you'd think you were on a college campus or in a park. Billie dumped the brochure and box in her purse and grabbed her keys, then asked, "Since you and the counselor have all the answers, now what?"

"I wish I knew," Cole said.

She rolled her eyes with disgust, then got in her Prius and drove off.

CHAPTER 2

Billie heard the pings on her phone, but she ignored them. It wasn't either of her children's ringtone, and she figured anyone else could wait. Cole, who'd slept like a hibernating bear all night, didn't budge. She had gone to bed at her usual ten o'clock but hadn't fallen asleep until after midnight. A news report about the rise in opioid deaths kept playing repeatedly in her head. Dylan said he was staying with friends, although he wouldn't tell her who or where. Whenever he called, she tried to follow the counselor's advice and not nag or cry, but yesterday had been hard. His classmates were attending junior prom, a date that had been circled on their calendar for months. It was a milestone her son was missing and another reminder of the detour their lives had taken. Even watching back-to-back episodes of *Martin* didn't lift her spirits. When the opioid story came on, she sunk into a deeper funk.

She had just drifted off to sleep when she heard her phone. *Who sends a group text at four o'clock in the morning?* she thought, seeing she had thirty-seven minutes until the alarm went off. Thirty-seven minutes and two snooze button slams later, Billie stumbled out of bed, trying to get to the toilet before the first of the day, bloody gush came. She knew about fibroids, or at least thought she did, but no one prepared her for the never-ending period.

One of her most popular radio show guests was an herbalist, and Billie had tried dandelion root and nettle to shrink her fibroids. Her mother had urged her to get a hysterectomy. But Billie's doctors wanted to try medication first and if that didn't help, fibroid embolization. Her insurance wouldn't pay for surgery until less invasive methods had been tried. Not that she planned to have more children, but she was always in favor of avoiding surgery.

The phone pinged again, and this time Billie answered. Kelly, her coworker, had forwarded the announcement that KBLK had been sold, effective in thirty days on June first. There was also a text from the station manager informing them of an employee meeting at eight-thirty.

When Mr. McNeal died last year, rumors circulated for months that his family was looking to sell the station. But Mrs. McNeal said too much of her husband's blood, sweat and tears were tied up in the station and she would never sell it. However, she died six months ago, and apparently her children didn't share the same devotion. They had sold the station to Love Media Group, a company that owned five hundred stations of all formats across the country.

Billie shouldn't have been surprised. KBLK was one of a dwindling number of independently owned radio stations and an even smaller group of Black-owned radio stations. The business had changed dramatically since her start twenty years ago as a college intern, answering phones and working with the promotions department. When she graduated, she was hired as a Program Assistant, a fancy term for grunt work and meant she filled in wherever needed.

As the youngest employee at the station, Billie introduced them to the music of new artists like Rihanna and Ne-Yo. The owner noticed her enthusiasm and when the on-air 11:00 PM to 5:00 AM time slot became available, she was selected. She had enjoyed curating her own playlist, discovering new bands, and giving them exposure. When she started, the FCC required stations to be staffed any time they were on the air to monitor the transmitter. Thanks to technology, music, commercials, weather forecasts, even dee-jay adlibs, were now pre-recorded to be played overnight. The station was closed, and the computer "DJ" ran on autopilot.

With so much technology, they were rarely all at the station at the same time. So to see everyone underscored the seriousness of the meeting. The new managers announced how happy they were to welcome KBLK to their family and they were all valued employees. Billie heard *blah, blah, blah.* She knew this was their perfunctory pitch and all their jobs were on the line. She was one of the senior people at the station, but instead of giving her security, her seniority made her vulnerable. Time to dust off her resume.

Billie rarely drove during rush hour. She knew many people commuted over an hour each way to work. Those had been her most loyal listeners. The radio station was thirty-five minutes from her house and since her shift started at dawn and ended in the early afternoon, she rarely had to sit in traffic. *I don't know if I could do this every day*, she thought as she sat in five o'clock traffic on the Golden Gate bridge. She was coming from her third interview with Ignite Marketing, and if she got the job, this would be her regular routine.

Her initial job search had been more selective, and she only applied for positions within an hour of her house, and no more than a ten percent pay cut from the radio station. She focused on jobs in media, but the industry had shifted toward syndicated shows and celebrity DJs. *Nothing against Steve Harvey or Ryan Seacrest, but don't they have enough jobs and money,* she wondered. Her college major was journalism, but the outlook for newspaper jobs was worse, and she couldn't even get interviews in that field. She had a master's degree in education, but had let her license expire so all she could do was sub. When she researched substitute teaching, she would earn less as a sub than she was getting from unemployment. *Surely, I can do better,* she thought.

As weeks passed, and her severance package dwindled, she broadened her geographic boundary and acceptable pay range. She had lost count of the number of applications she'd submitted. News reports claimed unemployment statistics were historically low, but you couldn't convince Billie of that. Most job applications were online, and she was surprised that most of her interviews were virtual. *Technology has replaced some HR person's job, just like mine,* she thought. The arduous job search was real to her now, not just one of her radio show topics.

A temporary agency helped her reword her resume to focus on her leadership, communication, and marketing skills. However, she was competing against younger millennials and generation Z workers with second nature computer skills and ties to younger consumers. Another disadvantage she hadn't expected was her social media footprint. Background checks now included more than calling previous employers and a drug test. Her advocacy for social justice and environmental causes was well known, but not an asset when trying to get into corporate America. Her credit score was only fair because they had maxed out their credit cards to pay for Dylan's treatment.

She'd had three interviews with Ignite. When she saw their name on her phone, she was hopeful that her job search was finally over.

"Ms. Jordan, I'll get right to the point. You have excellent credentials and your interviews were great. I fought hard for you. You're the type of person we need, but senior management viewed your arrest record as a liability."

"What are you talking about?"

"It came up in our background search. You were arrested twice in 2012."

"That was in connection with a protest about Trayvon Martin's killing, and they arrested twenty of us. Plus, I was never charged, so I wasn't found guilty of anything."

"I'm so sorry."

"Can you explain this to them? Or can I? The application only asked if I had ever been convicted of a felony. I forgot all about those bogus arrests but would have disclosed them had I been asked."

"They've offered the position to someone else."

"This is so unfair. What happened to innocent until proven guilty and the First Amendment right to free speech?"

"I'm on your side, that's why I called you. They usually send an email to unsuccessful applicants. I suggest you get that expunged."

Billie was furious, but things were making sense now. Others had probably seen the same thing. At least this company had let her know. When she investigated, the minimum time for an expungement was 120 days. By then they would be in the poor house.

CHAPTER 3

Billie was headed to the airport, her first time outside all weekend. She'd been cooped up in the house due to an ozone alert. Cole was returning from his grandmother's eightieth birthday celebration in Texas. Billie was supposed to go but she got invited to a second interview with the Gates Foundation. She was having little luck in her job search, and a few days in Calderville would have been a pleasant distraction. She knew asking to postpone the interview would be the same as saying she wasn't interested. The cost to change her ticket was exorbitant and she wouldn't arrive until almost midnight Friday, so Cole went alone.

It was just as well that she hadn't gone. From the looks of the pictures Cole texted her, they were having a great time. She loved Cole's grandmother, Lovey, but wasn't in a celebratory mood. Dylan hadn't answered her calls or texts all week and she was frantic with worry.

It was so hazy, drivers drove with low beams, even though it was midday. She had tried to listen to KBLK but disliked the changes the new owners had made. KBLK had been more than her employer, the station was tied to her family. Cole loved getting press passes to Oakland A's games. Her kids got to go backstage at concerts, and they always had discount tickets for Six Flags, the zoo and the Space and Science Center. Maya met one of the owner's sons during a company picnic and they dated for almost a year. Even her mother had swooned at the chance to meet Jesse Jackson.

She changed the channel and played solitaire in the cell phone lot until she got her husband's text that he was ready. They exchanged a quick peck as he put his carryon bag in the backseat. "From the plane you can really see the impact of the wildfires. It's breathtaking, and not in a good way."

"I spent the weekend inside. I finally have time off and wildfires are polluting the air and we're urged to stay inside. They don't expect any improvement until later this week," Billie said.

"Everyone asked about you. Uncle Amos said you didn't come because you didn't want him to beat you in chess." Cole's uncle, Amos Jordan, lived with Cole's grandmother, Lovey, and had been like a father to Cole and his older brother, Monroe, after their parents died in a car accident. Amos took them fishing, went to their ball games and taught them about girls—although he may not have been the best teacher since he'd been married and divorced twice.

"How did your interview go?"

"Hard to tell. It was a 'don't call us, we'll call you.' Was Lovey surprised?"

"Nope. Can't hide nothing from that old lady. But she was still ecstatic all weekend. After the banquet, she was doing the Electric Slide like she invented it. The resolution from the pastor did surprise her and she was genuinely moved."

"I'm glad you enjoyed yourself."

"I did. Calderville is so different than when I lived there. It's growing, and they even have a Black man running for mayor. Monroe showed me some new housing developments, Premier Paper is expanding, and a new EV battery factory may be coming. He says lots he bought years ago have tripled in value."

Monroe was four years older than Cole. Growing up, Cole had idolized his brother. When she first met him, she thought, *this is your great big brother?* Monroe was older, but Cole was taller. Monroe had a receding hairline and like many shorter men, he was louder and more aggressive than he needed to be. He had been a star running back, and led the high school football team to a state championship. In Texas that was a revered accomplishment.

He attended Calder State and hurt his knee during the third game of the season. He left school, joined the Air Force, and participated in the invasion of Afghanistan. When Monroe was discharged, he used his GI bill to go back to Calder State, majoring in education. He taught and coached a few years, but he had always been handy with tools. He worked on houses, bought a few real cheap, fixed them up and sold them, making a good profit. Eventually, he made more from fixing and selling houses than from teaching, and when the school district closed some of the older schools, he resigned. His construction firm was now one of the largest Black-owned businesses in the county. Marrying the heir to the only Black funeral home owner in the county also helped his cash flow and lifted his community standing.

"I've got something to ask you," Cole said. "Please keep an open mind."

"That sounds ominous."

"Nothing bad. Monroe took me all over and introduced me to a few Calder State trustees. They offered me a position."

"And you're considering it?"

"Monroe and a few frat brothers have previously asked me about coming to Calder State, and I always dismissed it. But this would be the department head position. Plus, you're not working now…"

Calder State Agricultural and Industrial Institute was founded in the early 1870s by the American Missionary Association. The association purchased 200 acres from a former plantation owner to build a school for freedmen and their children. Construction was paid by the United States government through the Freedman's Bureau. Calder State became a source of pride for the Black residents and most of the teachers in the Calderville colored schools had been Calder State alumni. The name was changed in the 1950s to Calder State College and enrollment peaked in the 1970s. Once African American students were allowed to attend larger, better funded schools elsewhere, numbers declined. However, in recent years, the school was experiencing a renaissance with increased alumni support, and an aggressive expansion plan.

"You didn't answer my question."

"I can't consider it without you. Maybe this is the time to make a move. The university system is cutting back due to state budget cuts, so I'm going to be stuck teaching Economics 101 forever and won't ever get tenure. And you just mentioned how the air, wildfires, and traffic make this a difficult place to live."

"I may complain, but California is still the best place in the world. I've never lived anywhere else. I've never wanted to live somewhere else. We've made our home here."

"Home is wherever we are. We could sell our house and buy one twice as large for a third of the cost. There's no state income tax, no polluted air, and no long commutes."

"Aren't they trying to secede from the United States?"

"That's ridiculous. It's some fringe group. They're harmless."

"That's what they said about that cult in Waco, and it didn't end well. But it sounds like you've already given it a lot of thought."

"There's a few things we'd have to work out, but—"

"Isn't one of those 'things' our son?"

"The change would be good for Dylan. It would give him a fresh start and a slower pace of living with more family support. With me working at Calder State, he gets a big tuition discount. Just think about it."

The holidays were usually Billie's favorite time of year. November and December had been her mother's busiest time because she worked at Sears Department Store during the Christmas holidays after her hospital shift. Many days Billie babysat her sister and didn't see her mother until ten o'clock at night. She didn't feel bad not having the Norman Rockwell holiday, because she didn't know any other life. But for her children's sake, she was determined to make the holidays magical and about family.

They rose early Thanksgiving morning for a pancake breakfast, then spent the day at the Union Mission serving homeless veterans. They went Christmas tree shopping the day after Thanksgiving and spent the rest of the weekend decorating it and putting up outside lights. KBLK did a live broadcast with the Salvation Army for its toy drive, and Kendra and Dylan loved helping collect the toys. She'd heard the new owners had made a donation instead. Billie knew $15,000 would make an impact and the nonprofit could use it, but it wasn't the same as getting the community involved. Billie and the kids made cookies every few days, and they took family pictures in matching pajamas and sent them out as Christmas cards. Two years ago, was the last year they'd sent family Christmas cards, and their world had changed dramatically since then.

Their holiday traditions were now memories. With a quiet house and no young people, she hadn't bothered to put up a tree or bake cookies. But today the tide was turning. Kendra had called and said she'd be home a few days after Christmas, and Billie had received a job offer. Before Thanksgiving, the Salvation Army manager called to discuss the annual toy drive, and when she mentioned she didn't work for the station anymore, he encouraged her to apply for their Outreach Director position. He agreed that community involvement was as important as a financial donation and wanted someone to spearhead year-round events. She applied, interviewed, and today learned she had gotten the job. They would bring her on after January 1.

As she finally turned on her street, her curtains were open and other than the porch light, which was on a timer, her house was dark. Since Kendra was coming, she figured she would at least put up some lights.

Christmas morning was quiet. Maya invited them over, but Cole said he wanted to stay home. He spent his time either watching football or holed up in his office working. She and Cole agreed not to exchange gifts, and since it was just the two of them, she wasn't cooking a large meal. All those years serving the homeless, this year she wondered if Dylan would be getting served somewhere. But she had received the best Christmas gift, Dylan had called, and she was going to see him tomorrow.

Billie hadn't seen him since October. He showed up at the house on a Wednesday morning, after Cole had left. She fixed him pancakes, eggs, and veggie-bacon. She placed two hundred-dollar bills in his pocket and hugged him tight, then dropped him off at the Fruitvale BART station.

Dylan called Christmas morning, and when Billie asked if he needed anything, he mentioned that he was short for his share of the January rent. She offered to pay the rent, but he said he needed cash because he and his roommates pooled their money. He had turned the location tracker app off on his phone, and she had no clue where he was living. Hearing he wasn't homeless and not living alone gave her some comfort.

She told Cole she was going to a Black Friday sale to get something for Kendra and left him planted in front of the TV watching a football game. She set her GPS to route her to their meeting spot. She rarely came downtown, and with all the construction, she needed to know the best route.

They were supposed to meet at noon, but she was so anxious, she had come early. It was almost one o'clock and she was still waiting on him. She hadn't noticed that she was in a loading zone parking spot, and a policeman gave her a ticket. Rather than move and risk not seeing Dylan, she stuffed the ticket in her glove compartment. As the officer drove off, she saw two people emerge from the BART station, wearing baggy Oakland A's jackets, and did a double-take when she realized one of them was Dylan. He always kept his hair short for swimming, but today he had a lumpy two-inch afro, and a scrawny little mustache.

Billie rushed to meet him and hugged him tightly, forcing her tears not to flow.

"Mom, this is Amy," Dylan said, as he stepped back from his mother, and grabbed the purple-haired, tongue tattooed, waif of a girl's hand.

"I loved you on the radio. It's great to meet you." Billie managed a weak smile, as she took short breaths to limit inhaling this girl's strong funk. "I loved the Relationship Show. You guys kept me laughing. Was that real? Some of those stories were so wild, they had to be made up for ratings. Dylan said you interviewed Bruno Mars. He is so cute. What did—"

"Excuse me. Can I have a moment with my son?"

"Yeah, yeah. Sure," she said, dropping Dylan's hand.

"Get in and sit with me a few minutes. I promise I won't kidnap you," Billie said. "Do you mind sitting up front with me?" she asked as he opened the back door. As soon as he got in the front seat, she handed him an envelope. She embraced him again, even though she realized Amy wasn't the only one with a strong odor. "You've lost so much weight," she said with tears in her eyes.

"Mom, don't cry," he said while putting the envelope in his pocket.

"I said I wasn't going to nag you, but I wish you'd come home, at least until you finish school. I worry about you so much," Billie said as she grabbed a tissue and blew her nose. "How are you feeling?"

"I'm okay. I would tell you not to worry, but I know you won't listen."

"That's my job."

"Speaking of job, I'm sure you miss the radio station, but I'm glad you're finally getting a chance to take it easy."

"Taking it easy doesn't pay the bills, but I guess it was time for me to do something different. I'll be starting at the Salvation Army on January 1."

"That's great. How's Dad?"

"He's fine. He misses you," she said while rubbing his hand.

"I miss you too. Don't be surprised to look up one day and see me at the door."

"That's what I hope for every day."

"It's starting to drizzle," Dylan said. "Me and Amy need to get back before it starts raining hard."

"Are you and Amy dating? How old is she?"

"We're just friends."

"I hope so. You know if she's under eighteen, you can be arrested."

"She's not like that."

"They always say that until something happens. I'm sure her parents are as worried about her as we are about you. I can give you a ride."

"I don't want to take you out of your way. We'll be okay."

"Wait a minute," Billie said as she fumbled through her purse. "Take this."

"Thanks Mom," he said as he pulled McDonalds, Burger King, Smoothie King, and Subway gift cards from an envelope—all his favorites. Billie abhorred fast food, but that was a debate for another time.

Amy waved, then she and Dylan headed down the street. Billie watched them until they reached the corner and went inside Burger King.

"You're going to need another suitcase," Billie said as they loaded Kendra's shopping bags into the trunk. "The fee for a second suitcase will probably wipe out most of your After Christmas Sale savings."

"The airline gives a discount for active military. My bags are free."

"I never knew that, but I guess that's the least the country can do for young people risking their lives on the other side of the world for economic power conflicts between greedy men."

"Mom don't start. I'm a housing specialist, one of the least likely positions to deploy. Thanks to summers working with Aunt Maya, I had a background in real estate that most recruits don't have."

"Do you want to pursue real estate after you leave the military?"

"I'm not sure. I'm on a waiting list for the air traffic controller program, but I'm thinking of staying in the housing field. I like doing something where I'm not cooped up in an office all day. I've started taking classes toward a bachelor's degree. If I have a degree, I'll get a bonus, plus I can apply for Commissioned Officer School when I reenlist."

"Reenlist?" Billie asked with horror.

"I'm considering making the military a career. I can stay for eighteen more years, retire and start my own real estate company, all by the time I'm forty."

Her daughter's transformation still amazed Billie. She had seen pictures of Kendra in uniform and couldn't believe that was her little girl. The teenager who had left home the day after she turned eighteen, was now a young woman. She didn't have to remind Kendra to turn the lights off, make her bed, or eat her vegetables. In a true sign of maturity, this time it was Kendra, comparison shopping and declaring some items overpriced.

"I'll be so glad to start working next week," Billie said. They were on a tight budget and had been dipping into their savings. After having checked their available credit, she made an exception and charged a few outfits for her new job. Billie usually wore brightly colored, bold Afrocentric prints and designs or T-shirts and jeans. She had a jewelry box full of earrings, but generally rotated between three pairs of gold or silver hoops, for the three holes in each ear. Her wedding ring and a Rolex were the extent of her jewelry. She received the watch from her mother, who had received it from a boyfriend, but when they broke up, she gave the watch to Billie. Kendra helped her put together a few interchangeable outfits appropriate for her new career.

It had been a long time since Billie and her daughter had gone shopping together. In the last years before leaving, Kendra was in the "don't want to hang with mom" stage. Billie felt betrayed when Kendra enlisted in the military. It was as though Kendra was embracing the opposite of every-thing she had tried to instill in her daughter. While they argued constantly in the months before Kendra left home, today they had not only spent an enjoyable day together, but they were also attending the Warriors game this evening.

The shopping trip had been a pleasant distraction. Billie had gone several hours without checking her phone for a call or text from her son. However, as they entered the house, the weight of Dylan's absence dampened her uplifted mood.

Since Christmas, she had tried several times to call Dylan,

but his phone went to voicemail. He had turned off the locator tracking on his phone and when she checked her bill, she noted he hadn't made any calls in five days, which worried her even more. The last numbers he had called were to an Arizona area code. Billie had no idea who he knew in Arizona.

They picked up Thai food on the way home. As they brought the food into the kitchen, Billie asked Cole, "Have you heard from Dylan today?"

"No," he answered, while helping Kendra with her bags.

"His phone is off," Billie said. "It was going to voicemail, now there's a strange buzz when I call."

"Kendra, is there something in the settings I can adjust so my calls will go through?"

"No, Mom. When he wants to contact us, he will."

"I'm so worried."

"You girls better eat quickly. We need to leave to get to our seats before the game starts," Cole said.

"We can't go to a basketball game, when Dylan is who knows where. At least before, with the phone location tracker, I could see his movements. Now there's nothing. We should file a missing person's report."

"He's not missing, he doesn't want to be bothered. He'll be okay," Kendra said.

"Honey, my boss gave me these tickets because they were going to be out of town. It's not right for me to accept them and not use them. These tickets are hard to get, and I'm sure he would have given them to someone else."

"I couldn't enjoy myself worrying about him."

"Sitting around the house isn't going to make Dylan call or come home any faster. When he needs a few dollars, he'll show up," Cole said. "No news is good news."

"I'm not going to some silly game when our son is missing, and I don't see how you can want to go either."

"I am so sick of our lives revolving around Dylan,"

Kendra said as she tossed her fork in the sink. "Today we had a good time. It was the first time in a long time you and I did something without having to schedule around Dylan. Dylan has a swim meet. Dylan is sick. Dylan needs—"

"Your brother has a problem, and we're his family. We must be there for him, just as we would for you."

"Mom, face facts. Dylan is a drug addict. He uses drugs and he uses us."

"Don't say that," Billie snapped.

"He's made the choice to live his life this way, and we need to live our lives. I should have followed my first mind. What the hell was I thinking? Some friends went to New York City for New Year's. I should have gone with them, but I wanted to spend it with my family. That doesn't mean I want to spend it talking about Dylan."

"Dad, are we still going? We can eat at the game."

Cole grabbed his keys and he and Kendra walked out.

Billie was coordinating her outfits for her first week on the job when she received a call from an unfamiliar number. She quickly answered, hoping it was Dylan.

It wasn't her son, but it was almost as devastating. The Outreach Director position had been put on hold. The Salvation Army manager said one of their large grants was not being renewed, and they would not be able to hire her. "Sorry for waiting until the last minute to call you," he said. "We were counting on a couple additional funding sources, but those didn't materialize. The grant may be renewed at midyear, but I know you can't wait around for that. I am so sorry."

Not as sorry as I am, Billie thought. She poured a glass of wine then turned the TV to the Warriors game.

"Congratulations," Cole said, when he came in. "You successfully ruined our daughter's trip. She changed her flight to the first one tomorrow, and it will probably be a long time before we see her again."

"I wonder what karma I'm reaping," Billie said as she poured her third glass of wine. "Dylan is missing. My daughter isn't speaking to me, and the Salvation Army called. They lost a large grant and won't be able to hire me for at least six months and maybe not even then."

"Well, I got a phone call too. While we were at the game, Monroe called and said he had just gotten out of a trustee's meeting and Calder State was willing to increase their offer, but they need a decision, or they'll give the position to someone else."

"You can't be seriously considering it."

"Our credit cards are at the limit, and the way our savings is dwindling, we'll never be able to retire. Maybe it's not karma, but a sign that this place isn't working for us anymore."

"You do what you want. I'm not leaving Dylan alone in California."

CHAPTER 4

Billie and Cole spent New Year's Day in a cold war. Cole was planted on the couch watching sports and Billie in their bedroom rotating between binge watching HGTV dream homes and trying to read her library book before it was removed from her Kindle. She also completed her application to the school district to be a substitute teacher.

When Billie started at KBLK she was having so much fun she almost forgot it was her job, but the limited hours didn't pay many bills. She got student loans to get a master's degree in early education. By the time she graduated, she had worked her way up to the weekend mornings DJ. Her first teaching assignment was as a second-grade teacher. The hours paired perfectly with her radio job, and she worked both for ten years. The state had a budget crisis in 2011, and she received a layoff notice. The station manager knew about the layoffs and offered her a full-time weekday slot. Layoffs were averted, but Billie had already accepted the full-time radio position. She let her certification expire and had never considered going back to the classroom, until now.

Billie's phone rang, but she didn't recognize the area code. She figured it was a telemarketer and let it go to voicemail. Within seconds, Cole's phone rang too. He always answered because students often called. It was the emergency room at St. Vincent hospital in Phoenix. Dylan had come in and said he was on his father's health insurance, but they needed consent and information before they could treat him. Cole put the phone on speaker and asked, "What is he there for?"

"Due to privacy concerns, the hospital can't discuss that on the phone."

"Is he there with you?" Cole asked.

Billie rushed to his side, and whispered, "Ask if we can speak with him."

They were told Dylan was in the waiting room, and patients couldn't use hospital phones. "I'll get you a copy of the insurance information and we're on our way," Cole said, breathlessly.

Billie wondered, *how did he get to Phoenix and why was he there*? She had so many questions, but at least she knew where he was. She quickly packed a bag, while Cole booked the next flight to Phoenix. The price was expensive, but they would be with their son within four hours. Other than a few curt statements during the flight, neither spoke.

They rented a car, drove directly to the hospital, and found their son in the waiting room, sitting in the corner, leaning against the wall. He was sweating, and his eyes were beet red. Cole marched to the admitting clerk and stated, "This is heartless. You leave someone obviously ill to languish because you don't have insurance information?"

"Sir, if we admitted every addict going through withdrawal, we wouldn't be able to serve any other patients."

They waited seven hours in the emergency room before Dylan finally saw a doctor. The doctor ordered tests of his heart, blood, chest and kidneys and determined that Dylan's vomiting, sweats and headache weren't life-threatening. He did have an abscess on one of his molars that was causing his ear and headaches. Of course, the primary diagnosis was opioid

abuse, and he was released with a recommendation to immediately enter a treatment facility.

They stopped at a Subway and bought sandwiches and
soup, then headed to a hotel. Dylan ate three spoonful's of
soup, then vomited. Billie tried to clean him, but he curled
up into a fetal position and cried out, "I'm hurting so bad.
Please get me a couple Vikes or Roxys, just enough to make
my head stop hurting."

"Honey that poison is what's making you sick," Billie
said.

"Dad, can't you do something?"

"We'll help you any way we can, but we're not getting
you pills," Cole said.

"You never cared. Why are you even here? Get the fuck
out."

"I'm going to the front desk to ask for more towels,"
Cole said. Billie noticed tears in his eyes as he closed the
door.

Dylan moaned a few more minutes, as his face glistened
with sweat. Billie wet two towels and put a cool one on his
forehead and used the other to gently wipe the spittle from
the corners of his mouth. He drifted off to a fitful sleep after
that.

He slept off and on for three days. They took turns feeding him soup, wiping his forehead when he sweated pro-
fusely, and wrapping him in blankets when he shook with the
chills. They cleaned his vomit and diarrhea, and Cole paid the
housekeepers to leave extra sheets and towels. Cole went to
Walmart and bought him some clothes. On the fourth day,
Dylan asked for pancakes. It was six o'clock in the evening,
but Cole found a diner that served all-day breakfast. This was
the first meal he ate that didn't come back up.

They watched him eat with the awe of parents watching
their first newborn. When he finished, he asked, "What day
is it?"

"Thursday," Cole said.

"That's four days," Dylan said. "And by looking at your faces and this room, I can tell it hasn't been a good four days. I'm sorry for putting you through this, and I don't ever want you to go through this again."

"We don't either. Now that you're feeling a little better, you're coming home with us. We'll get you into the best treatment center and..."

"No, Mom. It can't be at home. It reminds me how much of a failure I am. How much I've disappointed you."

"You could never be a disappointment to us," Billie said.

"I know I am. I'm a disappointment to myself. How could you be proud of this?" Dylan asked, while scratching his arm.

"Falling down isn't the problem, it's not getting back up," Cole said. "Once we get home, we'll be able to..."

"If I return to Oakland, I'll end up doing the same old thing. Amy and I were both ready to get clean and thought if we went somewhere else, we could start fresh. She said she knew someone in Phoenix, so she rented a car, and we drove down there. But her friend had moved and after three days, she figured out her parents had canceled her credit cards. We dropped the car off at the airport and were sleeping in the baggage claim area until she got arrested for stealing suitcases. Her parents paid the fine, found New Day Treatment Center, and got us enrolled."

"The hospital wouldn't admit you without our information. How did you get New Day to admit you without notifying us?" Cole asked.

"Amy's parents handled everything. She told them she wouldn't go without me. We'd been clean almost two weeks, at least I thought we were. The men and women were separated most days. It was the first time in so long that I felt half-way normal again. I was swimming every day and had started GED classes. Whenever I saw her during free time, she always said we should leave, but I talked her into staying. I didn't find out she was gone until she didn't show up for free time two days in a row. When I asked about her, they told me she'd run away.

I heard they found her on a playground bench, passed out with a needle in her arm. I didn't even know she was shooting up. We were just smoking and snorting. They arrested her for public intoxication and possession of a controlled substance. Since her folks weren't covering my bills anymore, New Day said I couldn't stay. They bought me a bus ticket to Oakland, and obviously, I cashed it in. I'll spare you the ugly details, but somehow, I found my way to the hospital. I don't want to end up like Amy."

"You should have had New Day contact us," Cole said.

"New Day is one of those rich folk places. You guys don't have that kind of money."

"You let us worry about the money. We'll find a way," Billie said.

Billie and Cole went to New Day, met counselors, and signed paperwork to admit Dylan into their six-month program. The counselor said they usually require self-pay clients to pay half up front, but since Amy's parents had paid for treatment for thirty days, they would apply that deposit toward their down payment. Ordinarily, Billie and Cole would have been too proud to accept money from some unknown white couple, but this was not the time for pride.

While waiting at the airport, Billie rewatched one of Dylan's videos from last season on her phone. After four staccato whistles, the swimmers stepped into their blocks. Dylan was in the middle lane. The referee instructed them to "take their mark." The horn blasted and the swimmers shot into the water like torpedoes. Dylan's head bobbed up and down and his arms parted the water with the strength of a lumberjack. The butterfly stroke was his best event, and he won his heat. His coaches said he had Olympic potential and Billie and Cole signed him up for an insanely expensive summer training camp. But now they would be spending that money on drug rehab. She hoped Dylan had been scared enough that he would follow through this time. They had spent thousands on the rental car, hotel and plane tickets but they were happier than they'd been in months and slept soundly on the plane.

Billie had spent most of the day traveling ninety minutes both ways to an interview for a job she didn't want and knew she wouldn't get. But to keep her unemployment benefits she was required to maintain evidence she was actively seeking employment. Billie had been home about two hours and was supposed to be preparing dinner but had lost her motivation after sitting in traffic. She ordered Chinese instead.

"Hey babe. How was your interview?" Cole asked when he came in.

"A waste of time. I'm over halfway through my unemployment benefits. I just knew I'd have a job by now, but each interview seems stranger than the last. Today the interviewer was infatuated that I had interviewed Bruno Mars and spent twenty-five minutes asking me about him. Then he asked two job related questions and told me the company was moving to Las Vegas and anyone hired would have to move."

"Well, I have good news. We heard from New Day. They've accepted our payment plan."

"Great. Now we can apply for the home equity loan."

"How would we repay the loan? It starts with interest only payments, but that's still a new monthly bill. And with the state deficit, I won't be getting a raise anytime soon, plus our health insurance premiums are rising," Cole said.

"I know things will be tight, but I still have a few weeks of unemployment benefits left. Hopefully, I'll find a permanent job soon. What else can we do? We must help Dylan. He's the priority right now."

"We can't help him if we're broke and lose our house."

Their decision to do a cash-out refinancing last year, now seemed short sighted. They repaid Cole's student loans, replaced the roof and remodeled the kitchen. The roof and kitchen did increase their home's value, but it also increased their mortgage payment. "What about my 401K?"

"There's a hefty tax penalty. That's a last resort and best saved for an emergency."

"I'd call this an emergency. I don't see another way."

"There is another way—Texas."

Billie sighed heavily and rolled her eyes.

Cole continued. "It's the only thing that makes sense. We're sitting in the key source of our son's recovery. Instead of fantasizing about the houses on HGTV, you can build the house of your dreams. We'll put in that pool you've always wanted. You won't have to get up before dawn to get to work or fight traffic. The only thing holding us here was Dylan, but he's not even in California, and it doesn't sound like he wants to come back. You're apprehensive because you've never lived anywhere else. You'll love Texas."

Billie glanced at the stack of bills on the kitchen table and reluctantly conceded that her husband was right. Moving to Texas seemed to be admitting that their seemingly perfect life was gone and would never be regained. She thought of her yoga affirmations and decided to view a move as a new beginning rather than a sad ending.

She poured a glass of wine, then said, "I guess you're right. Just know, I'll never be a Cowboys fan."

CHAPTER 5

The first time Billie visited Calderville, she expected to see tumbleweeds, oil derricks, and big ranches like Southfork. Instead, it resembled the small town in southern Louisiana where her great-aunt lived, with houses ranging from shotgun style to grand antebellum. On the surface, it was a charming, quaint, sleepy, southern town. Its sleepy façade belied the history of discrimination and injustice. Texas was among the last states to enforce the integration of schools, and the Calderville school district was one of the last Texas districts to implement the desegregation law.

Billie and Cole couldn't have been more opposite in their upbringing. Billie had always gone to integrated schools, lived in a large west coast city with her mother and sister, and at various points in her upbringing had been Catholic, orthodox Muslim, a member of the Nation of Islam, and lived in a commune with twenty-five other Faithful Believers. While a member of the Nation, her mother changed her name from Doris to Zuri. Her mother took night classes and eventually graduated with a nursing degree. But after her mother's divorce, and while in nursing school, they moved so many times, Billie lost count.

Cole was raised by his grandmother in a household that

varied in size but was never less than seven. He spent Sundays, Wednesday evenings, and Saturday afternoons in church. His grandmother, who they all called Lovey (no one could ever tell her why), still lived in the aluminum-sided bungalow where Cole grew up, west of the railroad tracks, where Black people were confined until the latter part of the twentieth century. She paid off the mortgage with the proceeds from her daughter's insurance money. Monroe and Cole understood the attachment to their mother, but still tried for years to convince Lovey to move to a newer, larger house. She refused. When her neighbor died, Monroe bought the old house next door and had it torn down. He added an addition with a den, second bathroom, and covered patio to Lovey's house. She always had a small garden, but Monroe expanded it and when she wasn't watching her daytime stories, she was in her garden.

Billie and Cole had looked at several houses online. New industry was bringing higher income, out-of-town buyers who snapped up the limited inventory of newer (which meant less than thirty-year-old) homes. Any house over three hundred thousand dollars was considered high end and were either historic, vintage homes in the garden district, or new construction on the outskirts of town. In either case, there was limited inventory in that price range, and houses sold as quickly as they came on the market. Cole's frat brother was their real estate agent and urged them to come view a new development. He warned it would sell out quickly and they needed to act fast. Cole and Billie flew down that weekend.

She had visited numerous times with Cole, but now that she was going to be a resident, she viewed it with a different eye. They rented a car and made the ninety-minute drive from Dallas Love Field to Ross County. As soon as you crossed the county line, a navy-blue water tower cast a shadow across the highway and welcomed you to the home of the 1997 state football champions. Cole's brother Monroe had been on that team and residents still treated those team members like superstars.

Calderville's housing stock ranged from sprawling ranches to trailer parks, from historic dwellings to new construction. Billie loved the charming vintage houses in the garden district with ornate fireplaces, brick exteriors, transom windows and mature trees. She said they looked like houses from a fairytale and had several ideas to update kitchens and bathrooms and open up the floorplan. Most were owned by "old money" families and rarely came on the market. Cole wasn't interested.

"What's the point of being in Texas if we're going to live close to neighbors again? Rossbrooke Estates is a new development near the new interstate exit, with two acre lots, three car garages and an outdoor kitchen. I can't wait for you to see it."

They drove out to Rossbrooke Estates, south of town, to tour the models. "Is that a rebel flag?" Billie asked swiveling her head to get a good look as they sped down a bucolic looking highway. "That should be illegal. That's the flag of an entity that attacked the United States."

"Honey, don't start."

She knew about the six flags that had flown over Texas and had taken her children to the Six Flags amusement park outside Oakland several times. She knew Texans were proud—almost fanatical—of their history as the Lone Star state and you saw many more Texas flags than United States. Billie thought of the Confederate flag as a historical relic, or something hanging in an out-of-the-way cult compound, not flying beside a major highway.

The Rossbrooke Estates entrance had a fountain in the median of a maple tree-lined boulevard. They toured the models and Billie had to admit, she liked the large closets, kitchen islands, and stand-alone showers, which she wouldn't get in an older house. She knew this was the smart decision. They wouldn't have to deal with repairs and the lots were bigger. Their house would have a pool but having access to an indoor community pool was the deciding factor for Billie. Dylan would be able to swim year-round. The development was already half sold, and Cole convinced Billie they needed to act fast. They paid a deposit and were officially on their way to being Texans.

They spent the rest of the evening with his family. Uncle Amos barbequed everything that wasn't tied down, and pans overflowed with everything from beef brisket to goat. "You sure you don't want anything else?" he asked when he saw Billie's vegetable plate.

"No sir. I'm a pescatarian, so I'm not eating meat. But it does smell tempting."

"I think that's one of those white churches near the country club. I didn't know they couldn't eat meat though. I want you to have your strength, so you have no excuses when I put this whipping on you."

Their chess matches lasted hours, and their win-loss record was about even. Although you wouldn't know it if you listened to Amos's trash talking. After two and a half hours, Billie insisted they move inside, because the mosquitos were feasting on her legs. Cole finally declared himself the referee and called the game a tie, as other family members were leaving.

Sunday, they attended church with his grandmother then hung out with the family. Billie and Amos resumed their chess game, and Amos won. "You gave it a good try, young lady." Hearing someone call her 'young lady' was almost as good a feeling as winning. She was the oldest in her family and it was a pleasant change to feel youthful, even if only for a minute or two. They left that evening and stayed at a hotel near the Dallas airport so they could catch an early flight on Monday.

Billie had turned her phone off during the flight and when she checked her phone upon landing, she had a missed call from Sunrise Bank and Trust. The employment agency encouraged her to apply, even though Billie wasn't optimistic about her chances. She had a virtual interview and was surprised when they contacted her for a second interview, in-person, but that was over three months ago, and she hadn't heard from them since. Since they were moving to Texas, she almost didn't respond, but out of courtesy returned the call. He was complimentary and said he thought she would be a fantastic addition to their community liaison team. *Just my luck*, she thought. *They would call after we've committed to move.*

"I would be thrilled to join your team, but my husband received a great offer and we're relocating to Texas."

"You and everyone else it seems," he said. "Sunrise has a national footprint, and we have similar positions throughout the country. I'll transfer your application and interview results to our southwest region. They may be interested."

Within two hours, she had spoken with the manager for the Sunrise Bank and Trust East Texas region and received a job offer. He said it was hard to get candidates with her qualifications. As a Community Development Liaison, she would be responsible for increasing awareness of government assistance programs for low-and moderate-income residents, small businesses, and engaging partners to work with the bank in community development projects. The interviewers had been impressed by her passion and community involvement at the radio station.

Even though they had placed a deposit on a new house, the move had still seemed surreal. But now she had a job. It was real. She was moving to Texas.

CHAPTER 6

Billie and Maya were on their second glass of merlot and debating about the upcoming mayoral election when their mother finally showed up for the Sunday brunch at Gelila's Place. Billie knew it would be impossible to find Ethiopian food in Calderville and was making the rounds of her favorite restaurants before they moved.

"What a treat," Zuri said as she hugged each daughter then sat. "We don't get together often enough. Thanks for suggesting this."

Her mother was right. She had always taken for granted that either of them was a short drive away. The furthest she'd ever been from her mother was when she attended UC Berkeley, and stayed in the dorms, a whole ten miles from home.

Maya ventured further and went to USC in Los Angeles for two years pursuing an accounting degree but came home pregnant much to their mother's disappointment. Maya's baby, Imani, was born eighteen months after Kendra, and people often commented that they looked like sisters. Maya worked a few odd jobs before working as a receptionist at a real estate company. After seeing how the business worked, she took her broker's license test and passed. Now she made more money than Billie and counted several pro athletes and actors as her clients. The sisters often met for lunch, went to plays and concerts. Billie envied her sister's glamorous lifestyle and Maya thought Billie had the perfect family. They supported each other and despite opposite views on everything from men to politics were best friends. Once she moved, there'd be no more impromptu brunches.

After they ordered, Billie made her announcement.

Maya almost choked on her wine and said, "You're doing what? You mentioned it, but I didn't think you guys would actually go through with it."

"Everything happened so fast. Cole had accepted a position starting in the fall, but a vacancy for an adjunct position opened and Calder State administrators asked him if he was interested. He won't be under contract until fall semester, but it will give him a chance to get acclimated to the school."

"Sounds like a good opportunity, but Texas?" her mother asked. "My grandparents rode the Sunset Limited out of Louisiana and said they wanted no more parts of the south. They wouldn't even live on a street with south in the address."

"Have you not been paying attention to the news?" Maya said. "They have book banning, abortion is illegal, and the weather is either drought or floods."

"We have wildfires and earthquakes—either place has weather events," Billie said.

"What about Dylan?" her mother asked.

"He's doing well in Arizona and says he doesn't want to return to Oakland. The counselor agrees. Sometimes it's good to get a fresh start in a new place."

"You can't run away from problems. Drugs are everywhere," Maya said.

"We're not running away, but we'll be in a better position to help Dylan financially. Rehab is expensive. We can get twice as much house for a third of the cost, and there's no state income tax."

"There's got to be another way. You've always been a city girl. Can you even fly there?" Maya asked.

"It's only ninety minutes from Dallas—we drive that long from place to place around here sometimes."

"You've been through a lot recently. Worrying about Dylan has had you on an emotional rollercoaster. Plus, I know losing your job at the radio station was hard. They say you shouldn't make major life decisions after experiencing trauma," Zuri said.

"We've thought everything through, and this seems like the best option right now. A lot of people are moving from California to Texas. They even have Facebook groups. Look on the bright side. You'll have somewhere new to visit."

"It won't be in the summer. Baebee, it was so hot when I went to Dallas a few years ago, the makeup in my purse melted," Maya said.

"I have more news. I got a job. Sunrise Bank called and when I told them I was relocating, they offered me a position in Texas."

"Are you sure about this? You'd be going from a small, progressive, black-owned company to the epitome of conservative capitalism. You've never worked in corporate America," Maya said.

"What's so different about it? A job is a job."

"Don't go in there thinking you can change things. Lay low for a while. Leave your Kente cloth in the closet, and only wear one pair of earrings," Maya said. "Also, you might want to pull your hair into an updo in the beginning."

"In the words of India Aire, *I am not my hair.*"

"That's what I'm talking about," Maya said. "Those folks probably never heard of India Aire. You're used to wearing Black Lives Matter shirts and Nikes to work."

"You'll need to cover those tattoos I told you not to

get," her mother said. "And I love your natural beauty, but you should wear a little lipstick."

"Not that matte pink you've had for years," Maya said, digging in her purse. "Take this fire engine red tube. It will brighten up your face."

"You two make me sound like Eliza Doolittle. I know what business attire is," Billie said.

"Your hair is part of your corporate attire. It's unspoken, but like Sharon vs. Shaquanda—one will be perceived differently. Hold up a minute, I need to take this call."

She smiled as she heard her sister discussing a property sale. She could tell by her tone that her sister was speaking with a white person. Maya could code-switch in a second. Working at the radio station—Billie never really had to, authenticity was an asset. "Your sister is right. The playing field still is not level, and things are going backward instead of forward. All the progress we made is being undone by ignorance, greed, and apathy."

"Without your efforts, I wouldn't even have this opportunity. I remember going with you to see Nelson Mandela speak when he got out of prison. I didn't understand it all, but there were a lot of people there and you let me miss school, so I knew it was a big deal. I helped you distribute flyers for the Million Woman March, and I soaked up your stories about studying under Angela Davis and meeting James Baldwin. You made your impact your way and I'm looking forward to carrying on your work. Instead of talking about what others are or aren't doing, I can have an impact from the inside."

"Don't think you'll be able to have much influence," Maya said, as she slid back in her seat.

"They've seen my resume and heard online clips from my shows. I'm sure they wouldn't have hired me if they didn't want the real me. So can you list our house?" Billie asked.

"Of course. Even though I don't think this is a good idea, if you're going to pay someone, it may as well be me. When can we do a walk-through?"

"You know what the house looks like."

"But I wasn't looking with my realtor eye. Your sister Maya can overlook the shaky banister and outdated wallpaper in the bathroom, but your realtor Maya cannot. We'll need to come up with a punch-list of items that need to be fixed before you list the house."

"We don't want to put any money into this house. The whole point is to get as much out of it as we can."

"If you spend a little on the front end, you'll make more when you sell. You'd be surprised at the nitpicky things buyers focus on."

"I thought it was a seller's market. We get unsolicited mail and phone calls all the time from companies and people wanting to buy our house," Billie said.

They had lived in the house fifteen years. It was Billie's first time living in a house. The closest she'd come was a duplex her mother rented during her first year of high school. Zuri said the owner kept raising the rent and after two years, they moved back to an apartment. Billie and Cole started out renting, but by the time she was pregnant with Dylan, Cole said he wanted his children to have their own house, and they began house hunting. Maya had been promoted to Associate Broker and Billie and Cole were her first customers. Their budget didn't stretch far until they received a surprise twenty-thousand dollar check in the mail from Monroe, with a note that said, *for my niece and nephew.*

Billie felt that was too generous and didn't want to accept it, but Cole said, "They don't have kids and can afford it." Billie was still skeptical until she saw and fell in love with a three-bedroom Tudor style house in Maxwell Park. Monroe's gift helped them qualify. While Billie loved watching

HGTV and getting new ideas, she still loved their home and hadn't planned to move.

"Those are investors who quote a low price, then fix them up and flip for a quick profit. Maxwell Park is an in-demand area, your house will probably sell quickly. Make sure this is really what you want to do."

What choice do I have, Billie thought. She loved California, but she also loved her family. And it looked like their future was in Texas.

Billie and Cole loaded their rented Kia and headed to New Day. They were closing on their Texas home on Monday. They could have completed the transaction remotely via DocuSign, but their initial lot choice had sold, and they wanted to view their second choice again. It also gave them an opportunity to include a weekend trip to visit Dylan on their itinerary. His counselor had been urging them to come to a family session and to attend a Nar-anon meeting. They had done a few virtual family sessions and were pleased to see Dylan looking happier and healthier than he had in a long time. However, they hadn't attended a Nar-anon meeting before.

"We're not the ones with the problem. How is that going to help him?" Cole asked. "It's another tactic to justify their outrageous price."

"I'm not that thrilled about it either, but we don't want to appear uncooperative. Since we're going to be there, we can't really get out of it."

When Dylan walked in the room, the three of them hugged and didn't say anything for several minutes. "Something smells good," Cole said as he stepped out of the hug and discreetly wiped a tear from his cheek.

"Don't let the smell fool you. The food here isn't that great," Dylan said.

"Want to go eat somewhere?" Cole asked.

"Can we leave?" Billie asked.

"As long as you sign some papers and we're back by seven," Dylan said.

They went to IHOP, then returned for a family counseling session. On Sunday they went to brunch and the Heard Museum. They had avoided a Nar-anon meeting as long as they could and finally went to one that evening.

During a last tearful hug with their son, Billie and Cole praised him for his progress, took selfies, and promised to return as soon as they could.

"So what did you think about that meeting?" Cole asked as they drove to the airport. The meeting had been like an episode of "scared straight." They heard from parents whose children were in and out of jail, living on the streets and even stole from them. One mother said her daughter would sleep with men for money and had been raped and beaten more than once. She was thankful when her daughter was arrested because at least they knew where she was. They all said they never thought it would happen to them and wondered what they could have done differently.

"I feel bad for those families, but I can't see Dylan stooping that low. He's accepted responsibility, and this time he's serious about rehab," Billie said.

"I'm even more convinced that Texas is a good move for us. We can all get a fresh start," Cole said.

They boarded their plane with a renewed sense of optimism and comfort.

"Welcome to flight number 833 to Dallas. The pilot has informed the crew that we're trying to leave early to get ahead of stormy weather. The cabin door has been closed, so please find your seats as soon as possible and fasten your seat belts," a flight attendant announced.

Cole squeezed his wife's hand as they prepared for take-off.

★ ★ ★

After breakfast burritos and sweet tea, Billie and Cole met at their realtor's office Monday morning before heading to Rossbrooke Estates. "Glad you're here early, we've hit a snag in the closing. We always run a final credit report before closing. The bank wants to make sure your financial condition hasn't changed since the initial application. That's why we tell clients don't buy a car, change jobs, or do anything that's going to alter your credit score."

"We followed your orders," Cole said.

"Then maybe fraud is going on. Your scores dropped 80 points due to two new credit cards that are already at their limit."

"That can't be right. Neither of us has any new credit cards," Cole said, while looking at Billie with a raised eyebrow.

"Don't look at me. I didn't open anything."

"Here are copies of the reports from all three credit rating agencies. You'll need to put an alert on your file, then call Capitol One and American Express to report the fraud."

"What does that do to our closing?" Cole asked.

"Unfortunately, we won't be able to close today. We'll reschedule, once we get proof that the charges are fraudulent. Maybe we can close Wednesday."

"But I just started a new job. I need to be at work tomorrow," Billie said.

"There's so much red tape involved in fixing stuff like that," Cole said. "We don't have the time or money to get bogged down in a paperwork nightmare."

"Don't worry. You're not liable for fraudulent charges and getting them removed won't be hard. It may take a few days to work everything out though."

They spent two days at Lovey's house and Billie and Amos had marathon chess sessions while Cole got started on his Calder State duties. They finally heard from Capitol One and the fraud department was able to track down the origin of the new credit cards. Research revealed the one card had been used six times for cash advances in Los Angeles. They could prove they weren't in Los Angeles and the closing was rescheduled.

"Congratulations, and welcome to Texas." Billie and Cole shook the closing agent's hand, as he handed them an envelope with their closing documents, house blueprint, and a Welcome to Ross County brochure. They had been able to get the fraudulent credit cards closed and removed from their credit report.

They were almost the official owners of a two-acre corner lot on Pecan Lane. Billie liked the subdivision because it had sidewalks and there were nine house plans, so the houses wouldn't all look the same. It was in an unincorporated area ten miles from the Calderville city limit and Cole's family acted like they were moving to Maine. "Man, I'll need to pack a lunch to come see you way out there," Monroe had said. Once the realtor did the final walk-through and their credit report was updated again, the sale would be final.

Billie had never lived in a new house and was still in awe of all they were getting for the price. They added upgrades for solar panels and an enclosed patio since Billie hated bugs. Construction would begin within ten days, with completion expected in six months.

They had been talking about this move for months, but it was now becoming real to Billie. They went to a Calder State baseball game and ate Tex-Mex every day. She knew Cole was doing his best to ensure she had a good time. He could barely contain his excitement about moving.

On their way to their eleven o'clock flight, they stopped at their lot for one last glance. "This will be a new start for us," Cole said as he grabbed his wife's hand and strolled across what would be their front yard. "I know it's a big change, but you'll love Texas. It's quiet here, and breathe in that fresh air," he said, inhaling deeply. "No air you can see. No bumper-to-bumper traffic. And we'll have more money and can finally travel like we always said we would."

"We've signed the papers honey. You don't have to keep giving me the sales pitch."

"I'm thrilled, but I want you to be happy too."

"I just want us to get settled and started on this next phase of our lives. The house is going to be beautiful. I want lots of crepe myrtles, and a small garden. Once Dylan gets straight, I'm sure everything will be fine."

They arrived home late Thursday and because of the time change, to her body it was even later. The delayed closing pushed her start date back until Friday. Even though she had only worked one day, it had been a long week, and she was glad when five o'clock came. Billie had sat in front of a computer monitor all day, getting a username, an email account, and access to several databases. She had a migraine and couldn't wait to get home.

A FedEx truck was in her driveway when she drove up. "I almost missed you," the driver said as he asked her to sign for the envelope. It was from the credit card company. Capitol One researched the fraudulent credit card trans-actions and needed Billie and Cole's signatures on a fraud affidavit to press charges against the perpetrator. They had been instructed to sign and return the documents as soon as possible to complete the mortgage company's file. Attached to the affidavits, were copies of the fraudulent purchases ranging from three dollars at Dunkin' Donuts to hundreds of dollars of cash advances. Two of the purchases were captured on the store's security camera. The pictures were fuzzy, but there was no mistaking who was using the card, and tears welled in Billie's eyes. It was Dylan.

CHAPTER 7

"I've got good news," Maya announced as soon as Billie answered the phone. "I've sold your house."

"It's not even on the market yet."

"I shared the info with a few brokers in the office and we've already received two offers. Both are above the listing price we agreed on. One is twelve thousand more, but they want to close within thirty days."

"I don't know if we can move that fast."

"Both are 'as-is' offers. You won't have to do any repairs or bother with staging. That saves you a few thousand dollars. But there's a chance you could get a higher offer when we make the listing public. Think about it, but don't take too long."

Twelve thousand now versus a few months from now was critical to their cashflow, especially since they now had an additional twenty thousand in credit card debt to pay. Dylan's treatment payments were hellacious, plus there were added costs for trips for family counseling that included airfare, car rental and hotel. She could have participated online, but this was a small price to pay to get her son back.

After reviewing the credit card charges, they explained

the situation to their realtor, and they couldn't press charges. Fortunately, they were still able to qualify because Billie wasn't working when they completed their original application. So even though their credit score was now lower, so was their debt-to-income ratio. There was more paperwork, but the sale was still finalized. However, they were now on the hook for an additional twenty thousand in credit card debt. She and Cole didn't mention it to Dylan. The charges were made months ago, and they chalked it up to the past. Hopefully one day all this would be a distant, ugly memory.

"What is there to think about?" Cole asked when she told him about the offers.

"It will take a herculean effort to move in a month. And if we do, where will we live?" Billie asked.

"Monroe has a place we can stay until our house is finished. He offered a while ago, but I didn't think we needed it. It's not fancy, but we won't have to sign a lease."

"Have you seen it? It's not rat-infested or raggedy, is it?"

"I think it's only a few years old. It's a mobile home."

"Mobile home, as in a trailer?"

"Yeah. He owns a couple of trailer parks. A few years ago, he tried to get me to invest with him. I should have. I didn't know how much money they generate."

"Do they have real bathrooms? And aren't those things made of formaldehyde? You know, the material that causes cancer."

"According to you, everything causes cancer. It's only a couple months. He has a two-bedroom unit available. And yes, it has a regular bathroom. Go to the MJ Rentals website and look for Lakewood Terrace. When you see the pictures, you'd never know it wasn't a house or apartment. And here's the best part—it's free. If we don't take it, he's going to rent it out."

"I'm still skeptical, but I guess we can get air filters and lots of house plants. It's hard to argue with free."

"I'm in your driveway," Maya said when her sister answered her phone. "I came by to put up the yard sign. Even though we're under contract, the sign is good advertising, so I'm still putting one in your yard. I thought you would be at your hair appointment, or I would have called first."

Billie had been elbow-deep in boxes and Hefty bags and was glad to take a break.

"The house looks the same," Maya said as she stepped inside and looked around. "You do realize we close in three weeks?"

"I didn't know I'd be working when we agreed to the quick closing. I'm behind on everything."

"So how was your first week, Miss Banker Lady?"

"I've never been so bored. I did online orientation all week. I'm not used to having so many health insurance and retirement plan choices. The radio station was family-owned, and they didn't even offer insurance when I started. Maybe there are advantages to working for a big corporation. But instead of learning about banking, I've been watching stale videos about sexual harassment, conflicts of interest, and workplace safety. You can't skip ahead because they ask questions at the end of each section. Every evening, I planned to pack at least one box when I got home, but all I can do is grab something to eat, then collapse into bed. Who knew sitting all day could be so tiring?"

"That's why I love selling real estate. I'm not cooped up in an office."

"What are you doing the rest of the day? How about helping me pack?"

"No thank you. I don't fraternize with my clients."

"Very funny."

"I don't want to impede your progress, so I won't stay. Call me later," Maya said as she walked to her car.

The days were passing quickly, and Billie wasn't getting through her 'to-do' list as fast as she needed to. She checked the time as she returned to her daughter's room. Kendra had left her closets and drawers practically empty when she moved out almost two years ago. Billie had filled two boxes. Other than the Steph Curry and Ice Spice posters on the wall, anything indicating this room had belonged to a teenage girl were gone. She did find a box in the closet with old CDs and DVDs. She also found several Army, Air Force and Navy brochures in her desk. Billie hadn't even known her daughter was considering enlisting until the Navy doctor's office called to verify insurance during her physical. She regretted not being more present for her daughter and often replayed the last weeks before Kendra left.

"It's almost time to go honey, you need to hurry up," Billie had said, a few weeks before her graduation. "We're going to meet your father there."

"I'm not going," Kendra announced.

"We've already discussed this. The counselor said it's important for the family to be involved in Dylan's treatment."

"Daddy said I didn't have to go."

"That must have been before he knew the counselor's treatment plan. We must…"

"I'm not going to listen to some stranger tell me about my brother. He was in pain and found a way to stop it. Then he went back to the swim team too soon. He only did it because you guys were so excited about it. He believed he wasn't enough without being a star athlete."

"That's not true. He loved being on the swim team. We encouraged Dylan, but didn't push him."

"Your encouragement feels like pushing. If you'd been

paying attention, you would have known something was wrong. I knew."

"You knew your brother was taking pills? Why didn't you tell me?"

"Since when do you listen to me or anyone else, including Dylan? Just like I've been telling you for months, I'm going to the Navy the day after my birthday. You act like we're robots to mold as you wish and don't have our own feelings."

"Kendra, can we not do this right now? Dylan is in crisis. Let's handle one drama at a time. When you have children, you'll understand the desire to encourage them to make good choices."

"Like I said, I'm not going. Dylan knows I'm in his corner, so you guys go encourage and help him. Lucky for me, you don't care enough about anything I do to encourage me."

Those words stung, but at that moment, Billie didn't have the time or energy to spar with her daughter. True to her word, right after her birthday and four weeks after graduation, Kendra left for basic training at Great Lakes Training Center outside Chicago. She hadn't even invited them to her basic training graduation and didn't come home on leave for a year. Her barren room was her statement of independence.

Dylan's room was a statement of a life interrupted. The closets and drawers were overflowing. He had always been a passionate sneakerhead, and shoe boxes were under the bed. It was a hobby Billie didn't understand, especially for someone with no job. But Dylan did odd jobs and found money to keep up with the latest sneaker trends. When he stopped buying new shoes, Billie and Cole figured he was moving to another phase, hopefully one less expensive. They didn't know he was selling his coveted sneakers for pills until Kendra told them after he fell at school.

Several of his larger trophies had already been packed away when she cleaned out the basement. His drawer was full of ribbons, certificates, and other awards. There were also college scholarship letters. He had been offered full rides from all the large California schools as well as swimming powerhouses like University of Pennsylvania and Michigan. His last coach was now at the University of Texas in Austin and Dylan had been leaning toward that school. They had planned a campus tour to Austin, with stops at Baylor in Waco, Southern Methodist in Dallas and Sabine Christian College about an hour east of Calderville. How ironic that they were going to Texas, but under such different circumstances.

She'd hosted substance abuse counselors on her talk show several times and still didn't recognize the red flags. They called it intentional blindness—not noticing gradual changes. Kendra was the rebellious one. She broke curfew, was suspended for smoking at school, and had a boy in the house when she thought her parents were at work. While they were keeping tabs on their daughter, their son was slipping into darkness.

It had been hard to accept that Dylan had a drug problem. The first inkling they had that anything was wrong was a failing report card. He attributed it to missing so much time with his injury. He had studied online while he was out, but it wasn't the same as being in the classroom. This sounded reasonable, and they arranged for tutoring. He had loved being a jock, so when he lost weight, they thought it was because he was unable to work out. By the time he returned to class, swim season was over. He managed to pass his classes, but barely. That summer he returned to the lifeguard job he'd had the previous summer. Within three weeks, he quit, or so they thought.

The swim season started in November. He made the team, but his times were slow. However, he never appeared "out of it," was always respectful, and came home when he was supposed to. Actually, he was spending too much time at home. He wasn't eating everything in sight like he usually did, and frequently came home from school exhausted and went to bed. While cleaning his room, Billie discovered a stash of pills and several prescriptions. They blamed it on his injury and after stern admonitions from Cole, which included grounding and limited video game time, they thought they had things under control. Until the coach called. Dylan was on camera, going in a teacher's purse. The School Resource Officer searched his backpack and found several prescription bottles. They also found out he hadn't quit his lifeguard job—he failed a drug test. They could no longer ignore the obvious, their son had a problem.

Cole never blamed her for Dylan's drug use, but he always said she was too soft on him. Even Kendra complained, saying her parents were easier on her brother. Billie had attributed Kendra's comments to sibling rivalry, she said the same thing about Maya.

Billie was only four years older than her sister, but that four years made a world of difference. Her mother was never very strict, and they had an almost sisterly relationship. This was fun when Billie could see "R" rated movies and her friends couldn't, or when her bedtime was whatever time she went to bed. But it also meant at times Billie was the shoulder her mother leaned on and cried on, and she absorbed her mother's devastation and anger about the divorce. When her father came to pick the girls up for visitation, Billie refused to go. Two years later, he remarried and moved to Berkeley Hills. Maya loved going to his house, but Billie refused to go, and never opened any cards or gifts he sent.

Maya didn't seem fazed about the divorce, was popular, and made straight As. Billie had been a late developer and was envious of her younger sister's C-cup breasts, hips, and smooth caramel complexion. Pregnancy gave her the curves she'd never had growing up along with some unwanted pounds.

She shed the roll around her stomach and cellulite on her thighs when she switched to a vegan diet and maintained her weight with weekly spin classes and morning yoga at home. Billie's sandy skin meant she was more susceptible to sunburn, and her mother insisted she slather herself in sunscreen, while her sister was already outside playing. Her hair had always been coarser and kinkier than her sister's and was another source of envy. The texture was perfect for locs, and she had finally learned to love her hair. Her mother handled them differently because they needed different things, which is what she thought she was doing with her children. But as she packed the remnants of her son's teen life in boxes, she wondered if she had done the right thing. Could she have averted this nightmare they were now living?

Billie wiped the sweat from her brow as she taped a box of books to be given away. She had enough Warriors and Raiders paraphernalia that she could wear a different shirt or jacket every day for weeks. Her niece, Imani, would inherit most of them, as Billie was only keeping a few pieces. She had a shred stack and filled two blue recycling garbage bags with pieces of bank statements, tax returns, and old bills. She should have been finished hours ago, but her rinky-dink home shredder was slowing her down. In the past, they stacked old papers, and she had taken them to the radio station and shredded them there.

Browsing through old photos was also slowing her down, but Billie couldn't resist viewing pictures from what had seemed like an idyllic family life. As she went through unlabeled folders, she found the kids report cards, more of Dylan's swim medals, and Kendra's spelling bee ribbons.

In another folder were documents she had forgotten about—their divorce papers. Only two years had passed, but it seemed like a lifetime ago. She had found out about Cole's affair when she was helping him clean out the office he shared with two other instructors. Since he'd earned his Ph.D., he was given his own office. As she was emptying his drawers, she found a birthday card with a picture, obviously written by a lover.

"I forgot that was in there," he said when she slapped it on the table in front of him.

"Obviously," she replied.

"Before you get upset, you need to know that is old news. I realized I was wrong and broke it off, months ago. It was nothing."

"But you kept the card, and the picture doesn't look like *nothing*. Pictures don't lie."

Since the affair was over, he acted as though her anger was unwarranted. That made her angrier. They went to counseling, which turned into "pick on Billie" sessions. She couldn't get him to understand her feelings. Cole had been working on his doctorate and spent a lot of time studying, or at least that's what he told her he was doing. Since she had missed the signs, she became suspicious of any unexplained time away from her. He thought they were moving on and became defensive when she questioned him.

"Either you trust me, or you don't," Cole said after he found her looking through his phone. "This is bullshit."

"Don't you dare try to play that game with me. I'm not the guilty party."

"I get it. I screwed up, but I'm not going to live like a suspect the rest of my life. If you want to try to make this work, fine. If not, let's not waste time."

"Wow," she said, shaking her head. "You're giving me ultimatums. I need some time. I'll get you a blanket and sheets."

"I'm not going to let you treat me like a second-class husband. I'm not sleeping on the couch."

Billie had agreed to work things out, but she was still hurt and didn't think Cole should just expect to say he was sorry and for her to act like nothing had happened. They barely spoke for the next two weeks and when he told her she needed to "get over it," she replied, "I'll show you how I get over it." She filed for divorce.

After several weeks of back and forth negotiating between their lawyers, they met in downtown Oakland to sign the divorce documents. Billie hadn't expected to be there long and only put enough for one hour in the parking meter. Cole and both lawyers were seated at the conference table when she walked in. He barely nodded when she spoke. She noticed he wasn't wearing his wedding ring. She had seen these scenes in movies and read about it in books. She knew over half of all marriages end in divorce, but still never expected it to happen to her. Yet here she was.

"Here are the documents we discussed," Billie's attorney said as he slid the papers to Cole's attorney.

"After further review, we'd like some changes," his attorney said.

"What kind of games are you playing? These documents were finalized over a week ago. You should have shared your concerns with me prior to this meeting," Billie's lawyer said.

"Mr. Jordan wants his equity from the house."

"You want to sell the house?" Billie asked. "I thought we agreed it was best not to disrupt the kids' routines."

"We suggest a home equity loan, or that she do a cash out refinance to pull the money out now," his attorney said.

"You know I can't afford to pay a larger mortgage payment by myself."

"Ms. Jordan will pay less in taxes filing head of household and will have a larger interest deduction, so her take home pay will be about the same."

Billie stood and said, "Cole, I cannot believe…"

"I didn't know rents were so high when I agreed to

move out," Cole said. "Rent is as much as our mortgage payment. We're taking income that supported one household and splitting it in two. I don't want to disrupt our family, but I don't want to live under a bridge either."

"As usual, you're being selfish," Billie said. "I cannot believe…"

"If you two will give us about thirty minutes, maybe we can work something out," Cole's attorney said.

"I'm going to put more money in my meter." Billie went to the Starbucks on the corner, then sat in her car to wait for her attorney's call or text. She played solitaire on her phone as she tried to calm her simmering rage. Her phone rang, but it wasn't her attorney. It was the school. Dylan had an accident and was being rushed to the hospital. She called Cole. He had gotten the same phone call, and they agreed to meet at the hospital.

Dylan had slipped during swim practice and hit his head on the side of the pool. She called the hospital, but they wouldn't give her any additional information over the phone. She and Cole arrived within minutes of each other. Dylan was undergoing an MRI, and they were directed to a waiting room. Finally, a nurse came and told them they had completed the MRI and Dylan was being transported to a room. They could meet him there. All sorts of thoughts had gone through Billie's mind, and when she entered his room, the left side of his face was bandaged like a mummy and he was hooked up to an IV drip. He had waved at them when they entered the room.

"Your son will have a nasty bump on his head for a few days and a headache, but no injuries were noted on the MRI."

"Thank goodness," Billie said.

"But there is another issue. His blood tests came positive for hydrocodone, indicating opioid analgesic misuse. That likely contributed to his fall."

"What do you mean?" Cole asked.

"Were you aware that your son is abusing opioids?"

"He was prescribed pain pills a few months ago after a swimming injury. I guess it's still in his system," Billie said.

"Mrs. Jordan, hydrocodone passes through the system within four days at the longest. It showed up in his blood and urine, which indicates recent usage. We can refer your son to treatment. It's easier to find a center if he's admitted directly from a hospital."

Billie and Cole were shaken. This happened to other people, not them. The divorce, which minutes earlier had been the biggest crisis they'd ever faced, was replaced by the urgent need to save their son. They rushed out of the office and neither mentioned the divorce again. Her attorney mailed the unsigned documents, and a bill, which they still had to pay. Billie tossed the envelope in the shred box, amazed at how close they had come to splitting up. Dylan's addiction saved their marriage. Would they be able to save Dylan?

CHAPTER 8

The sign said: WELCOME TO TEXAS. Billie and Cole were driving through El Paso on the third day of the journey to their new home. They'd spent the first night in Los Angeles. It was only six hours from Oakland, but they had decided to turn the drive into a mini vacation. "I want to spend one more night in California," Billie said.

"You act like you're going to Siberia," Cole said.

"I just want to admire the ocean and smell the salty breeze. It will be a while before we're back on the coast."

They spent the next night in Phoenix, visited Dylan, and attended a family counseling session. He seemed in good spirits when they left and told them he'd be joining them soon. When they entered Texas, they were still ten hours from their destination and decided to get a hotel. They had driven to Texas once, when the children were small. Now she remembered why they only did it once. Most of the drive was boring, flat, and brown. They listened to the Comedy channel, National Public Radio discussions, the 70's, 80's, and jazz radio stations. "You can drive from coast to coast and never listen to a local radio station," Billie observed. "No wonder local radio is struggling."

Finally, they reached the Ross County sign, and ten

minutes later they arrived at Lakewood Terrace. Cole drove her through the mobile home park of about thirty trailers. Three double-wide trailers near the entrance had higher pitched roofs and faux brick skirting which made them look like traditional homes. "Those must be the units I saw on the website. The rest look like barracks," Billie said. They circled around the neighborhood and were back at their unit which was close to the front. Three steps led to their front door, and they entered the single-wide unit with a bedroom on each end. The front door opened into the family room and twelve feet away was the dining, and kitchen area, the epitome of open concept living. All the walls were white, and some had beadboard on the bottom half. There was one bathroom with one tub and one sink. Other than in hotels, she and Cole had never shared a bathroom sink. They would also share a full-size bed. Something they hadn't done since college.

"These closets are tiny and little of our furniture will fit in here. We mapped it out to scale but seeing it in person is different. Let's keep one recliner and the loveseat. Everything else can go in storage," Billie said. "What day do they pick up garbage and which day is recycling day?"

"We have to take our garbage to the dumpsters in the back, and there's no recycling."

"Then where do we drop off recycling?" Billie asked.

"I think the closest is in Tyler, about two counties over."

"That should be illegal," Billie said. "I thought Texans were so big on..."

"Yeah, that's a real shame," Cole said, as he wrapped his arms around her waist and began kissing her neck.

"I thought you were so tired," Billie said, as she put her arms around his neck.

"I am. I need some vitamin B, as in Billie. Don't we have a blanket in the car? Let's have a welcome to Texas party."

While Cole went to the car, Billie opened the bedroom

door and hollered. "What is it?" Cole said, after rushing back inside.

"What's that miniature dinosaur looking thing running across the floor?" Billie asked.

"That's a lizard. They're harmless."

"I'm not living with lizards. This place needs to be exterminated."

"You are such a city girl," Cole said, shaking his head. "Now where were we?"

"I can tell you where I'm going. Out of here."

Cole hung his head in mock disappointment, threw the blanket over his shoulder, and followed his wife to the car. They were staying at Lovey's house until their furniture arrived. Uncle Amos was sitting on the front porch with a can of Coors, as Cole pulled up in the yard, next to his grandmother's Kelly-green Nova.

"Hey, Unc. It's not even twelve o'clock. How do you drink beer like that?" he asked, pointing to two empty beer cans on the armrest.

"Lots of practice, nephew," he said with a burp. "Excuse me."

"Since the moving truck won't arrive for two days, we should go to the clerk's office tomorrow to change our driver's licenses," Cole said.

"You go ahead," Billie said. "I'm going to Walmart to buy a few things for the trailer, or I guess I should say our place. There's plenty of time to get licenses."

Not as much time as she thought.

SECTION II

Fish Out of Water

CHAPTER 9

Water Drop Alert – Ross County Water Works
A rare spring freeze is in the forecast. Everyone can help reduce the risk of bursting pipes and low water pressure. Take shorter showers and try not to wash dishes or do laundry, until the alert is lifted. Let's all do our part.
Save time, pay your bill online. rcw.com.

"That was Monroe," Cole said as he put his phone in his pocket. "He said pipes burst at the treatment plant and Lovey doesn't have running water. She and Uncle Amos are staying with him. He was checking to see how we were."

"Tell him we're cold," Billie said, rubbing her hands together.

"Nothing he can do about that," Cole said. "Unless you want to go to his house too. We've got enough buckets around here to flush the toilet. This cold snap should be over tomorrow, so hopefully our pipes hold on at least one more day."

The weather forecaster had been a relentless hype man, warning about the coming freezing temperatures for a week. Today it finally came. This was the coldest March ever, and farmers who had already planted were going to suffer losses. The children were out of school and the bank was closed.

But with remote work, there was no snow day, and she was still expected to work. However, Billie found it hard to concentrate as she gazed outside. Two inches of white, fluffy snow covered the ground. Bushes and tree limbs had a silver shimmer and were bent over, looking like a scene from a doomsday movie or another planet.

She could count the times on one hand she had seen snow. On the rare occasion that it snowed in Oakland, it melted by the end of the day. This snow was expected to hang around. The thin trailer walls were losing their battle against the record-low temperatures. She had on a jogging suit, turtleneck, T-shirt, and socks. They hung blankets over the doors to block the cracks and the fake fireplace was running on high. To avoid frozen and burst pipes, they were advised to keep their cabinets open and let water drip from the faucets overnight. "With all of our modern technology, this is the best solution to avoid freezing pipes?" Billie asked. "This is an irresponsible waste of water that borders on criminal."

"Do you want to save the planet, or be able to flush the toilet?" Cole asked.

"We should be able to do both."

"I don't remember it ever being this cold this late in the season when I was growing up," Cole said.

The snow was pretty the first day and began melting when temperatures reached thirty-three degrees for a few hours. But as the sun set, the wet streets froze and turned into an ice-skating rink, more dangerous than during the actual storm. They heard cracking sounds, which was the weight of ice breaking tree limbs. "The water pressure is low, but at least the pipes haven't burst. I hope we don't lose power," Cole said.

"This fake fireplace is cute, but if you're not standing right in front of it, you can't feel the heat," Billie said as she took a cup of green tea from the microwave.

"That gives us an excuse to snuggle together," Cole said, while pulling her toward him. "I'll warm you up."

"You are still the sexiest man I know, but I have an appointment this afternoon and if you warm me up, I'll need a shower to clean me up. We barely have water and..."

"I know. I know. You take the fun out of everything," Cole said with a sigh.

"Boiling water and wearing a turtleneck to bed isn't fun to me. Of everything I heard about Texas, snow was not on the list. What else haven't you told me?"

"As you would say on the radio, stay tuned," Cole said and left the room.

CHAPTER 10

Billie checked her watch for the third time in two minutes, hoping the meeting would end soon. Sunrise Bank was everything Maya had warned her it would be. There were meetings, and meetings about meetings. She was assigned a cubicle in the Tyler office and shared it with Lydia Hayes. Lydia was out of the office on Billie's first day at the office and it was obvious Lydia hadn't planned to share the space. Billie slid Lydia's stacks of paper, folders, and family pictures to the side to make room for her meager possessions.

They met on Billie's third day in the office. "Hello. I'm Billie, looks like we're cubicle mates."

"My name is Lydia, but you already know that since you moved my name plate."

"I made room for my things. If I'm encroaching let me know and maybe they can find me another spot."

"Good luck with that. When they closed the Calderville branch, they split us between existing offices. I was assigned here."

"You live in Calderville?" Billie asked, "So do I. I read there had been some consolidations."

"There were three branches in Calderville, and I had my

own office. Now not only have I lost my office, but I have to drive forty minutes to come share my windowless cubicle."

"In California, it could take forty minutes to drive ten miles, so this commute doesn't bother me. Plus it's my understanding they don't want us hanging out in the office. I have a list of prospects to call on."

"Get real. Sunrise isn't going to do any of the stuff you come up with. Don't waste your time."

"I already have appointments. I only came in today because my internet at home is acting up and I'm getting behind in my emails. I don't see how you keep up. Every day my inbox has something from legal, marketing, human resources, and the tech team."

"You don't have to read them all," Lydia said. "That's so they can say they told us about x, y and z, and we can't say we didn't know. Just scan the subject line."

"You can do that, but I'm new here. I don't want to miss anything."

"Bless your heart. I guess I was eager and energetic when I started too."

"I don't have a banking background, so I want to make sure I understand everything. Plus, I get emails that don't even belong to me, so the Help Desk told me to come in. I get messages for bjohnson and bjones all the time."

"Bjohnson, I think that's Betty over in Waco, and Bill Jones is the area president. His messages might be pretty juicy."

Gossip had not been much of a part of her radio career. The staff was small and were like family. They knew most of each other's business anyway, so there was no need for gossip. But in her brief time with the bank, she was learning the gossip grapevine was strong. Her official title was Community Relationship Liaison. She wasn't replacing anyone. This was a new position created to improve the bank's compliance with the Community Reinvestment Act, a federal law requiring banks to meet the credit needs of borrowers in their chartered communities, particularly low and moderate-income borrowers. The bank had earned an unsatisfactory grade during its last examination. She had interviewed numerous community activists on her show, who were exposing biased practices by some banks. Despite millions of dollars set aside by large banks, little was changing. Maybe she could be more effective on the corporate side.

As a Community Relationship Liaison, or CRL, she was tasked with reaching out to organizations and businesses in underserved communities the bank could lend to, partner with, or buy from. Management gave her a prospect list, but she preferred generating her own. This was the perfect job for a newcomer. She learned that Premier Paper Company, usually referred to as PPC, an insurance company call center, and a potato chip factory, were the largest private employers in Ross County. Billie planned to meet with each of them to determine partnership opportunities.

While those companies had sprawling, well-maintained buildings and operations, Downtown Calderville looked frozen in time, with more unoccupied buildings than occupied. Calderville was founded on farming and slavery and thrived due to cotton and the town's proximity to the railroad and the Neches River. The town continued to prosper after slavery, but agriculture suffered the one-two punch of the boll weevil, then the Depression, and the town began a slow decline. Reminders of that time included empty art deco buildings, a boarded-up movie theater, and former stores with tattered canvas awnings. Many of the storefronts were covered with murals. Names like Woolworth's, First Mercantile Bank, and Calder's Dry Goods were faintly visible on faded brick buildings.

Mostly government offices, city hall, the post office, the Chronicle newspaper, and the public works administration were the main occupants. The growing areas were located closer to the interstate and Walmart. The empty buildings reminded her of Oakland, but not in a good way. Homeless people would have occupied those buildings back home. A lack of affordable housing, gentrification, and economic disparities had generated an intractable homelessness problem. But here it looked like everyone had a place to go. Calderville had less resources, but had figured out how to take care of its people.

Billie had one more appointment on today's list. As part of her job duties, she met with small business owners to determine what, if any services the bank could provide them. She'd met with a daycare owner and florist that morning and was on her way to a medical transport company. In each instance, she was able to connect them to a Sunrise product that would save them money, such as the ability to accept online payments for the daycare, and a seasonal line of credit for the florist.

"Good afternoon, I'm looking for Adrian Butler," Billie said when she entered the reception area.

"Depends on why you want him. If you're a bill collector or salesman, he's not here. If you're a new customer, or with the Publisher's Clearinghouse Sweepstakes, you've found him." She had expected a woman, not this good-looking, fit, pecan-colored man, with a thin mustache and one earring.

"How about, none of the above," Billie said, as she placed a business card and bank brochure on the front counter. "I'm with Sunrise Bank and Trust, and I have an appointment to discuss how we can serve your business."

"My name is Adrian Butler and I'm the owner," he said as he read her business card. "So was my loan approved?"

"I'm not aware of an application. I'm a CRL Officer, but I can check when I return to the office."

"I don't mean to be rude, but unless you're here to discuss my loan, no need in us meeting."

"Sunrise offers other services. I can..."

"I already know. You want me to put money in your bank so you can pay me little to no interest and then upsell me a bunch of stuff I don't need and nickel and dime me to death."

"Mr. Butler, I can assure you, Sunrise..."

"When I made this appointment, it was to discuss a loan application. My business doesn't need a CRL or CDL, or whatever you called it. If they aren't going to send a loan officer, I'd appreciate you and your bank not wasting my time."

The bell on the door jangled as someone came in. "Hey Mr. Butler, I can come back if you're busy."

"Ms. Jordan and I are finished." Adrian said. "Have a seat."

Billie gathered her purse and bag and walked to the door. She wasn't used to professional rejection. When she reached the door, she turned around, just in time to see Adrian throw her business card and brochure in the garbage. *This job is going to be harder than I thought.*

It didn't take long for Billie to realize that Lydia knew what she was talking about. Billie's initial zeal at unearthing potential partners had been zapped as her recommendations went through numerous committee reviews before coming back with a "no." The company's financial statements were incomplete, the business was too new, or their impact wasn't broad enough. There was always a reason, and when she made a recommendation which addressed the first exception, there was a new one.

One of her first proposals was an expansion of the Boys

and Girls Club near Lovey's house to include an indoor swimming pool. Since Dylan was a swimmer, this project hit home for her. The project was not approved and instead they green-lighted an indoor pickleball court close to her house. She did get one outreach event approved, a financial literacy workshop on the Calder State campus.

Billie enjoyed not being tied to a desk, but that also meant she could be called on to represent Sunrise. Today she and Lydia were participating in career day at Tenth Avenue Middle School. As she walked across the parking lot, students were lined up and Billie assumed they were returning from a fire drill. She and Lydia had prepared remarks and then were engaging the students in a bingo-like game of financial terms with prizes. Lydia was already in the office when Billie entered.

"We need to push your time slot back an hour," the secretary informed them. "The rain disrupted our bathroom break time, so we're trying to catch up. I'll let the principal know you're here."

"Okay," Billie replied, although she had no clue what the lady was talking about. As she sent a few quick emails on her phone, the principal entered with another man behind him.

"Welcome to Tenth Avenue," Principal Moore said. "We can preach to our young people that they can be whatever they want, but it's even better for us to show them. The only thing most of them know about banking is the little man in the Monopoly Game, so thank you so much for coming. And Adrian, thanks for coming again. The students enjoyed your presentation last semester. Most of them had never even heard of a medical transport company, let alone considered owning one."

"Pleasure to see you again Ms. Jordan," Adrian said.

"Hello. I'm surprised you remember my name, since you threw away my business card."

After an awkward silence, the secretary said, "As soon as the sixth graders are all in, we'll get started."

"What's going on?" Billie asked.

"Bathroom breaks are scheduled every two hours by grade, but it was raining so hard, we didn't want to take them outside earlier," Principal Moore stated.

"Outside?" Billie asked.

"Yes. Didn't you see that row of Porta Pottis next to the parking lot?"

"I assumed there was construction going on."

"This is an old building, and our water pressure is too low to properly flush toilets, especially on the second floor."

"You're kidding. The bathrooms don't work?" Billie asked.

"Don't worry. If you need to use the restroom, I'll show you the teacher's lounge," the secretary said. "We don't have enough pressure for the building, but if we limit usage to a few restrooms, we don't have many problems."

"I'm not concerned about me, but the kids have to go outside?" Billie asked. "What happens when it's cold? And doesn't that take away a lot of instruction time?"

"You're not saying anything we haven't presented to the school board, state officials, Ross County Water Works, anyone who will listen. They're studying it," Principal Moore said, using air quotes.

"This is appalling," Billie said. "There should be some way the bank can help. We'll see what we can do."

"Leave me out of that 'we'," Lydia said when she and Billie were alone.

"But people need to know what's happening. This is where the bank's input is needed, not some Bingo game. Let's prepare..."

"Stop right there Angela Davis," Lydia whispered. "You're still on probation, so I advise you to keep a low profile. Plus, you don't want to get stuck in this department.

I'm five years from my social security, so it doesn't matter to me, but you're still young. When I came to the bank, they didn't have Black folks in officer positions. I've hung around and done okay, but things are different now. Racism continues to exist, and the good-ole-boy network is still alive, but there are more opportunities. This is a good place to get your foot in the door, then apply for a position in another department. This department is not the path for upward mobility. They stick us here to show a good face."

"Rather than trying to leave the department, we need to get them to elevate it. Doesn't the bank do better when communities are thriving?"

"Senior management doesn't give a hill of beans about this department. It's not seen as a profit center. We're here so they can check a box for the examiners."

"Maybe we're here so we can make a difference."

"You're not listening," Lydia said, shaking her head. "Do what you want. I'm not getting involved in any political stuff. I'm not trying to make waves."

"Clean water and sanitary bathrooms for children shouldn't be political. They don't care because they don't live here. But you and I have a vested interest in making Calderville better."

"The only vesting I'm trying to do is in my retirement account. You're on your own."

CHAPTER 11

The worst part about living in the trailer wasn't the lack of space or privacy but going to the laundromat, something she hadn't done since college. Billie had never had an official "wash day." She washed a load or two when she had time, or when a pile started to form. Now she had to plan her washing. There were a few washing machines and dryers in the Lakewood Terrace community room, but they were either being used, didn't work, or some creepy looking guy was there whenever she went to wash. Lovey said to bring their laundry to her house, but that meant Billie would have to sit around and talk or watch the stories and judge shows with Lovey, Uncle Amos, or whoever happened to stop by. What was usually an effortless task could turn into an all-day chore. So, she usually took her computer and worked while at the laundromat. She didn't like putting her clothes on tables that other people's germs had inhabited, but it was the best of the three options.

She had gone to the laundromat around ten o'clock so she could be finished and back home for her one o'clock Zoom meeting. But the change machine wasn't working, and she only had enough exact change to do two loads. So, after washing and folding two loads, Billie left. *I'll try again tomorrow*, she thought.

They were sharing a bathroom, didn't have a dishwasher, and Wi-Fi was undependable. But whenever she felt discouraged about the cramped trailer, and leaving Dylan, she'd take a ride out to Rossbrooke Estates. The development looked like a construction zone with mounds of dirt, dozers, and dump trailers. The cold weather had put the builder behind, but the project manager assured them they would work to make up lost time and the house should still be complete within six months. This timeline would have them moving at the start of the next semester. The first few times she drove by herself, she got lost because the reception was spotty, and her GPS didn't work. *I find my way around the Bay Area, surely, I can maneuver around this little town,* she thought. But now she knew the way and had even found a shortcut.

As she drove slowly, admiring the houses already completed, she noticed blue lights in her rear-view mirror. She pulled over to let the police car pass, but to her surprise, the car pulled over behind her. *What in the world could he be stopping me for?* she thought.

As the officer approached the car, she let her window down. "Good afternoon," he said. "Your license and registration please."

"Why are you stopping me?" she asked, while handing him her driver's license.

"I'll ask the questions," the officer replied.

"By law, you must state the reason you're stopping me before asking any questions. I really shouldn't even have given you my license," Billie said, squinting her eyes to read his badge. "Officer Robert Walls, I'm going to..."

"What are you doing around here? I see you have a California license."

"You still haven't told me the purpose of this stop," Billie said.

"For one thing, you changed lanes without signaling. Also, it looked like you weren't wearing your seatbelt."

"There's no one else out here, so I guess I forgot about my turn signal, and I always wear my seatbelt. Now that you see I have it on, can I go?"

"You seem very irritated, ma'am."

"You are very irritating," Billie said, as she grabbed her phone.

"Keep your hands where I can see them."

"This is ridiculous and you are being recorded."

"Get out of the car."

"I don't have to get out."

The trooper pulled on the door handle. "Step out of the car."

"You don't have the right to do that."

"Step out or I'll remove you."

"Remove me? I wish you would put your hands on me. I'll own this backward town," Billie said as she called Cole.

"I'm giving you a lawful order. Get out of the car now." The officer then reached into the car and stated, "I'm going to drag you out of here by that stringy crap on your head if you don't comply."

"Don't touch me. You don't have the right to touch me," Billie shouted.

"You are under arrest. You can get out on your own, or I can make you get out," he said as he pulled out a taser.

"Are you serious?" Billie said, shaking her head. "What are you arresting me for?"

"Get out of the car! Get out of the car now!"

"All right, all right," Billie said as she opened her car door. "Are you giving me a ticket?"

"I told you; I'll ask the questions."

"Wow. Wow. This is crazy."

"Get over there!" he said, pointing to the side of the road. "And get off the phone."

She laid her phone on the ground, and he walked back to his car. As she stood for what seemed like hours, sweat beads rolled down her cleavage. He dumped her laundry baskets on the ground and rifled through their clean folded clothes. A few drivers slowed as they passed, probably wondering what was going on, just as Billie was. Her phone rang, but she didn't dare move to answer it. What had seemed like hours was twenty minutes. A few more cars had driven by, then a gray pickup truck parked behind Billie's car. She'd never been so happy to see her brother-in-law. "Can you believe this shit-show?" she said to Cole.

"Hush," Monroe said as he walked to the police car. "Hey Rob. What's going on?" About five minutes later the police officer drove off. "Let's go," Monroe said, handing her license to her.

"What the hell just happened?" Billie asked.

"Rob can be a little overzealous."

"You know him? I want to report that jerk for an unlawful stop," Billie said while retrieving their laundry from the side of the road.

"Report him to who?" Monroe asked.

"That was a pretextual stop. That's illegal."

"Honey, it's illegal in California," Cole said. "I doubt if they have that law here."

"So we do nothing?" Billie asked.

"For now, let's get out of here," Monroe said. "We heard you on your phone. You could've been more agreeable."

"I told you to change your license as soon as we moved here," Cole said.

"So now this is my fault. I don't care what address was on my license. That does not give him the right to..."

"You know better than to argue about the right and wrong of it. We had 'the talk' with Dylan, I guess I need to have 'the talk' with you," Cole said.

"Why? He was wrong. I've never been so disrespected in my life. In Califor..."

Monroe shook his head and said, "This is not California, and the sooner you realize that, the better things will be."

CHAPTER 12

The city council meeting was starting in five minutes, and Billie put her phone on silent. She had practiced her presentation and knew most of it by heart. Sunrise had a standard presentation, but she revised and customized it for Calderville. Management wanted her to promote Sunrise's small business loan and construction loan products. She also planned to highlight their programs to assist low-income residents with home repairs, and down payment assistance. This was her first time presenting on her own. Lydia was present, but Billie was the only one on the program.

The first sign that this wasn't going to go well was when she overheard Councilman Barnes jokingly say he thought 'Billie' would be a man. Then she learned her talk was limited to four minutes, plus three minutes for questions and answers. She was originally told she had ten minutes, and her prepared presentation was ten minutes. She had been told a screen would be available. She arrived early to be sure she could work the equipment, but the screen wouldn't come down. Then she noted she was last on a long agenda.

The long agenda gave her time to revise her talking points as she sat through ninety minutes of committee reports about everything from zoning to animal welfare. The school water situation seemed more critical, but it wasn't even mentioned.

She managed to distill the key points of her presentation within her allotted time, thanked the small audience for their attention, and passed out business cards. When Fred Ramsey, the chairman, asked for questions, she was surprised when hands went up.

"My name is Adrian Butler and I'm Vice President of Ross County NAACP. President Douglas sends his regrets."

That's the medical transport guy again. How many jobs does he have? Billie thought.

"Your words sound good, but the fact is, Sunrise has treated this community like discarded toilet paper. How can Sunrise claim to provide development opportunities, when you closed the downtown and west side branch? The only one left is outside city limits and it's more difficult for older residents and those without transportation to get to. And my second question is…"

"Mr. Butler, you're only allowed one question. You may answer now, Miss Jordan."

Billie felt like she had been set up and wanted to blink her eyes and vanish like Samantha on *Bewitched*. She knew there had been closings, but not that they had adversely impacted lower-income residents. She managed to give the company response about community commitment, but even she knew they were hollow words.

The next question came from an older man in a clerical collar, with a salt and pepper afro and a conspicuous gold tooth.

"Yes, Reverend Collins," the chairman said.

"Miss Jordan, are you familiar with the Golden Rule?"

She hesitated, wondering if this was a trick question.

He answered, "Do unto others as you would have them do unto you. So I ask, would you want your water to be polluted, and your land made worthless?"

Billie wanted to say he had surpassed his question limit but stood stoic out of respect for this older man and because she had no idea what he was talking about.

"Premier Paper has already polluted our wells and the expansion your bank is financing will further devastate Grove City. I know everyone must make a living, but I would rather dig ditches than to participate in this corrupt land-grab. How you people can sleep at night is beyond me. In the book of Proverbs, we are told, *Do not withhold good from those to whom it is due, when it is in your power to act.*"

"We appreciate your comments, Reverend Collins, but we need to move on," the chairman said. "Submit your concerns in writing and someone will get back to you."

Reverend Collins and four people stood, began singing *We Shall Overcome,* and walked out.

After the meeting was over, Billie said, "That was some real John Lewis drama. What was that about?"

"That guy has a little church over in Grove City," Lydia said. "He and some of his members usually show up at meetings, and he even manages to get on TV sometimes."

"What's the issue with their water? I know there's a history of boil notices, but..."

"He's a troublemaker and keeps folks stirred up so he can get donations."

Billie remembered when she had been the so-called troublemaker. "I'd like to speak with him to at least see what his concerns are."

"No," Lydia said, grabbing Billie's arm. "We're here to represent the bank. His concerns about water are nothing the bank can solve. Let's go, it's starting to rain."

As they walked out, Reverend Collins and his members were in the parking lot singing *We Shall Overcome,* with locked arms. Billie walked up to Reverend Collins and extended her hand, "We haven't officially met but I'd like to..."

"Save it lady. We both know the bank isn't interested in

what's going on down here. You're just the newest flunky sent here so they look good on paper. Don't waste our time," he said and turned away from Billie back toward his group.

"But sir, how can we help if you won't..." Lydia jerked her from behind and as Billie stumbled, she bumped into one of the protestors, who fell on the concrete.

"I'm so sorry," Billie said, as she reached down to help the moaning older woman. The protestors circled the woman and began singing *We Shall Not Be Moved*.

Lydia pulled Billie out of the circle. "Let's. Go."

"Listen to your sidekick and get your ass out of here," the youngest protestor said. "We should sue you and your racist bank."

So much for southern hospitality, Billie thought and followed Lydia across the parking lot.

"Congratulations," Lydia said and dropped a newspaper on the cubicle counter. "We made the front page, and one of Reverend Collins' members shared a post and it has over two thousand views. Didn't I warn you not to go messing with those people?"

"This picture looks like I pushed her down," Billie said.

"And I'm right next to you. The rain has my hair looking like Don King's."

"This headline is misleading, and none of the statements are correct."

"They're not going to let the truth get in the way of a good story," Lydia said.

"The good thing is they have cameras all around there. Anyone who is interested can see what really happened."

"These days, people don't care about the truth," Lydia said. "Maybe you'll listen to me from now on."

★ ★ ★

When she got home, Cole was sitting on the couch, and the newspaper was on the kitchen table. "You've seen the paper," Billie said, swatting it aside.

"Me and everyone else in town," he said. "I left work early because I got tired of people mentioning it to me. This article sounds different from the version you told me yesterday."

"I told you, I stumbled, bumped into her, and we fell like dominos. The article reads like I attacked her, and the picture makes me look like a maniac pushing a little old church lady. Too bad they didn't have a microphone. That sweet old lady cussed me out and was using words I don't think are in the Bible."

"You're the one always saying pictures don't lie," Cole said. "The President wants to meet with me tomorrow to discuss what happened."

"That should be a short meeting," Billie said.

"You're used to forging ahead on anything you do, but things are more laid back here. I just need you to try a little harder to fit in and be a little less outspoken."

"I guess I should cut my hair and start saying y'all too," Billie said.

"You're overreacting," Cole said. "Lighten up."

"I tell you what, all y'all can kiss my grits," Billie said and went to the bedroom and slammed the door, causing the trailer to shake.

Cole sighed, rubbed his fingers across his temple, then went to the bedroom. "I'll make a deal with you," he said. "I won't ask you to fit in anymore, if you promise not to say, 'kiss my grits' ever again."

Like an inmate, Billie was marking off the days on her calendar until moving day. They were once again living in a packing zone. Anyone looking at the boxes and plastic totes lining the wall, would find it hard to believe they had only lived in the trailer a couple of months. They had managed in nine hundred square feet, but Billie was ready to occupy their new two thousand square feet house. After washing her hair, she went to the laundromat, then drove out to their house. The house next door already had sod laid down, and Pecan Lane was looking like a neighborhood and not a construction site. Seeing their house, reminded her that the trailer was temporary. She was grateful Monroe had arranged the trailer for them, but was ready to move.

Billie entered through the double doors and announced herself, getting a kick out of hearing her voice echo through the twenty-foot cathedral ceiling in the foyer. She loved walking through the house, picturing where their furniture would go, having arranged and rearranged it in her mind several times. In some rooms, she wanted new furniture but hadn't mentioned it to Cole. They were on a strict budget until they got Dylan's situation settled.

His counselors said he was making satisfactory progress. He was remorseful and hopeful for the future during their virtual family counseling sessions. She knew he was in the best place right now but couldn't wait for them to be together again. He had always liked visiting and playing with his Texas cousins. Perhaps he could even enroll at Calder State, since Cole would get a tuition discount.

After visiting their house, she went to the storage unit. Cole had told her about the open house for the newest campus building, and her boss asked her to represent the bank since she lived in town. She agreed, but he hadn't told her it was such a stylish affair. Billie would have worn the plain tan pantsuit she'd worn to work if she hadn't run into her sister-in-law, Joellen, during her lunch break, who was returning from Dallas, picking up a new designer dress for the open house.

She brought two clothes bags from their storage unit yesterday and had pulled together a decent ensemble. But her shoes weren't where she thought they were, and she made a last-minute trip to Walmart for sandals. Billie had done shows railing against Walmart and the negative impact they had on small businesses and wages. However, with Walmart the only game in town, other than Family Dollar, she had no choice.

Due to her last-minute shopping trip, they were running late. Then Cole had to take the long way around, because Main Street was flooded. "What happened?" Billie asked.

"Probably a water main break," Cole said. "Pipes over here are old, happens all the time."

"Then why don't they fix them?" Billie asked.

"I'm sure they never thought of that," Cole said dryly.

The program had already started, and Monroe was speaking as they walked in. "Thank you to the choir for leading us in the Calder State hymn. On behalf of the board of trustees, welcome. This three-story classroom complex will house our expanded engineering, cybersecurity, and robotics programs. We've had a ten percent enrollment increase for the fall term, and many incoming freshmen have expressed an interest in these majors. With our state-of-the-art facilities and strong corporate partnerships, such as Premier Paper Company and Sunrise Bank, we're confident these programs will provide students a solid foundation for the future and position Calder State toward even greater heights."

Even though she was a new resident and not an alum, she felt a connection through her association with the bank, and was proud to be part of an organization that was helping an HBCU. She didn't have the platform of her radio show but had found another way to build community.

Monroe made closing remarks, thanked everyone, then gave the mic to the alumni association treasurer who made an appeal for donations. *This is as bad as church*, Billie thought. She was surprised to see Cole take their checkbook from his pocket and write out a check. She didn't have her glasses on, and couldn't read the amount, but whatever it was, it was an amount they couldn't afford.

As several faculty and board members introduced themselves to Billie, Cole walked up with the alumni treasurer. "So, this is your wife? Pleased to meet you," the thick, cinnamon-colored woman, with smooth, permed hair said. "It's Billie, right? What is that short for?"

"Uhhhh, it's not a nickname," Billie replied with a furrowed brow.

"Honey, this is Serena Nash. We had a few classes together in college."

"That was until Coleman left us for the bright lights of California. What a full circle moment for you to be back at Calder State. We're glad to have you back and we appreciate the generous donation from you both."

Billie smiled and wondered, *just how generous have we been?*

"Coleman tells me you were a DJ. How exciting. We have a campus radio station. Would you be interested in speaking with our students?"

Billie was familiar with K100, the college station. Whenever they visited, she would listen and they usually had game play-by-play, depending on the sports season, smooth jazz, or rap. College stations were run by interns and faculty and provided real-world experience for students. "Sure, I was an intern myself and would love to speak to the students. Maybe I can even get the bank to be an underwriter."

"Great. Dr. Harland is the department head and he'll be pleased to have you. I'll give Coleman his information. Tell them I referred you."

"So, *Coleman*, how generous were we?" Billie asked as they were driving home, dragging out his name as she said it.

"I wrote a check for one thousand dollars."

"A thousand dollars? And you did it without checking with me? Do we have a pot of money I don't know about?"

"I know. I know. It's kind of like tithing. Department heads are expected to support the school."

"I don't want to hear anymore complaining about a budget. Looks like *Coleman* is more generous than the Cole I know."

"The teachers back then called me Coleman, so she did too."

"I see," Billie said, with raised eyebrows. "Did I just meet an old girlfriend?"

"Very old. Not that she's old," Cole stuttered. "You know what I mean. We dated for a short while, broke up, and I hadn't seen her until recently."

"Maybe I need to find Serena's secret. You wrote that check before she even finished talking, without a complaint or grumble."

"She runs the Calderville Public School finance department and has been a great treasurer. Alumni membership has increased by almost a third, and she's trying to double it. We'll be able to give more scholarships and increase our endowment. Serena is a real go-getter."

I wonder what else she's trying to go-get, Billie thought.

CHAPTER 13

"Babe, get up. We're going to be late. If we get there late, we'll have to sit on the front row."

"*You're* going to be late," Billie said as she turned over. "I told you I'm not going."

"Lovey is expecting us," Cole said.

"I have nothing against church, but I don't see why it has to last two hours. Numerous studies show no matter how interesting the topic, a listener's optimum attention span is ten minutes and twenty minutes is the maximum speech length. Last week the preacher talked for fifteen minutes, before he even introduced the title of his sermon. Besides, I'm sleepy. Did you hear that baby crying all night? By the time I fell asleep, the roosters started crowing and the baby began crying again. I hope everything's all right."

The trailers were barely ten feet apart, and you could smell what the neighbors were cooking, hear if they had an argument, and hear crying babies.

"I didn't hear a thing," Cole said as he yawned.

"Figures, you always slept soundly when Kendra and Dylan cried. It seems like yesterday they were babies, now they're both gone. I know we raised them to grow up and be independent, but it wasn't supposed to be like this. Kendra was supposed to go to college, and Dylan..."

"Don't go getting all melancholy. Kendra is doing great, and Dylan will find his way."

"I wish I could be as certain as you."

"We must have faith. I bet you'd feel better if you came to church with me."

"I see how you snuck that in there. I just don't feel like it today," Billie said.

Whenever they visited, it was understood that they'd attend church and Billie didn't mind. She wasn't a religious person but did believe in a higher power. Given the evil that had been done in God's name, from the crusades to slavery, Billie felt mankind had corrupted religion as a tool to control others. She knew church on Sunday was always a family affair, but now that she lived here, she didn't plan on making it part of their weekly routine.

"It's bad enough the choir stretches every two-verse song out to ten minutes, and they take up two collections and the preacher is long winded. But to sit there for two hours with that stained glass white Jesus is too much for me. I'm not a Bible scholar, but even I know the Bible does not describe Jesus as a white man. Plus, its's too hot. I know that's the church you grew up in, but my family spent Sunday mornings in the park or cleaning the house. I'm not doing this every week. We're not visitors. We need to establish our own routines."

"Church could be what's missing from our lives. I enjoy spending this time with my family and seeing so many famil-iar faces. It's like time has stood still and a return to a time before I had bills and a job."

"I'm happy you get to relive your childhood, but that doesn't mean I have to do it with you."

Billie dressed then pulled out oat milk and raisin bran

cereal. She had on her gospel jazz playlist, but the baby's crying distracted her. She grabbed her phone then went and knocked on her neighbor's door. They waved a few times in passing, and Cole had helped jump her car battery. Her young neighbor came to the door with the baby on her hip. "I couldn't help hearing the baby cry all night. Is there anything I can do to help?"

"She won't sleep longer than fifteen minutes. I've changed her, fed her, and walked her. When I checked her temperature, it was ninety-nine. The urgent care clinic isn't open on Sundays, but when I called the emergency number, they said not to be concerned unless it reached 102. I called my mother-in-law, and she said the baby is probably teething. She said she'll stop by after church. I don't know what else to do," she said, practically in tears.

"Do you have a stroller? Let's take her outside for a bit. It rained briefly last night and there's a nice breeze this morning. The movement and change of scenery will soothe her." Billie remembered nights trying to soothe Dylan. Then when he was quiet, she woke up in a panic, nervous because the baby had been so quiet.

"What's her name?"

"Jenna Willette. The 'Willette' is after her father, Will. He's in the Gulf working on an oil rig the next three weeks. My son, Willie, is with his grandparents this weekend. I was supposed to meet them at church. And my name is Shaun."

"I'm Billie. Nice to meet you."

Billie knew her way in and out of Lakewood Terrace, but had never walked the neighborhood. When Cole told her they'd be living in a trailer until their house was complete, she imagined the trailers along the highway outside of Stockton, where seasonal migrants were housed. They were old and crammed on top of each other. When he showed her pictures, she was more amenable to the idea, and it was hard to argue with free. The pictures showed nice trailers, but didn't show how close they were to each other. As they walked, she noticed most had patches of grass and some in the back even had chickens strutting around. A few ladies came outside to admire a now quiet Jenna, dressed in a frilly peach-colored dress with matching ruffled socks and a bonnet. "This is what I had planned for her to wear to church. She's growing so fast; I may as well get some use out of it."

As Billie and Shaun walked, she learned they had both followed their husbands to Calderville. Shaun and her husband met and lived in Houston, but when she became pregnant with their second child, he convinced her to move to his hometown where they would have help with the children, since her parents were both deceased and his parents and siblings lived in Calderville. His father was the pastor of Bethel Fellowship in Grove City and there were many friends, cousins, and church members they could call on for babysitting. Also, she could stay off work longer, since the trailer rent was less than half what they paid for their Houston apartment. They both liked yoga, and neither were Cowboys fans.

After forty-five minutes, they rounded a corner and were back on their street.

"You have my number now," Billie said. "Call me anytime. Sometimes we try to do things on our own, but I bet your in-laws, and their church members would love more visits with your little angel."

"It's hard right now. I'm potty-training Willie, but they have big time water issues on the west side, and it seems I have to start all over whenever he stays over there any length of time."

"I'm learning water is an ongoing issue in this county. That boil notice was a nuisance. Thank goodness it's over," Billie said.

"Let's hope so. I'm going inside, and hopefully she'll stay asleep. I don't know how to thank you," Shaun said. "You were a lifesaver."

Shaun would be Billie's lifesaver soon.

Billie and Cole sat in lawn chairs on the patch of grass next to their trailer, sipping sweet tea like an old country couple. Several people stopped to talk to Cole, who knew everyone. Other than Shaun, Billie hadn't done more than wave at her Lakewood Terrace neighbors. One new friend was Shaun's son Willie, who always had something to show Billie, from a picture he'd colored to a puzzle he put together. Billie suspected he was a little jealous of his baby sister. She felt closed in with just her and Cole in the trailer. She couldn't imagine the stress of such a tight space with two small children. He was good company, and very smart. She had helped him learn his Easter speech and she was touched when he invited her to church to come hear it. She had been so busy when her children were small, she barely remembered Dylan at this age.

"I know you're not into church, but it's a holiday. Everyone goes to church on Easter," Cole said when she told him she wouldn't be joining him.

"With everyone there, no one will miss me. Plus, Willie personally invited me."

"That's pretty dirty, using a cute kid against me," Cole said.

She had passed the Grove City sign numerous times, but today's trip to church would be her first visit to Grove City. After the parking lot outburst a few days ago, she'd done some research. Grove City was a former freedmen's town formed during the 1860s, as an oasis from daily discrimination and harsh treatment. As an unincorporated area, Grove City never had water or sewer lines, trash pickup, reliable ambulance and fire service or sufficient streetlights. The town survived on well water for over one hundred years and was a tight knit community. Many who grew up there said their well water tasted fresher than the water in Calderville. But that resource was now damaged and most blamed runoff from the nearby paper mill. Grove City became unlivable, property values plummeted, and younger residents moved away.

As Shaun maneuvered through the pothole-filled roads, Billie couldn't imagine why people were attached to the rundown village. It was a ten-block section hemmed in by railroad tracks on the east side, the freeway on the west, an old cotton mill on the north, and thick woods to the south. They pulled onto a gravel lot next to the church. There had been heavy rains all week and her heels sunk into the muddy grass as she made her way to the walkway. The white cinderblock building was well kept. Monkey grass on both sides of the walkway led to the front door of a sanctuary with a middle aisle, and ten pews on either side. It was early, but already warm and fans were strategically placed throughout the sanctuary. They stepped over several extension cords as they found a seat up front. The children's Easter program was during Sunday School. Only a few children needed coaxing, and Willie spoke loud and clear. Billie hadn't really looked around at the crowd, but when it was over, Shaun took her to meet the pastor.

"Daddy Will, this is my neighbor, Billie Jordan."

"You're kidding," Billie said.

"So, you've come to see how the other half lives," the pastor said, with a slight grin that flashed his gold eyetooth.

"You two know each other?"

Daddy Will was Reverend William Collins. "We've met."

★ ★ ★

After church, Billie went to Lovey's house. She had turned down the Collins' dinner invitation and was starving. The front yard was full of cars, so she parked on the street. As she was walking up the street, she met Serena, who was leaving. "Hello Billie. We missed you at church." She was wearing a lavender, sateen dress, carrying a to-go container, and looking like she had just done her make-up. "I promised a neighbor I'd go to her church today," Billie said. "Whatever you have in that container sure smells good."

"Miss Lovey is still one of the best cooks in town. I got a little of everything to take home, and I got a piece of my red velvet cake. I made it but didn't want to cut it at home."

Billie shifted her feet, feeling self-conscious about coming empty handed, but also because she had to use the restroom. She refused to use the Porta Pottis at the church. "That's one of Cole's favorite desserts. It was hard to find in Oakland."

"I know. Coleman ate two hunks when he came over the other day. It's my son's favorite too. He just left to go to the house and pack. He's headed back to Dallas, or I would stay longer," she said. "Maybe we'll see you at church next Sunday."

Billie gave a slight nod as Serena walked away, as she wondered why Cole would be at her house.

"Hey babe. How was the program?" Cole asked as she entered the house. Several family members were in the living room watching the game, and she felt a twinge of nostalgia. Back in Oakland, they spent most spring Sundays watching the Warriors. It was one of the few activities they did as a family as the kids got older. Since it wasn't the Warriors, she wasn't interested in the game and instead followed the sweet smells coming from the kitchen.

After eating yams that she knew contained a month's worth of sugar, garden fresh turnips and greens that melted in your mouth, and heavenly potato salad, Billie began nodding off. Rather than add her utensils to the overflowing sink, and to stay awake, she decided to clean the kitchen. She stretched, then turned the small kitchen TV to a Lifetime movie and began scraping plates. "I'll help you," Joellen said when she came inside to get a bottle of water. "How are you adjusting to our little town?" she asked.

"I miss California, but I'm getting used to it," Billie replied. "Cole loves being around family."

"Monroe is excited to have his little brother close," Joellen said. "Don't hesitate to call me if you need anything."

When they finished the dishes, Joellen said, "Let's take a selfie. You aren't in any of the pictures." Billie and Joellen leaned back and smiled as Joellen stretched out her arm to take the picture. "I'll send it to you."

Joellen sent all the pictures she had taken, and a clear pattern emerged. She sent pictures from church, in the backyard, and in the house. Any picture that Cole was in, Serena was next to him, and Billie was almost certain she saw claws.

CHAPTER 14

The weekend volunteer radio position was turning out to be more work than Billie had anticipated. She received a small stipend and could have declined the extra duties, but she enjoyed working with the students, knowing that she was once in their shoes. The department head assured her when homecoming was over, the workload would slack up, and they really appreciated her help. She'd attended several homecoming weekends with Cole, but now had a new appreciation for the work that went into making that event happen.

Calder State homecoming was Ross County's biggest event, and even though it was months away, hotels were already full as far as thirty miles away. She was busy preparing promotional ads, doing interviews and working with the sports announcers. She'd interviewed the college president, band director, president of the alumni association, and Ross County chamber of commerce president for public service commercials on area television stations. Due to her Oakland connections, she had been able to get the singer Keyshia Cole and rapper Starlight to perform at the Friday concert. She had interviewed Ms. Cole several times. Starlight was from Oakland and Maya had dated his uncle.

The laid-back Texas lifestyle she and Cole anticipated had not materialized. Cole stayed busy with his classes and fraternity activities, and, helping the baseball team—which was leading their division. Billie was getting accustomed to her Sunrise Bank position. She was putting in more than forty hours a week, but other than the countless meetings, she liked her job.

The volunteer radio position was consuming her non-work hours. She had encouraged the students to develop a call-in show. This would help them gauge their audience and gain experience for increasingly popular all-talk radio formats and podcasts. She told them about her show *Let's Talk About It*. They decided to call their show *Calder State Conversations*, and the call-in lights stayed lit during their first two shows which were about dating apps. She also shared ideas to generate more ad revenue.

She was learning her way around Calderville—the places and people. She was also learning to say 'no.' The station manager had texted her and asked her to follow up on a few phone calls. Billie left the text unanswered. Tonight, the Warriors were on TV playing an east coast team. They rarely got to see their team anymore, and she and Cole had plans to watch the basketball game.

On her way home, she swung by their house construction site. While the outside looked finished, it was only a shell. The contractor said they were waiting for materials. The house completion date had been extended due to supply chain issues related to port congestion, a labor shortage, and longer shipping times as ships navigated around warring middle eastern countries. These were the type of issues she used to report on as news director, but she was no longer on a twenty-four-hour news cycle. Billie didn't really care about labor issues and middle east conflicts; she just wanted her house finished.

When she got home, the trailer felt like a sauna. She

turned on the air conditioner, then went to change clothes. One thing about living in a trailer, it didn't take long to cool off the nine-hundred-square-foot space. One unexpected benefit of moving, they spent less money eating out. There were several fast-food places, but vegan options were limited. When they first moved, she had binged on vegetable plates at the two soul food restaurants in town. They served different specialties each day, from red beans and rice to cabbage salad, and both knew her by name. She was eating hot water cornbread like cookies, and fried green tomatoes like potato chips, and gained ten pounds. Cole had gained weight too, thanks to almost daily visits to Lovey's house. At eighty years old, she still cooked like she was feeding a houseful every day. Billie began cooking more at home and she and Cole planned to begin walking on the Calder State track but hadn't done it yet.

It was too hot to turn on the stove, so she planned to prepare salads, adding grilled chicken and boiled eggs to Cole's salad. He came in as she was washing fresh spinach. "Hey babe. Now that you're here I'll put garlic bread in the toaster oven, and we can eat in ten minutes."

"I'm headed to a frat meeting. I mentioned it this morning," he said as he grabbed a Dr Pepper from the refrigerator.

"Didn't you meet a couple days ago?" Billie asked.

"That was the graduate chapter, tonight's meeting is with the undergrads. I didn't know being an advisor would be this time-consuming."

"You should still eat something before you go," Billie said.

"I stopped by Lovey's and ate. I'm stuffed."

"Great," Billie said. "Let me know when you can squeeze me in your calendar."

"Now you're being petty," Cole said.

"Petty because I want to spend time with my husband.

Petty, because you got me down here in this backward village, living in a raggedy trailer while you run off with your buddies? This move was supposed to be good for us, but it looks like you're the only one benefitting."

"That's not true and you know it. In California I never begrudged your time with your mother, sister, college and high school friends. And we wouldn't have moved if you had been against it. This is different for you. You're homesick and I get it. Things will..."

"Don't patronize me. Go to your meeting."

"I won't take on anything else the rest of the week. I promise."

Billie dumped the spinach in the sink, went to their bedroom and slammed the door, shaking the trailer. When she heard Cole leave, she returned to the kitchen. Cole was right, but she couldn't help feeling left out.

She washed a small bowl of grapes, then sat and surfed through the channels. She heard a car drive up, looked out the window and saw Cole. She figured it was either the shortest meeting on record, or he had returned to keep her company. She rushed to the door and opened it before he could insert his key. She planted a soft kiss on his lips. "I'm so glad you came back," she said. "I'm sorry."

"I'm sorry too," Cole said. "I know living here hasn't been easy for you and I'm afraid it's about to get harder."

"Harder? What in the world are you talking about?" Billie asked as Cole closed the screen door behind him.

"Ross County Water Works just issued a boil notice. Monroe called me. I'm surprised you didn't get a notice from the radio station."

Billie dug her phone out of her purse, then said, "You're right. I have five missed calls and a string of text messages. My phone was still on silent from my meeting earlier today. And I just washed this spinach and grapes. I guess I'll have to throw them away."

"I'm going to go stock up on bottled water before everyone runs out," Cole said.

"And I'm going to the radio station to see what they need me to do," Billie said as she put on her sandals. "We had the boil notice during the spring freeze, but nothing like that is going on now. I wonder what happened."

"Monroe said some samples identified E. coli. This happens when the reservoir overflows. They've already started treating it and the notice shouldn't be very long this time."

"This time?" Billie asked.

CHAPTER 15

The Calderville Chronicle
News For You Since 1922

A Sunday morning power outage at a treatment plant caused water pressure to fall below the level required by the Texas Commission on Environmental Quality. The plant is operating on generators and working to restore full service. Officials from Ross County Water Works believe the water is safe but per regulation, any time water pressure drops below 20 psi, a precautionary boil water advisory is required. Symptoms of water borne illness can include diarrhea, nausea, vomiting, cramps and fever. Infants, children, the elderly and those with compromised immune systems or chronic illness are most at risk.

When Billie entered the radio station, there was no hint of impending disaster. Marcus, the student production manager, waved from the broadcast booth. "I didn't expect to see you today," he said.

"I heard about the boil notice, and came to see if there was anything I can do."

"We've been through this before and everything is under control. A campus-wide alert has been texted to students and distribution of bottled water and hand sanitizer has already begun."

"What about people off campus? We have a lot of older residents who don't get emails or texts, and by the time they get the next *Chronicle*, the advisory will be old news. We should play an announcement on the station. I'll pull something together."

Billie turned on the computer and pulled a more detailed boil notice announcement, changed the date, and programmed it to run every ten minutes. Residents were advised to wash dishes in boiled water or use paper plates. Only fruits and vegetables washed with boiled or bottled water were to be eaten. They could flush toilets, wash hands and bathe as usual if they didn't swallow water. They were to brush teeth only with boiled or bottled water. They could cook with tap water if the food had been boiled at least one minute. This was handy advice, but most students didn't have a way to boil water. Some kept electric hot plates and microwaves in their room, although they weren't supposed to.

As she checked the announcement archive, she was amazed to learn how frequently boil notices were issued. Low water pressure meant no air conditioning, no working toilets or water fountains, and the last two weeks of class were virtual. She learned the treatment plant had been in disrepair for years and many pipes leaked constantly. She emailed copies of a couple of the announcements to Cole, then answered a few emails. Marcus emerged from the booth and asked, "Shouldn't I get Dr. Harland to approve this?"

"I copied him on the email. I'm surprised he's not here. This is a major disruption, but everyone seems so non-chalant."

"This isn't new, but my guess is things will get fixed quickly. With graduation in a few weeks, they can't afford for the campus to be in disarray. Viola Davis is the commencement speaker, and the auditorium will be packed."

"That's like people who only clean for company. What about those who are here every day?"

"You're preaching to the choir. Not much we can do about it though."

"This is going to be the next topic on *Calder State Conversations.*"

"Unless you're sharing information, Dr. Harland won't approve anything related to the water issues. The trustees don't want to advertise our problems. That hurts donations and recruitment," Marcus said.

"This situation would never be tolerated at Texas Tech, or Sam Houston State. We're not going to get anywhere keeping quiet."

"I know you mean well, but that's just the way it is around here."

"Oh yeah?" Billie asked as she grabbed her keys. "We'll see about that."

It was day four of the boil notice, and Billie's daily routine included getting up thirty minutes earlier than usual to boil three large pots of water. She used buckets of tap water to flush the toilet and hand sanitizer to clean her hands. Thanks to Monroe, they had cases of bottled water, and jugs of boiled water lined the walls. She used bottled water to brush her teeth. Then she poured the just boiled water in the tub with two jugs of boiled water, so she could wash up. This routine was time-consuming, so Cole bathed at night, and she bathed in the morning.

"This reminds me of bathing in a number three washtub when I was a kid," he said.

"What the heck is that?" Billie asked.

Cole shook his head and smiled. "You are such a city girl."

"Then what am I doing in this wilderness?" she asked.

The saying, *you don't miss your water until your well runs dry* had a new meaning for Billie. They had a clothesline across the second bedroom to hang dry a few things she hand washed. It was a hassle to wash dishes, so they were relying on paper plates and plastic utensils. She had even started drinking some of Cole's sickly sweet Dr Peppers, so they wouldn't use up their bottled water. Billie hated that they were generating so much waste. But she tried to keep a positive attitude, since others had an even heavier burden. Shaun and other of her Lakewood Terrace neighbors had young children to cook for, dress, and keep clean.

Young children are a lot of work, but at least you know where they are, she thought. Dylan's calls were more infrequent, and his location tracker was off. Cole kept saying no news was good news. Billie hoped he was right.

The line for water was around the block. Sunrise was one of the companies providing bottled water, water filters, body wipes, buckets, and bleach, and they asked her to participate in the distribution. Billie selected the first shift. This was the coolest time of the day, if eighty degrees and high humidity can be called cool. The idling car engines also added a few degrees. Distribution started at eight o'clock, but cars were already lined up around the block at daybreak. There was even an elderly lady in line with a wagon. Billie's shift was supposed to last until 11:00 AM, but they always ran out of water within two hours. She was only working a few hours a day but was exhausted by the time her shift was over. She thought of her ancestors who planted, picked, and chopped cotton, tobacco, and sugar cane. *How in the world did they endure,* she often wondered.

The boil notice was lifted in Lakewood Terrace after five days, eight days on the west side of town. Classes had been virtual for the week, and some students received vouchers to

stay at area hotels. As Marcus said, this was not a new occur-
rence, and once water was restored, things quickly went
back to normal. But Billie remained in investigation mode.

She had been consumed by her water research. The water
treatment plant had been constructed in the 1960s, and the
pipes were part of a larger, deteriorating underground infrastructure. Newer parts of the county like Rossbrooke Estates
had new pipes and its own water tower. State senators had
unanimously approved legislation to create a billion-dollar
water supply fund to pay for upgrades to water infrastructure.
Legislators disagreed on details of the proposal, and it kept
getting pushed aside for "priorities," like banning books and
eliminating diversity, equity, and inclusion programs. Ross
County Water Works was impotent, and the more she learned
the more indignant she became. The more she shared her
findings with Cole, the more frustrated she became at his
lack of interest. "The boil notice is over. Let it go," he said.

"It's not over, they've merely put a band aid on it," Billie
replied.

She had waited to do the show until she was more
familiar with the water situation. She didn't want it to be an
emotional rant. The Ross County NAACP president and a
doctor from Dallas were her guests, and she and Marcus
asked the questions. There was no way to gauge ratings, but
based on student reaction, she knew the show had reached a
large audience.

Driving home, she was reminded of the feeling she had
after some of her KBLK shows. Doing things that made a
difference, made up for the relationship drama silliness she'd
had to do. "Cole did you hear the show?" she asked as soon
as she walked in the trailer. "We had a great response. The
phone lines stayed lit."

"I heard the show. You do know I work for those, what
did you call them—handkerchief head Negroes."

"Other public colleges have their own water systems.

Calder State trustees should demand the same. Portable toilets and showers and prepackaged meals should not be part of the college experience."

"A lot goes into running and sustaining an institution like Calder State," Cole said. "I'm sure the trustees are doing their best."

"If this is their best, we're in trouble. Anyway, it's Saturday morning. They probably weren't even listening," Billie said, while looking in the refrigerator. "I'm hungry." As she washed lettuce and cherry tomatoes from Lovey's garden for a salad, they heard a knock on the door.

"How're you doing?" Billie asked as Monroe came in.

"I've been better," he replied.

"I hate to add to your load, but I was going to call you," Billie said. "There's a small leak in the second bedroom."

"You are my load. I heard the show this morning. What were you thinking?"

"I was hoping we'd start a conversation to get something done about the water situation."

"You are milking the bull if you think you're going to show up with your braids and black power shirts and miraculously change things around here," Monroe said.

"I don't know anything about milking a bull, but aren't we supposed to be encouraging young people to challenge inequities and make things better? An HBCU would be the last place I expected to find complacency and apathy."

"What you label complacency and apathy, I call pragmatic. Talk is cheap. Until you have to meet a multi-million-dollar budget and capital campaign you're just blowing hot air. The trustees know you're family and asked me to speak with you. You need to back off."

"I will not."

"You are so hard-headed. Can't you control your woman, baby bro?" Monroe said, while turning to Cole.

"Who do you think you're talking to? I'm not a child who needs to be controlled."

"I'm not going to argue with you," Monroe said as he walked toward the door. "Your services are no longer needed. Cole can turn in your campus ID."

"I cannot believe you let him talk to me like that," Billie said, after he came back inside from talking with his brother.

"It's hard to defend you when you're being unreasonable."

"Wanting to take care of the young people parents have entrusted to..."

"You can get off your soapbox. We all agree, this is a bad situation but insulting and accusing school administrators who have devoted their careers to Calder State, especially in public, doesn't solve anything."

"Other than Jesus Christ, you're supposed to be on my side."

"I thought you said you were working too many hours anyway."

"That's not the point."

"It's done now. Let's just move on," Cole said.

Billie didn't say anything but had no intention of moving on.

CHAPTER 16

Billie and Cole were meeting with the contractor to pick a different backsplash and kitchen tile since their original choices were out of stock and would take ten weeks to arrive.

After picking the tile, they viewed the back yard. The spot for the pool had been marked off and dug up. "Dylan is going to love this," Billie said.

"When I was a kid, the Westside YMCA had the only pool in our neighborhood. Only rich white folks had a pool. I never dreamed I'd have one at my house," Cole said. "I also never dreamed I'd have such a smart, pretty wife."

"If you're trying to butter me up, it's working," Billie said, with a smile.

"Good," he said. "I don't have classes this afternoon, and I think we have some making up to do."

"Why Professor," Billie said in an exaggerated southern accent. "Are you—oh my God," she hollered. "Cole, what is all this?" she said jumping around and swatting her leg. She had stepped in a bed of fire ants.

Cole brushed off her legs then said, "Baby, let's get out of here." She pulled off her sandals and pants, ran to the car and poured bottled water on her legs.

"I'll stop at the drug store and get alcohol."

"What the hell kind of ants are these? My legs are throbbing and feel like they're on fire."

"I'll go to Lovey's instead of the store. She'll have what we need." They ran into a water main break on Seventh Street, with water gushing thirty feet in the air, and Cole had to turn around. By the time they got to the house, Billie was covered with red welts. Lovey wiped Billie's legs with cold ammonia compresses and gave her Benadryl. After an hour, she threw up, and her neck was swelling.

"Some folks are allergic to fire ants," Lovey said. "She's got hives. This girl needs to see a doctor."

Cole pulled off Billie's t-shirt and dressed her in one of Lovey's house dresses, then took her to the urgent care office, but it had a ninety-minute wait and Billie seemed to be fading by the minute. She was groaning and couldn't hold her head up. He called his brother to get them a sheriff escort to Ross County General Hospital. It turned out Billie was part of the three percent of the population with a severe fire ant allergy.

Billie scanned the receipt and diagnosis from her emergency room visit and forwarded it to the HR department. She had missed four workdays. She appreciated their understanding, but did feel slightly irritated and disrespected. The radio station never required documentation for sick leave. If you said you were sick, you were sick.

She was trying to fit in, but even the insects were conspiring against her.

CHAPTER 17

"Y ou've been so helpful these past weeks. Will and I want you to come to Jenna's baptism," Shaun said, as she returned the book she had borrowed.

"At Reverend Collins' church? I don't think so. As you Texans say—we don't set horses too well," Billie replied.

"My father-in-law is passionate about Grove City. Don't take it personally."

"If you think it would be all right, I'd be honored to attend."

Despite not being a religious person, Billie was moved by the service. Mrs. Collins played the piano and had the six-person choir rocking. Reverend Collins knew everyone by name and mixed just enough humor, fire, and brimstone to hold her attention. They hadn't baptized Dylan or Kendra, and she could probably count the number of times they'd taken them to church. They did teach them right from wrong and the golden rule. She wondered if things would have turned out differently if they had been church-goers. But she knew from her radio show that church people had as many, if not more, issues than those who didn't attend church. Still, she admired the peace these people seemed to have.

"Miss Billie, we're having dinner at our house," Reverend Collins said, after service. "You're coming, aren't you?"

"Of course she is," Mrs. Collins said, grabbing Billie's hand. "This is a joyful day. It's not burning up hot and we have plenty of food."

Billie thought of the left-over spinach wrap she had waiting for her. Cole was likely already at Lovey's house. She'd told him she would stop by on her way home if she got out of church before he did. "You can at least come get a to-go plate," Mrs. Collins said. "We're not taking 'no' for an answer. We really appreciate you helping our little Willie."

"It was my pleasure. My children grew so fast, I don't even remember them at that age."

"Yes, we often forget to be thankful and enjoy the gifts God has given us, and children are a gift."

"Do you have a few minutes?" Reverend Collins asked. "I need to go across the street to Mrs. Green's house to give her communion. She's in a wheelchair and can't always get to church. Then I'm going to take you on a tour."

"Dad, she's not interested in seeing a bunch of overgrown lots and empty houses," Will said.

"She doesn't mind, do you?"

Billie really wasn't interested but figured it couldn't hurt. *Maybe I'll see something that Sunrise can do*, she thought.

Reverend Collins began the tour before they even left the parking lot. "My grandfather was pastor when that cornerstone was placed in 1950, when the men of the church built this brick building. The cemetery behind the church has headstones of formerly enslaved persons, and many of our members can trace their families here. Have you heard of Monty Wells?"

"The football player? Of course. He was on the Raiders championship team when they were in the AFL. I interviewed him and a few other older players."

"That was his mother's house over there."

"He's from here?"

"Born and raised. When he got his contract, he moved his mother to California. Sometimes they come back for Family and Friends Day. He gave a lot of money to Calder State and paid for our first paved basketball court," Reverend Collins said, pointing to a rusty, leaning basketball goal with a few strings hanging from the rim in an overgrown lot. "At one time, there were four churches here. We're the only one left. We had a pool hall, ten-cent store, and a couple juke joints. We didn't get street signs or emergency services until the 1980's. Some may have considered us a backward settlement, but we were self-sufficient and content. We didn't bother anyone, and no one bothered us. Around 1970, Premier Paper Company opened. My father was one of the first Black men to work out there, and I joined him as soon as I graduated from high school. It was good money, but not long after I started working there private wells around here had brownish water with a metallic odor. We boiled it, added a drop of bleach, and kept on with our daily lives.

"I worked at PPC for three years, but I thought there was more for me, and moved my family to Houston, only to be wiped out by Hurricane Alicia. So, I came back and moved to town, that's what we called Calderville, only to have different water issues. I've taken that as a sign the Lord wants me to help his people with water, literally, and also figuratively, since water in the Bible represents salvation and renewal."

For ninety minutes, Reverend Collins immersed Billie in the history of Grove City. Billie now knew that Morgan Street, was named after Earl Morgan, the first pastor of Bethel Fellowship Baptist Church. The majestic magnolia trees along Lincoln Street are what's left of the thick groves that the city was named for. The overgrown lots, old, rusted cars, and abandoned, corrugated tin roof buildings, were remnants of families' lives, and she understood why many wanted to hold on to their families' land. She had come for the baby's baptism—a symbol of renewal, but she was the one who had been converted.

CHAPTER 18

The quarterly Water Works board meeting was held at the county courthouse at three o'clock in the afternoon. The courthouse was the centerpiece of the town square and the imposing white building with columns and flared staircase that resembled a facade from the Gone with the Wind movie set. A statue of Hugo Calder greeted visitors to the building. The historical marker praised the founder's courageous trek from Alabama and perseverance to build a town in what at the time was wilderness. The marker didn't mention the twenty-five slaves he brought with him who actually did the cutting, clearing, planting, and harvesting that birthed the town. Nor did it mention the indigenous Caddo people who were already in the area and forced to move to a reservation in Oklahoma. Billie thought of the rallies she had participated in, protesting monuments that negatively depicted Native Americans and glorified Confederate soldiers and slave owners. America's biased history irritated Billie, but that was a cause for another day.

During the campus radio show, Billie and Marcus urged residents to become more involved with the Water Works board on an ongoing basis, and today she was practicing what she preached. Marcus had planned to meet her at the meeting, but with finals coming, said he really needed to study and would join her next time. The agenda had been posted on the website and citizens were allowed to ask questions at the end of the meeting, but had to be present from the meeting's start and signed in. She was required to give her address and driver's license information or water bill account number. She signed in as a representative of Sunrise Bank and Trust. Maybe there was government funding or other programs the bank could help the city access. An older couple were the only two other observers at the meeting. She had expected to see more, but shouldn't have been surprised. Back in Oakland, if an issue was in the news, school board, city council, and county board of supervisors' meetings were standing room only. However, it was difficult to sustain interest. But at least those meetings were in the evening at a time more accessible to working people.

When the members came in, she was surprised to see her sister-in-law. Billie knew her as Joellen Jordan, so seeing the name Joellen Barnes on the list didn't register. The meeting opened with prayer. They spent ten minutes approving corrections to the previous minutes, then reviewed new contracts, new hires, heard an engineering report, and after forty-five minutes, took a break that was supposed to be fifteen minutes, but ended up being closer to thirty. During the break, Joellen came to Billie's chair. "Hey there. I'm surprised to see you here. I can think of more interesting things to do than attend a Water Works meeting."

"I'm doing research for a bank customer. I didn't know you were on the board."

"I use my maiden name for business dealings. Let me know what you're looking for. Maybe I can help and save you from attending these boring meetings," Joellen said.

When they finally reconvened, the chairman, Fred Ramsey, mentioned a three-sentence audit summary, discussed a possible rate hike, then asked if there were questions or concerns from the guests. The older man sitting in front of Billie went to the microphone and said, "I've had problems ever since you changed the billing system, and installed them dumb, smart meters. My last bill was over five hundred dollars, obviously an error. When I called, I was told someone would come look at my meter, but until then I had to pay the bill, or my water would be cut off. I'm on a fixed income and don't have a spare five hundred dollars lying around. I've called numerous times and been told someone would come to look at my meter, but no one has come."

"I'm sorry to hear that. We will ensure someone gets in touch with you. Here is my personal cell phone number," Chairman Ramsey said as he handed the older gentleman a business card. "If it doesn't get resolved, call me directly. We have no other speaking requests, so we will adjourn."

"Wait! Wait," Billie stated and stood. "I signed in to address the board. Billie Jordan, my name should be on the list."

Chairman Ramsey scanned the list then said, "Speaking opportunities are only open to county residents."

"I am a resident. My address is listed on the form. Joellen, I mean Ms. Barnes, is my sister-in-law. She can vouch for me."

"Your driver's license didn't match the address, so we'll have to verify your residency. Assuming everything checks out, you're more than welcome to address our next meeting." He picked up his gavel and adjourned the meeting.

Billie was washing breakfast dishes and clearing the table so she could work from home. She saw her brother-in-law park his pickup in her carport and went to the door. "Cole's not here," she said through the screen door.

"I know. I came to see you," Monroe said and walked inside. "I hear you went to the Water Works meeting yesterday."

"News travels fast in this town."

"The Water Works board is terribly busy. Whatever

your concerns are, I'm sure they're already working on it. You badgering them will only slow them down. We may not have the fancy restaurants and tall buildings you had out there in Frisco, but we take care of each other."

Billie was still cringing from him calling Oakland, Frisco. Her hometown was always in San Francisco's shadow, even though it was a great city in its own right. And only old people and rappers called it Frisco. "It took them forever to restore water to everyone. I don't see how they could be any slower."

"You're new around here, so let me make it plain for you—don't go sticking your nose where it doesn't belong. I'd appreciate it if you stuck to your job and let other people do theirs."

Monroe's visit had the opposite of his intended impact. Billie became even more determined to continue her probe of Ross County Water Works. She handled her Sunrise business, but instead of breaking for lunch, she did a Google search on each board member, current and the prior ten years. She also researched current and former contract awardees. Remembering her news director skills, she tried a LexisNexis search. To her surprise, she still had access. LexisNexis had been her go-to when looking to verify or supplement news stories. They had the largest database of legal and public records related information.

Billie canceled her afternoon appointments, so she could keep searching before her username was revoked. She hurriedly put a casserole and sweet potatoes in the oven, returned a few phone calls, then got back to her search. The database was a good source for potential customers, and she learned of organizations and companies that she didn't know had local ties. One surprising discovery was that Ross County Rentals, the company that had the portable restroom contract with the school district and Calder State, had the same mailing address as MJ Rentals, the company that owned

Lakewood Terrace. She cross-checked those names on the Sunrise system and realized they were all owned by her brother-in-law.

Billie saved as many pages as she could since she didn't have a printer. It was a tedious process and took longer than she'd planned. She smelled something burning and realized her dinner was ruined. She opened the oven and smoke filled the trailer. Her dinner wasn't the only thing heating up.

Section III

Like Oil and Water

CHAPTER 19

Late mornings in Lakewood Terrace were Billie's favorite time of day. The early morning hustle of folks going to work had passed and it was before the heat of the day and the nonstop whining of window air conditioners. She was working remotely, something she'd never been able to do while working at the radio station. She loved the flexibility, but it also meant she snacked all day. There was a lot of open country around, but no sidewalks, and she hadn't gotten back into her exercise routine, and it was showing. She resisted the urge to eat another apple muffin and settled for a peach. She had intended to work out before breakfast, but Cole had another type of workout in mind, and thankfully her fibroids hadn't bothered her at all. She had gotten her herbalist to ship her some dandelion root from Oakland.

With no extra bedrooms or dining area to serve as an office, the kitchen was also Billie's workspace, and she tried to keep the dishes washed. She had washed more dishes this year than she had in years, and it was wreaking havoc on her nails. In Oakland, they always used the dishwasher, and when there weren't enough dishes, one of the kids became the dishwasher.

Good Morning America was going off and she was ready to

start her workday, when she saw her brother-in-law drive up and park in front of her door.

"As you can see, Cole's truck isn't here, so that means you came to see me," Billie said through the screen door, while wiping her hands on a dish towel.

"To what do I owe this honor?"

"You don't like me very much, do you?" Monroe said.

"Some things don't need to be said," Billie replied.

"I won't be long," Monroe said and walked inside. "Apparently you've gotten some of the students stirred up and they're still doing stories about the water, even though it's been resolved."

"Resolved for how long?" Billie asked. "My water still smells funny, and there are still schools without adequate bathrooms. If we keep it in the news, we can make changes."

"Changes are being made. Just because you aren't privy to all that's going on, you shouldn't assume people aren't working on the issue."

"Then share that news. Students want to know that something is being done."

"We've gotten good exposure from our baseball team and are expecting the largest incoming freshman class ever," Monroe said. "We've been working on all this a long time. Now because you've stirred up some radical kids, parents may reconsider their decision to send their children here."

"If the water is bad, they should."

"The water is fine."

"Is that why you have a filtration system at your house?"

"You are so self-righteous. I don't see how my brother stands it."

"And you are so hypocritical, I don't see how Cole..."

"This isn't getting us anywhere," Monroe said, with a dismissive hand. "Here's the bottom line, you need to come on the radio to clarify a few things and help put a positive spin on the administration's actions."

"I'm not going to take back anything I said. Besides, you fired me, remember?"

"If it was up to me, you'd stay fired. But Dr. Harland wants you to come back. Do a few shows with a balanced view, that's all we're asking. I shouldn't say asking, because we're going to do them with or without you. It will look better if you're involved, and it will be more beneficial for Cole."

"How so?" she asked with a raised eyebrow.

"To use your words, some things don't need to be said."

CHAPTER 20

"The baseball regionals are in Orlando next weekend. This will be Calder State's first ever invitation," Cole said.

"Is that your way of telling me you'll be out of town next weekend?" Billie asked.

"Some coaches are bringing their wives and kids and making it a vacation. You should come with me."

"Orlando wouldn't be fun without the kids."

Every year she and Cole had taken the kids on a big trip. They had visited about half of the continental United States, been to Toronto, Jamaica, Brazil, and two Disney cruises. Their next big trip was supposed to have been to the Olympics, but COVID-19 changed their plans. Even though most things went back to "normal" after the pandemic, their family didn't.

"With Kendra and Dylan gone, we need to reinvent ourselves as a couple. What did we do before we had kids?" Cole asked.

"We didn't have any money to go anywhere, but we didn't need it. In California we were a short ride from the beach, or the mountains."

"Let's take a quick vacation when I get back. How about a trip to the beach?"

"That would be great. I miss seeing the ocean," Billie said, with a glint in her eyes. "I'll check for cheap last-minute flights, then let Maya know."

"Not to California," Cole said. "I thought we could drive down to Padre Island."

"Texas?" Billie said, with a wrinkled nose.

"Yes. Texas has beautiful beaches. It's about a six-hour drive. That's less time than we would spend getting to the airport, through security and in flight. And it's cheaper. Just wait. You're going to be swept off your feet."

Truer words had never been spoken.

CHAPTER 21

Everyone said this May was one of the wettest on record, and the reservoir was on the verge of overflowing again. The Water Works board issued a boil water advisory as a precautionary measure to alert customers there was a potential for compromised water quality. No contaminants had been found, but they were still making bottled water available. There were four bottled water distribution centers in Ross County.

Today's site had been the Westside YMCA. Billie preferred this site because it was close to Calder State, so more students volunteered. She loved interacting with the young people, and they did most of the lifting. Today's distribution ended early, and she was looking forward to going home and sitting under her fan with a glass of sweet tea. Billie saw her sister-in-law drive up and waved to get her attention. "You can go home," Billie said. "Our shipment was short, and we didn't have as much water. We ran out already."

"I'm always assigned the first Saturday of the month, but when there was no line, I thought maybe I had my days mixed up," Joellen said.

"It's crazy that we've been doing this long enough to

have regular monthly assignments," Billie said, admiring Joellen's crisp white linen outfit, wrist full of jangling bracelets, and flawless makeup.

"Occasionally we'd have a boil notice if there was a bad storm. But the last year or so the notices are more frequent and last longer."

"You're on the board, can't you do something?"

"I wish it were that easy," Joellen said. "Everyone knows the issues and the solutions. Paying for the solution is the problem. But I don't want to dwell on problems. I've got to make a deposit at the bank, then I'm going to Dallas. I have a pass for a buyer's sale at the Fashion Market Center. Want to ride with me?"

"You don't bank with Sunrise?"

"No. My grandfather said when he was starting out, that bank was so racist, they wouldn't even let him open a checking account."

"I've heard a lot of those stories. Thankfully, it's a new day. I'll ride with you and log it as trying to court a new client."

Billie and Joellen had been in-laws for decades, but today was the first time they hung out without their husbands. They met at Billie's house, then left for their road trip. Their first stop was the funeral supply store, something Billie didn't even know existed. They went to a bookstore, stocked up on hair care products, had a late lunch at The Island Spot, and shopped at the trade mart until it closed. "This place is awesome," Billie said as they loaded their bags in the trunk. Even though they were on a tight budget, Billie splurged, justifying her purchases as investments in unique pieces for her corporate attire.

"Once you shop here, you'll never want to go to a regular store," Joellen said. "I have a pass for the home and interior designer sale next month if you'd like to join me."

"It's a date," Billie said. "I can get ideas for our house." They listened to the comedy channel on satellite radio and the return trip passed quickly.

"What is all this?" Cole asked, as Billie brought her bags in the trailer.

"I spent the day with Joellen. We went shopping in Dallas and..."

"Say no more," Cole said, shaking his head. "Monroe always complains about his wife's spending. I hope you weren't trying to keep up with her."

"Don't worry, prices were wholesale, so I got good bargains. You're always saying I need to make more of an effort to fit in. No better way to do that than hanging with my sister-in-law, who knows everyone. We've never really spent much one-on-one time together, and after twenty years I'm just getting to know her. I guess opposites really do attract. She seems very good-natured and thoughtful. How in the world did she end up with Monroe?"

Billie smelled grilled onions and garlic when she walked in. "Hey babe. I figured you'd be tired after driving to and from Dallas today, so I fixed dinner," Cole said. A spread of fish tacos, salad and fresh squeezed lemonade were on the card table that served as their kitchen table. It had taken him a long time to embrace her diet. He was still a meat and potatoes man, but he did try to find restaurants that served food she could eat and was willing to try new foods. The tacos smelled amazing, but what she really wanted was a drink.

Today she had her interim review with her supervisor in downtown Dallas. She arrived early and treated herself to a muffin from Vine's Vegan Bakery before what she thought would be a routine meeting. She replayed the conversation in her mind as she poured a glass of merlot.

"Billie, we're happy to have you on our team, and have been pleased with your work. Your enthusiasm and innovative approach have already generated tangible results."

"I appreciate your encouragement. And thanks so much for allowing me to take off next week for the cruise."

"We consider it good promotional exposure. However, we do have two other issues to discuss today. The first one has to do with your credit score."

"I'm not sure I understand," Billie said.

"Because we work in finance, we periodically pull our employee's credit reports. A low score can be a red flag, and your score is what we consider poor."

"My husband and I recently encountered unexpected medical and moving expenses," Billie said, as she felt her face flushing. "If you look at our history, you'll see we have always paid our bills on time."

"We understand things happen and have a program to help employees who find themselves in a financial hardship. You'll be registered for our Financial Literacy series. There are three hour-long videos, and we'd like you to complete them within thirty days."

Her supervisor delivered the news with a smile, but Billie was still humiliated. She had always been the responsible one in her family when it came to finances. She had worked since she was fifteen, wasn't a big spender, and was monitoring her credit score while Maya and her mother never met a credit card they didn't like. The last week of the month, she always scheduled a financial consultant on her radio show to help spread financial literacy. Yet she was now the one being counseled.

"And the last issue has to do with your social media footprint. You have very passionate views."

"I've always believed in the duty of the citizen to impact

and improve their community in any way they can. That's one reason I was attracted to this job."

"But your version of impact and improvement may not agree with someone else's. You aren't a back office or desk employee. You're visible in the community and in that role, you represent Sunrise Bank and Trust. Some may believe your personal views are radical and reflect the bank's views."

"It's my personal page. I don't even mention the bank's name."

"That may have been alright in California, but you're working in a small town now. A large part of our customer base will find your posts offensive. I know you can't undo what's already out there, and it's your right to post whatever you like. It is also our right to part ways with an employee that we feel may damage our brand."

"Are you threatening me with my job?"

"I'm asking you to think twice going forward. You're part of the Sunrise family now, and we make sacrifices for our family. I'm sure you understand," he said, glancing at his vibrating phone. "I need to take this call. Send me an email and I'll forward your proposal for an internship program with Calder State to HR. Drive safe."

He then spun around in his chair, indicating the meeting was over. To control her temper, Billie began counting to herself—employing one of the tactics she told her listeners to use. She didn't want to be labeled as an "angry Black woman" in addition to being branded as a radical who couldn't handle money. But she was angry, and she clenched her teeth so hard, her jaw was hurting. She went to her car and pulled up her Instagram account on her phone. The last thing she posted was a quote about the absurdity of banning books. *What could be more offensive than banning books?* On her Facebook page, she had liked and shared a joke about one of the senators.

Maybe some didn't care for her humor, but she didn't appreciate his dog whistling rhetoric.

She felt herself getting mad all over again as she told Cole what happened. "Can you believe that?" she asked and poured another glass of wine. "I didn't know suppressing my political views was part of my job description. I knew Texas was conservative, but I didn't know I'd be going back to the stone ages. Can they do that? I need to reread my employee handbook. I didn't see anything in there giving them the right to monitor and dictate my social media comments."

"And you won't. That doesn't mean they don't do it. Think about it in reverse. What if someone at the radio station had social media posts mocking Dr. Martin Luther King or John Lewis?"

"You're not comparing that uninformed, racist, insecure opportunist to..."

"I'm trying to make a point," Cole said with a heavy sigh.

"Someone with those views wouldn't be happy working at a black radio station."

"Well, that's how they feel—that someone who doesn't support their great senator wouldn't be working for their company, and more importantly, wouldn't be able to relate to their customers."

"This is ridiculous. I see where this is going. I'm still in my probationary period and they're starting a paper trail on me. I'm going to contact my employee relations rep tomorrow."

"Honey, he was all the employee relations you're going to get. Stay off social media for a while, then..."

"I don't care about Instagram, Facebook, or any other social media. It's the principle and I will not be intimidated by white fragility."

"Whoa—I'm on your side—remember?"

"Then I'll quit before they can set me up."

"That's an extreme response. Remember where we are," Cole said as he refilled her glass. "It will take a while for you to find another job, especially at the same pay. Also, people talk, and you may get blackballed. You've been spoiled working at the radio station. Most workplaces aren't that progressive."

"Maya warned me, but I didn't think things would get this petty."

"Let's forget all this corporate politicking. I have something more important for you. Look at this."

She opened the envelope he handed her and pulled out three filled notebook pages. The envelope had an Albuquerque postmark, and she recognized the neat script handwriting. It was a letter from Dylan.

Mom and Dad,

You are the best parents anyone could ask for. Kendra and I had a fairytale childhood and there's nothing you did to cause this or could have done to prevent it. So please don't blame yourselves. We learned in group that people are wired different. Some people struggle with weight while someone else can eat all day and not gain a pound. It's the same thing with drugs. Some people can take medications and have no side effects and others become addicted. I guess I drew the short straw.

But I never considered myself an addict. I was taking something doctors had prescribed, so it had to be okay. Eventually, I knew better, but the pills had taken over by then. It's hard to describe the feeling to someone who doesn't use, but the pills make everything feel chill. It's the feeling I had when winning a race, like I was the best and untouchable. But as time passed, I required more pills to get that chill feeling and function normally.

I still had all my dreams. I still wanted to try out for the Olympics—to make you proud. I just needed to stop feeling sick first. Do you know what my friends and I talk about most, after we get high together? What we'll do when we get clean. But when you're addicted, withdrawal feels like poison, and drugs are the cure. My stomach feels like it's burning, and like I need to puke my guts out. My muscles go into spasms, and my head is too heavy to hold up. It is hell.

I want to stop but cannot. I appreciate your attempts to help me get clean, though I may not always have welcomed them. But your efforts didn't work because they're based on the assumption that I have the power to stop. Your lectures make me feel even more ashamed and guilty than I do already, so I use and keep the cycle going. Willpower will not heal me—and neither will attempts to convince me that I'm hurting myself. I made promises that I would stop, but never kept them. Usually, I was simply telling you what you wanted to hear to get you off my back. Although sometimes I really meant to keep my promises.

I'm ashamed and hate myself for all I've put you through. When I think of the money you guys have spent trying to help me and the money I've spent getting high, I want to fall into a hole and disappear. This was not supposed to be my life. I don't want to be an addict as much as you wish you weren't a parent of one. There's a part of me that is terrified for you to read this, because this is the real me and I'm afraid if you know the real me, you'll give up on me. And after everything I've done, you have every reason to. But I hope you don't.

Your son,
Dylan

Billie read and reread the letter several times through tear-filled eyes. She was ashamed that she hadn't been able to see how much physical and emotional pain Dylan was in. Even though it was apparent he'd left New Day and it didn't sound like he had stopped using, Billie was comforted to know Dylan remembered what they had instilled in him and knew he was loved. It wasn't much, but it gave her hope that one day she would see her son healed and whole.

CHAPTER 22

Cole's text read: Have a surprise for you when you get home. Billie had been curious all afternoon. Her fibroid pain had subsided lately, and she wondered if he was planning a romantic tryst. Any other day she would have had more flexibility in her schedule, but she was being trained on a new system and had to stay all day. She was out the door at 5:01, and forty-five minutes later, she turned into Lakeview Terrace. When she saw the trailer she couldn't believe her eyes—Monroe, Cole, Amos and Dylan were sitting outside, with the grill smoking.

"Dylan!" she shouted as she got out of the car.

"Came to see my favorite girl," he said.

"He showed up at the house this morning," Amos said. "Lovey practically suffocated him, she hugged him so hard."

"I came to the trailer, but no one answered," Dylan said.

"You should have called," Billie said. "How did you get here?"

"I caught a ride with a friend. We can catch up later. Right now, I want some of this Texas barbeque Uncle Amos has been bragging about all day."

"This meat is so tender, even your mama will eat some," Amos said.

Billie eyed Amos's beer cans and remembered the counselor's words about substituting one drug for another. She also thought she probably should hide their wine bottles. "It's hot out here. You all should come inside. I'm going to go change my clothes," Billie said.

After changing and hiding the bottles, she was going to join them, but the Jordan men, as they were calling themselves, seemed to be having so much fun, she didn't want to interrupt. The reunion broke up around eight o'clock. Billie put sheets on the bed in the second bedroom and Dylan said he was going to bed early. She had many questions, but suppressed the urge to question him. Dylan was an unsolved riddle and she was learning to accept the parts of him that he wanted to share. Sometimes he called two or three times a day, then there would be weeks where they wouldn't hear from him. When he did call, he acted as though he hadn't just been missing-in-action, and everything was normal. Today had been like old times. Maybe New Day had been the answer they needed.

It was only eight o'clock, and Billie had been up cooking since the roosters crowed. Even though Dylan had left rehab early, she was relieved to see her son, but he looked thin. She cooked his favorite breakfast, pancakes, hash browns, and fried bologna. Billie was preparing lasagna for dinner and made a pineapple coconut cake.

"I thought I was dreaming," Dylan said as he walked in. "But my nose tells me it's real."

"Good morning, son," Billie said. "I should invent an alarm clock with aromas. I bet I could make millions."

"Are we having company?"

"No sweetie. Just trying to put a little more meat on your bones. I made all your favorites."

"Wow, I wish I had known. I told Uncle Monroe I'd help him paint some of his properties. He's picking me up in thirty minutes."

⋆ ⋆ ⋆

Billie took off work the first couple of days after Dylan's arrival. On her first day back at work, he was cutting the neighbor's grass when she got home. The past week, he had fixed the ceiling fan, repaired the leaky sink and fixed Shaun's stair railing. "I didn't know you were so handy. I'm glad you're keeping busy, but make sure your slave driver uncle pays you."

"It's pretty cool living in a small town. Everyone is super friendly. Stuff doesn't cost so much, and Whataburger is the best thing ever. There is one thing I miss though. This is the longest I've ever gone without getting in water. Is there a public pool around here?"

"The community building at the new house will have one. I'm sure there's one on the Calder State campus, but I don't know if it's public. Your dad can get you access. Also, I'll bet there's one at the country club. Ask Monroe, he's probably a member," she said as she reached for her phone. "I can call..."

"I'll look into it. You don't have to go to so much trouble for me."

"It's no trouble."

"I know I've made a tight space even more crowded. And you wouldn't ordinarily be cooking so much. I wish everything could go back to normal. I hate I've caused you so much..."

"Hold it, right there," Billie said, as she frosted the cake, the second one she'd made in four days. "Wherever we are is your home. There's always a place for you, whether we're in two rooms or twenty. We're not going to wallow in the past. Everyone makes mistakes. The important thing is to learn from them and not repeat them."

"Okay. But I do have one question."

"What is it?" Billie asked as she put her arm around his waist.

"Can I cut the cake?"

"Boy, get out of my face," Billie said, playfully pushing him away. She wrapped a piece for him to take with him and waved as he hopped in Monroe's truck. *How could such a loveable child end up in so much trouble?* she thought.

"When you said you guys were moving to Texas, I didn't think you'd like it. You always said it was too hot and the bugs were too big. But you seem to be fitting in. Even this trailer seems kind of cool, although I know it's a lot less space than you're used to."

Dylan had moved into the second bedroom, that had been their closet. Since Cole and Billie were gone most of the day, Dylan kept busy with odd jobs and volunteering at water distribution centers. Amos bought him a reel and they went fishing almost every day. His hair was cut low, and he wore jeans and a white t-shirt every day. There were a few boxes of designer sneakers in the storage unit, but he didn't seem concerned and had even bought a pair of Walmart sneakers.

They had been so relieved to see their son that neither questioned him about why he'd left Phoenix. By the second weekend, Cole was ready to talk, even though he and Billie had decided to let Dylan come to them in his own time.

"Son, we love having you here, but would like to know what happened. Didn't you have three more weeks?"

"But if you don't feel like talking, that's okay," Billie interjected.

"It's okay. When they brought me the paperwork to extend my stay, I saw the price. I knew it was expensive but not that much. I can't keep letting you guys spend money like that."

"We want you to get well," Cole said. "You let us worry about the cost."

"I feel better than I have in a long time. I'm so sorry to be such a disappointment."

"I'm disappointed, but not in you. I feel like we failed you," Billie said.

"I know I've hurt you and rather than see you in pain, I stayed away."

"But it hurt us more not to know where and how you were," Billie said.

"I have the tools to continue my progress and won't disappoint you this time."

"That's good to hear son, although we do wish you'd completed the program. But only you know if you're ready to stand on your own. To help you do that we're going to give you an occasional drug test. You're not opposed are you?"

"I understand why you don't trust me," Dylan said.

"It's not that we don't trust you. I believe the testing will be added incentive for you to resist temptation. We can't undo the past. Let's focus on making things better now and in the future. What do you see for your future?" Cole asked.

"I want to get my GED and driver's license, then maybe become a flight attendant. I'd like to travel."

"You can get a discount on tuition at Calder State," Cole said. "You should take advantage of the opportunity to get a degree at such a low price. Writing a plan can be helpful. That way you stay focused."

"We'll see. For now, I'll focus on the GED," Dylan said as he looked in the refrigerator. "Lovey's neighbor is picking me up. She wants me to help clean out her flower beds and trim her hedges. I'll be back in a few hours."

After he'd been gone a few minutes, Billie said, "A drug test? A plan? You're treating him like a criminal. Are you trying to drive him away?"

"He can't cut grass and plant flowers the rest of his life. I'm trying to guide him, and a plan will help him see where he wants to go and how to get there," Cole said. "Random testing will make him think twice about using again. Any job he tries to get is going to drug test him. You babying him has been the problem."

"Dylan has a medical condition. If he was recovering from any other disease, you wouldn't badger him about his recovery. You'd be glad he survived and let him do things in his own time. You've got to be a little easier and give him some slack and time to find himself."

"Black men don't have the luxury of easy and slack. If we don't teach him that, the world will. He'll thank me for providing structure."

Billie had meetings in Tyler, then left work and rushed home. She had planned to fry catfish for dinner, but when Cole came in she was sitting on the couch with a glass of wine. "I thought we weren't drinking in front of Dylan," he said softly.

"You don't have to whisper. He's not here."

"Who's got him working this late?" Cole asked.

"No one. He's gone. I guess he didn't want structure," she said and left the room.

CHAPTER 23

Billie cleaned the sticky card / kitchen table to get ready for her work Zoom meeting. Cole had returned from jumping Shaun's battery and Billie was cleaning up after having breakfast with baby Jenna and Willie. Rev. Collins had just picked up the kids and Cole was going to take Shaun to work. "She really needs a new car," Cole said, as he went to their bedroom to change his shirt. He'd left his phone on the counter and when it rang, Billie picked it up to turn it to silent. She saw that the call had been from Serena. She also saw a text he'd sent: *This is a feeling I was not looking for but has made me so happy. Can't wait to see you later. I'll be there at six.*

Billie wasn't a suspicious wife nor the kind to check her husband's phone or GPS coordinates. But this was more than a friendly text. After Cole's affair, she had put him out and had no intention of taking him back. Technically, they had been separated, but Billie understood the purpose was for them to clear the air and lower the tension, not to fool around. Just because he'd done a good job of covering his tracks, didn't mean it was okay. But they agreed Dylan was going through enough without having to deal with divorcing parents.

However, this time he wasn't even covering his tracks.

She had overlooked several red flags. Serena was always around, and her aggressiveness was obviously encouraged. In college, when Billie found out his given name was Coleman, he told her he hated to be called that, but when Serena said it, he seemed to melt like hot butter. These weren't red flags; this was a whole sheet.

Cole emerged from the bedroom, grabbed his phone, pecked her on the cheek and left while she was on her call. She managed to make it through her meeting, although she was steaming inside. The bank examiners were coming so she was busy all day, and by the time she turned her computer off at five thirty, she was deceptively calm and ready to confront Cole and whatever excuse he had this time.

"You must have had a busy day," Cole said when he came home. "I called you a few times, but you didn't return my calls or texts. I've got a frat meeting, so I hope you got my message not to cook anything. I'll probably..."

"I know you're not going to a frat meeting Cole," Billie said in a low, controlled voice. "How long did you think you could keep this from me? I saw your text this morning. To Serena."

"What text?" Cole asked, then his eyes brightened as he realized what she was saying. "I was going to tell you. I was waiting for the right time."

"The right time would have been before you dragged me thousands of miles from home to this hell hot Podunk town with rancid water and flying roaches. Before I sold my home to come live in a metal box and before I let you send my son away from home."

"I never knew. Serena and I dated a few months, then argued about something neither of us remembers and broke up. I moved to California, and she never told me she was pregnant. I don't think she even knew until months after we broke up. She got married and said she let the past be the past.

But her husband died last year and when I showed up in town, she figured Chris had a right to know who his father was."

"Chris?"

"My son."

The drama unfolding in Billie's life felt like a Tyler Perry movie. And the worse part, Cole seemed thrilled with this turn of events. Chris was a junior at Howard University, majoring in political science, with plans to attend law school. He was home on break, and he and Cole were making up for lost time.

"Thanks for being so understanding," Cole said. He and his new son had been in Dallas all day. This was the third weekend they'd spent together. Billie could have joined them but felt like the ugly girlfriend tagging along on a date whenever they were together. "We went to two Rangers games. I said I was a purist and didn't like domed baseball stadiums, but it was great not to fight the elements since it rained all weekend."

"Sounds like you two had a good time. Did you discuss the test?"

"No," Cole replied.

"Don't you think you should?"

"Serena has no reason to lie. Chris is over eighteen. She's not seeking child support."

"That's not the issue. I would think you'd want to be sure. And if her husband was your friend, how did he end up with your girlfriend?"

"She wasn't my girlfriend anymore."

"Don't guys have some kind of 'bro-code'? I wouldn't ever date one of my friend's exes. And for you to be such good friends, I don't recall you ever mentioning his name. A DNA test would remove any doubts."

"I don't have any doubts. If she says it, I'm sure."

"Well, I'm not. Not to disparage Serena, but if she was messing with both of you, there could've been another man in the picture."

"Serena wasn't like that and I'm not going to insult her."

"We can't upset the grieving widow by asking for something that would comfort your wife," Billie said, with indignation. "Ronald Reagan was never my favorite, but one thing he said I agree with—*trust but verify.* This goes beyond hurting Serena's feelings. My father had another family, and I know the mixed feelings children can have about it."

"Our kids are grown. It's not the same."

"So, which is greater, your desire not to insult your baby mama, or your desire to please your wife?"

Billie drove under the welcome arch and entered the world of Calder State College. The main entrance took her down a winding road past a grassy central commons area, with a center bell tower and fountain, made of bricks from the original building. Walkways, like spokes led to several ivy-covered red brick buildings. Billie parked in the visitor lot behind the Student Union building and headed to the cafeteria for her lunch date with Cole.

Mary J. Blige was playing in the background and large posters of historic African Americans from Texas were on the walls. This was so different from her college experience. Berkley was close to home, and she qualified for in-state tuition, so she never even considered attending an HBCU. Billie never felt out of place at UC, but she could see how being in an environment with a majority of Black students would be self-affirming and less stressful. Even the food choices were evidence of the culture, with peach cobbler, hot wings, baked macaroni and cheese, and greens on the menu, and Louisiana hot sauce a prominent condiment on every table.

After standing at the door for several minutes, someone tapped her on the shoulder. "If you're waiting for Coleman, he may be awhile. They're still in a department meeting, which started late, so I'm sure it will run long," Serena said. "You can sit with me if you like."

"No thanks," Billie said. She checked her watch and was about to leave Cole a text when she heard a voice say, "Hey Miss Billie."

"Marcus, it's good to see you."

"You too," he said. "We miss you. They were wrong, all day long, how they did you."

"No worries," Billie said. "I'm glad I could help."

"We're moving to the engineering building. We'll have more space, and updated wiring. Some of our equipment is on backorder, but we expect everything to be in place by homecoming. Do you have time to come see it?"

"Since my date stood me up, sure."

She'd been on campus several times, walking from a parking lot to her destination. Now as she walked the interior, among the students, she had an even greater appreciation for the school and became even more excited for Dylan to attend. *He will thrive in this nurturing environment*, she thought. They just had to get him past his current struggles.

After visiting the new station, she went back to the cafeteria to get the peach cobbler that was calling her name. When she got to the end of the food line, she saw Cole. He waved her over to the table he shared with Serena. "Hey babe, I thought you stood me up," he said.

"I was here on time. Serena said your meeting…never mind," Billie said, as she straddled the bench and sat next to her husband. "Want some of my pie? Although I'll have something even sweeter for you tonight," she said and kissed him softly on the lips.

Serena cleared her throat and picked up her tray. "I'll be going now."

"And we'll be cumming later," Billie said with a wink, as she fed Cole a forkful of cobbler.

He coughed, took a swallow of bottled water, then struggled to say goodbye as Serena stood.

"Leaving?" Billie said in a syrupy tone. "By the way, I meant to tell you I like your hair. It looks so much better."

Serena narrowed her gaze, took a deep breath and walked away.

"Was that necessary?" Cole asked as he cleared his throat.

"Yep," Billie replied.

CHAPTER 24

Billie was getting chill bumps and pulled the sheet over her naked body. Minutes earlier her sweat had mixed with her husband's as their bodies met in a familiar entanglement. But the abrupt ending had also become familiar.

As they both lay staring at the ceiling Cole said, "I don't mean to be insensitive, but isn't there a pill you can take to fix that?"

What used to be occasional discomfort that Billie would suffer through was now sharp pain that made sex almost unbearable. Some days were better than others, but the not-so-good ones were beginning to outnumber the good. "I guess I should find a local gynecologist. I need a new mifepristone prescription, and it's such a hassle here," Billie said.

"You never miss an opportunity to remind me that you're unhappy here," Cole said, as he got up.

"And you never miss an opportunity to remind me how selfish you are. Instead of being concerned about my pain, you want me to fix it."

"As usual, you're twisting my words. I don't want you to be in pain, but this isn't the moon. There are doctors here. Serena mentioned..."

"Have you discussed my health with her?" Billie asked, as she sat up in the bed.

"Of course not. At the last alumni meeting, she mentioned a new doctor who is opening a group practice near the hospital. But they're not from California, so they're probably not good enough for you," Cole said. "I'm going to take a shower. A cold one."

Billie got up and changed the sheets, since she had spotted on them. "Do you want breakfast?" she asked when Cole came out of the bathroom.

"No thanks. I'm meeting Chris for breakfast. He starts his new job today."

"Of course you are," Billie said and rolled her eyes.

Despite being vanquished from the radio station, Billie was still on the homecoming program committee since she secured a Sunrise Bank sponsorship. With eight weeks to go, Billie was headed to a mass meeting of all committees and committee members in the Calder State auditorium. She worked late and the meeting had already started when she arrived. Not wanting to disrupt others by joining Cole near the front, she sat in the back. Also, she knew the meeting would be long and wanted to tip out before the end. She'd missed a call from Dylan. He left a message saying he would call back around eight. She'd tried calling the number he called from but just got a fax machine sound. They'd spoken a few times since he left Calderville. He wouldn't say where he was, but he sounded strong and didn't ask for money.

While Dr. Harland droned on about the Alumni Foundation Reception, Billie left but stopped in the restroom first. All the stalls in the closest restroom had an 'out of order' sign, so she went down the hall. When she turned the corner, Serena said, "Hi Billie. You're leaving?"

"Yes, I don't want to miss Dylan's call."

"It's amazing, isn't it? Our sons are brothers. Chris always wanted a brother."

"Dylan never expressed any interest in having a brother," Billie said.

"That's not what Coleman said. He said..."

"Serena, I don't mean any harm, but it's not necessary for you to tell me about my son."

"We're practically family, so let me give you some advice," Serena said, then lowered her voice. "Your husband is very unhappy. If you're not careful someone may swoop in and take him from you."

"Cole is not a toy or a prize that can be taken."

"That's where you're wrong," Serena said putting a loose strand of hair behind her ear. "He is a prize, and the fact that you don't feel that way, tells me a lot. If he were my man, I'd treat him like a prize, and he'd feel like one."

"You are sad. Get your thirsty, bitchy, shifty, fake ass out of my face."

"You call me sad, but you're the one with an unhappy husband and a drug addict son. You aren't taking very good care of the men in your life."

"Let me phrase this with one of your Texas sayings, so you can't say you misunderstood. If I ever hear you disparage my son again, I'm going to knock your teeth so far down your throat, you'll spit them out in single file. And for the record, I don't believe Chris is Cole's son," Billie said. She turned around to leave and ran into Cole.

"Billie, what's going on?" he asked with a frown.

"Ask your wannabe baby mama. I'm going home to wait for a call from our son."

CHAPTER 25

"Babe, do you think your mother or Maya can go on the cruise with you? We finally got the championship schedule, and the team will be in Pine Bluff. This is historic. Calder State has never been to the conference championships. Even though most students have gone home, the hotels are sold out. We got a sponsor for three fan busses."

It wasn't a question and Billie didn't answer. The team had its best season ever and even people who usually didn't care about baseball were coming to the games. Working with the athletes had him on cloud nine, and it was almost as though teaching was the side gig and helping the baseball team was his primary job. Cole had even lost a few pounds working out with them. She was initially irritated, but cruising with Maya would be fun.

"I was about to hang up, it was taking you so long to answer," Billie said, when Maya finally answered the phone.

"I was washing my hair. This natural hair is too much work. I may go back to my perm, but I'm sure that's not why you called. What's going on?"

"I'm going on the Grown Folks Cruise again this year. Want to come?"

"Sure. Cole's not going?"

"There's a conflict with the baseball team. Besides, I think we need a break from each other."

"I'm sorry you and your honey aren't in sync, but that's good news for me. I'd love a free cruise. It is free, isn't it?"

"Yes."

"Then count me in. With Imani in school, I've lost my travel buddy."

It seemed like Billie had lost her travel buddy too. She was looking forward to hanging out with her sister, but still felt some kind of way about yet again being put on the back burner, especially when she dropped Cole off and saw Serena and Chris among the crowd, with packed bags.

Houston reminded Billie of home, with miles and miles of strip malls, gas stations, low-rise office buildings, and restaurants alongside Interstate 45. She had been within the metropolitan area ninety minutes, going in and out of the city limits and passing suburb after suburb. Everyone was in a pickup truck and passing her, just for her to catch up with them a half mile later. During these last months in Calderville she'd gotten rusty on driving in city traffic. She was only three exits from Hobby Airport, but it was taking forever as traffic had slowed to a crawl. But she had already received two notices that her sister's flight was delayed, so she would still arrive on time.

She and Maya were cruising out of Galveston in the morning. This was her fifth time joining the group, and they usually left out of Florida or California. It was a work assignment that didn't feel like work. They provided a balcony cabin, drink package and flight voucher. She and Cole looked forward to attending every year but hadn't expected an invitation since she was no longer with the radio station. So, she was pleasantly surprised to get an invitation. When the organizers learned she wasn't with the station anymore, they tracked her down and invited her to attend. She was already in Texas. She was cheaper than anyone else they could hire, plus she knew the routine. She didn't have any vacation days, but her boss allowed her to take leave without pay so she could attend, if her bank title and contact information was included in the cruise promotional information.

Their ship, *Integrity*, set sail at noon and she and Maya watched the shore become smaller and smaller as they enjoyed the gentle breeze from their stateroom balcony. Within an hour, Maya said she felt woozy, and Billie left her in their room and went to her first assignment—DJing the evening line dancing session. By the next morning, Maya had her sea legs, and they went to the breakfast buffet, then toured the ship. Billie had to host a late morning panel and she and Maya parted ways.

On previous cruises she had hosted panels designed to generate lively participation such as, do Black men prefer white women, and is monogamy dead. She roamed through the crowd with the microphone, getting audience responses. Since this was an election year, the organizers wanted to tackle more serious topics and she was assigned to moderate panels on immigration, environmental racism, and should Blacks support private school voucher programs.

Today's panel was a town hall on environmental racism. The organizers were impressed that she had actually attended her local water board meeting, but not surprised at the results. "Most of those board positions are used as prizes for campaign donors or family members. Water quality is a complex and critical issue. We wouldn't let just anyone provide oversight for a nuclear plant or hospital. Why do we allow water, our most precious resource, to be managed by incompetent cronies?" the NAACP panelist said.

An author from Flint shared her experience with their water crisis and Billie was in and out of the audience with the mic as others shared experiences. Cruisers from Helena-West

Helena, Arkansas, told stories about going weeks without running water and having broken pipes gushing water in the streets. Billie learned over half of the public schools in Baltimore use bottled water due to lead in school pipes, and even the nation's capital had a history of boil water notices. A Clean Water Coalition representative gave an impassioned speech and ended by saying, "Water quality information is public, but is often buried in flashy brochures or hard to navigate websites. Corporations pay lobbyists and political action committees whose agenda is to block any legislation that leads to more transparency, increased investment, and less pollutants. We don't have the money that they do, but we have you, the people, and that's how we will win this fight."

Billie was so engrossed, she almost forgot she was supposed to be moderating. Billie signed the Coalition petition and made a mental note to check for these reports when she returned to Calderville.

She tried to discuss the exhilarating session with Maya, but Maya said, "In the words of Evilene, the Wicked Witch of the West, don't bring me no bad news. I'm on this ship to have fun, not talk politics. Let's go eat again."

After stuffing themselves at a buffet, she and Maya went back to the lounge to dance off their food. "I'm looking at you. You're looking at me," Billie sang along with the lyrics as she moved in step with the crowd. "Mr. Sexy Man" was playing and even though she had just learned the line dance, she was keeping up with the crowd. The DJ segued into two more line dance songs, and she and Maya stayed on the floor. When a slow song came on, she and her sister made their way to their seats, after stopping a server and grabbing sangrias off his tray.

"I can't believe all this fun has been going on without me," Maya said.

"I've been trying to get you to come on a cruise for years," Billie said. She had been on this cruise several times, but this trip was different. When she traveled with Cole, they walked along the deck, danced in the lounge, and had great sex. It was a relaxing and romantic trip, and they rarely left the ship. She had a daily appointment to host a few panels and DJ in the lounge, but when those shifts were over, her time was free. This trip she was enjoying seeing sights through her sister's first-time eyes and participated in more group activities. They shopped, went on island excursions and played in the bid whist tournament. They tried pickleball, and at Maya's insistence, went to the spa, despite Billie's objections about the cost. "You only live once," Maya said.

As she was guzzling her drink, they both eyed a Terrance Howard look-a-like headed toward their table. He put his hand out, motioning for a dance. Maya scooted her chair back, but he reached for Billie's hand.

"Would you like to dance?" he asked.

Maya raised an eyebrow and scooted her chair back to the table.

"Uhhh, okay," Billie said. They'd danced about a minute, when the song went off and another slow song came on. Billie turned to head back to her table, but her partner guided her elbow back to the floor, put his arm around her waist and gently eased her into Babyface's rhythm. She hadn't slow danced with anyone other than her husband in years and was surprised at how easily they fell into sync. When the next song came on, also slow, she made no move to leave, and her partner did not release her.

During their three dances, she learned her partner was Julian Ward from Houston. He was part of the tech team employed by the cruise sponsor. She vaguely remembered him behind the monitors during her show, and they had briefly exchanged pleasantries. While she vaguely remembered him, she was surprised that he had paid so much attention to her. "I intended to talk to you after your show, but you disappeared before I could catch you. My good luck to see you here tonight." She wasn't sure if he was being nice or flirting. Either way he seemed harmless and when he invited her to lunch, she agreed. "I'll meet you tomorrow after your show," he stated when they returned to her seat.

"Sounds good," Billie replied.

"Sooooo Mrs. Jordan," Maya said when Billie sat down. "Would Mr. Jordan approve of you making a date with Mr. Fancy Dancer?"

"Things between us are complicated. Moving to Texas was supposed to be a fresh start, but all it brought is fresh drama. He has a son."

"Oh no," Maya said, reaching for her sister's hand. "How are you feeling about it?"

"I'm pissed, not just for me, but for my children. After Mom and Reuben divorced, it didn't seem like I had a father anymore. He treated his new family so well, it seemed like we were the outside kids."

"Men can be so low down, and I thought Cole was one of the good ones. I suppose he wants you to accept the baby with open arms. Tell him *Fences* was fiction and..."

"Chris is grown, older than Kendra. Supposedly this was something that happened before he moved to Oakland."

"You're saying he had a son before you were married? Girl, you had me ready to curse him and his baby mama out," Maya said, as she shook her head. "So, he has a love child. Why are you just now finding out?"

"He claims he just found out. Serena's husband died, and when Cole moved back home, she decided Chris should meet his biological father."

"The situation may be awkward, but I don't see how you

can be mad about something that happened before you met. They aren't trying to rekindle old flames, are they?"

"Whether they're trying or not, I see it happening. Chris is nice enough, but I suggested that Cole get a DNA test, to be sure. You would've thought I was asking them to donate a kidney and swear on the Bible. He refuses to even mention it to Serena."

"It's like the thrill of a new car. Give him time to absorb everything."

"I've been patient. They spend every weekend together. He even missed Dylan's family session to go to a baseball game with Chris. It's like getting a puppy, the more time they spend together, the stronger the attachment will become. I don't think it's unreasonable to ask for a DNA test."

"Maybe you should talk to Serena yourself."

"And offend Miss Perfect?" Billie said, clutching her imaginary pearls. "He's more concerned about hurting her feelings than me being upset. That's what really bothers me."

"This is a tough one, but in the big scheme of things; he wasn't unfaithful and he's trying to do the right thing. Eventually he'll realize making room for Chris doesn't mean there's less room for his family."

"And what if I don't want to wait for eventually?"

CHAPTER 26

221 Pecan Lane, Billie and Cole's new address, was finally complete. Their completion date had been extended so many times, she had stopped planning and just waited for the phone call. The house had passed inspection, and they had the final walk-through four days ago and received keys. The house was more beautiful than she imagined, and she loved the "new" smell.

Cole was out of town with the baseball team, and their official move in date would be this weekend when he returned. She had begun bringing carloads of stuff to the house. She coordinated with movers to bring their furniture from storage and utilities were already on. Waiting for Cole to return, she felt like a kid waiting for Christmas morning, but it gave her more time to clean the trailer that had been their home for ninety days.

Monroe was getting the trailer ready to rent and thirty minutes into putting in a new window unit, something he said would be a ten-minute task. Billie was in such a good mood, she could even tolerate Monroe, who, now that they were moving, was getting through the "fix-it" list she'd given him when they first moved in.

"Dylan was a lot of help to me when he was here. All of

Lovey's neighbors loved how handy he was. I'm glad he's getting himself straightened out and hope he comes back."

"Me too," Billie said, although she hated that Cole told his brother all their business. Dylan had returned to New Day on his own, and they were hopeful that meant he was really going to stick with it this time.

"I wish all my tenants left the units in as good a shape as you all have. I usually have to paint, replace flooring and re-landscape before a new tenant can move in. It helped that you don't have any pets or young kids. Folks don't control their children anymore."

"My mother always taught me to leave places better than I found them. We appreciate you letting us stay here. I never imagined housing would be so difficult to find."

"With so many new people moving in, we need more housing. I hope you're able to convince the bank to help with that."

"Rossbrooke Estates is new, and our section is almost sold out. They're already taking deposits for Phase II. It's amazing how much more affordable housing is here."

"Most people around here wouldn't consider four hundred thousand affordable."

"Then why is demand so great?"

"The new factories coming will transform this area. We beat out several larger cities. Plus, there are a lot of you California carpetbaggers coming here. All of that is driving up prices. But I'm not complaining, growth has brought us more streetlights, two new interstate exits and increased real estate values." As Monroe was rummaging through his tool bag, he turned and asked, "How's Mary?"

"Who?"

"Your sister."

"You mean Maya?"

"Yeah, Maya, with her fine self. Tell her I said hello and she should come visit."

Billie wondered why he'd be interested in someone he only met casually years ago, but didn't want to prolong his visit. She needed him to concentrate and finish, so he could get going. She only had a few chapters remaining in the new Stacey Abrams thriller and was looking forward to getting back to it.

"We're supposed to get some remnant from Hurricane Kyle tonight. They say it might be heavy. You want to come stay with us?" Monroe asked.

"I'll be fine. The weather announcers make every storm sound like the coming apocalypse," Billie replied. The hurricane had landed in Matamoros, Mexico, three days earlier, and was spawning tornados as it ambled north. Billie had earned decent geography grades, but never knew hurricanes impacted so far inland.

"We get more tornados, rain, and drought than we used to. They say it's due to global warming, so it's best to be prepared. Be sure to charge your devices. Call if you need anything."

It was hard to believe how much they had accumulated. Most of her household goods were packed away and rather than retrieve and unpack boxes that were in storage, she often bought a new juicer or waffle maker at Walmart. Her northern California wardrobe didn't work in the sizzling Texas heat, and she'd gone shopping a few times in Dallas. She'd also stocked up on towels, so she didn't have to go to the laundromat as often.

The trailer was an obstacle course with boxes everywhere. Billie had finished the second bedroom and started on the bathroom but ran out of tape. *That's as good an excuse as any to shut down packing for the day*, she thought. Monroe had stayed so long; she didn't feel like cooking the fish she'd taken out of the freezer and ate peanut butter and jelly instead. Lovey's canned muscadine grape jelly was divine.

Skies had been overcast all day, and it wasn't as late as it seemed. She remembered to heed Monroe's warning and made sure her computer, tablet, and phone were fully charged. She'd never lived in a place with such unreliable electricity. California had the record for the most power blackouts, but at least there was a reason. Electricity providers shut down the grid to protect power lines against wildfires during hot, dry days, and there were millions of people. Ross County was such a small place, it seemed like it should be easier to keep the lights on. But if it was too hot, the power went out. If it rained, the power went out. If it was too windy, the power went out. Now, a storm hundreds of miles away was a reason to plan for a power outage.

Billie made sure she had a flashlight, candles, and matches in an accessible place, then took a leisurely bath and read more of her novel. It was only eight o'clock, but she put on her nightgown and got in bed. She read a little while, then turned to a Lifetime movie. It started raining and the steady tapping of fat raindrops put her to sleep. She was awakened by a loud thunderclap. The change in air pressure made her ears pop. The toilet gurgled, then the lights flickered. She looked out her window and saw light rain, and the tree branches barely moved. But then there was loud thunder and constant flashes of lightning against an ominous pea-green sky. Suddenly the sky seemed to open, and bucketfuls of rain were coming down sideways. She heard sirens and hopped out of bed. She was dressing when the lights went out and heard what sounded like a rumbling freight train moving closer.

Billie knew what to do during an earthquake, get under a desk, cover your head, and hold on. She had been through countless fire drills and knew to stop, drop, and roll. But she was unprepared for a tornado. On the rare occasion of a tornado warning back home, they were told to go to the basement. But there were no basements here. Her first thought was to grab her phone, and then she remembered to grab a mattress and take cover in the bathtub. She dragged the mattress to the bathroom and as soon as she climbed in, parts of the roof peeled off. It sounded like the end of the world, and Billie prayed as high-pitched sirens blared.

After what seemed like hours, she felt like she was suffocating and moved the mattress just in time to see a barbeque grill fly through the pitch-black sky. The sirens finally stopped, and winds were dying down. She tried to get out of the tub, but couldn't move. Part of a wall had caved in, and she was stuck underneath it. A nail was piercing her thigh, and moving in any direction brought excruciating pain, then there was no pain. She had passed out.

Billie woke up in a dark room with a sliver of light streaming underneath a closed door. As her eyes adjusted to the dark, she saw Shaun in the chair next to her. "Where am I? What are you doing here?"

"You're at Ross County General Hospital. A tree crashed through your roof during the storm and trapped you inside."

Her memory was groggy, and Billie closed her eyes to try to remember. She couldn't fit all the pieces together, but the heart monitor sensors attached to her chest, the IV needle in her arm, and the tight bandage around her thigh, told her it was serious. "The last thing I remember is the sirens. I don't remember coming here."

"After the storm passed, everyone came outside of what was left of our trailers to escape falling debris and survey the damage. As we gathered in the street, I realized you weren't in the crowd. Your smashed car was on the carport, so I figured you were inside. We called 911, but got a busy signal, then put on hold. Will climbed over your broken steps and stumbled through the rubble. He found you in the bathtub, and he yelled that you were hurt. Some neighbors helped him remove the piece of wall that you were pinned under.

They got you in our car and we drove here, which was like navigating an obstacle course with all the downed trees and power lines. But thank God we made it. Will said if the wall had fallen two inches in either direction, you probably wouldn't have survived."

"I don't know how to thank you, but you don't have to sit here with me. You should be with Jenna."

"I don't mind. Besides, our place is a mess. We're staying with my in-laws."

"I need to call Cole," Billie said, trying to clear her dry throat.

"We talked to him. He booked the first flight, but the storms we had caused flight delays to the east, and he won't be here until around noon. Your mother called and she and your sister are coming too. They should arrive around the same time."

Billie had survived Hurricane Kyle, but now Hurricane Zuri and Maya were on their way.

Zuri tapped on the door, then she and Maya entered. "She's asleep," Maya whispered.

"Hey Mom," Billie said softly, as her eyes fluttered open.

"Are you alright? I was so worried," her mother said as she rushed to her daughter's side. "Where's Cole? Why are you here alone?"

"He had to take a trip for the baseball team. He should be here soon."

"He should've been here all along. He deposits you in this backwoods tornado magnet, so you can get blown around like Dorothy in Oz, and then leaves. I don't like that and I'm going to let him know. And what's going on with your hair?" she asked as she fingered Billie's locs. "It looks like straw, and I see gray streaks around your edges. I can't have a daughter with gray hair, folks will start thinking I'm old."

"Aisha, one of the students was doing my hair, but she went home for the summer. I'm thinking about cutting my locs," Billie said, wincing as she tried to sit up.

"That's the pain meds talking. You've been growing them for years," Maya said.

"How are you feeling?" Zuri asked.

"I'm sore," Billie replied. Her memory was still cloudy, but knowing they dropped everything to come to Texas confirmed how serious her injury was. She was sorry for the circumstances that brought them there, but seeing her mother and sister lifted her spirits.

The nurse came in to check her vitals. Then the staff worker brought in her dinner tray. Maya rolled the table close to her sister, then lifted the cover. "Baked chicken, mac and cheese, and green beans. Guess they don't know you don't eat meat or dairy. I'll go see if they have something else."

As Maya left the room, Cole entered. "Baby, I got here as soon as I could. Monroe picked me up from the airport and driving into town, it looks like a warzone. I'm so sorry you had to go through this alone."

Zuri tipped out of the room, to give them privacy and to search for a hotel. There were no vacancies within fifty miles.

"I couldn't help but overhear your phone call," Monroe said. "Everything around here is booked. You and Maya can stay at my house or with Lovey."

"We'll stay with Lovey," Maya said as she walked up.

"Hey Maya, good to see you."

"Hi Monroe."

"You'll have to share a room, but you'll have the best food in town."

Zuri and Maya spent the rest of the day with Billie. Zuri brought roses from the gift shop and did Billie's nails. Maya tightened and conditioned her locs. They watched two

Lifetime movies and left Billie comfortably snoring. For two days they hovered over Billie, befriending the staff, and ensuring she received their full attention.

Zuri and Cole were in Billie's room when the doctor came for his last visit and stated Billie could go home, with instructions for limited activity.

"The tornado hopscotched over southern Ross County and there was only minimal damage at the house," Cole said.

"Good, even if it's empty, I'll be glad to finally move in."

"Didn't you hear the doctor say you'll have to take it easy," Zuri said. "No moving, packing or unpacking."

"We're not quite ready to move anyway. There's no water."

"What do you mean?" Billie asked.

"The water tower was hit and there's no running water in Rossbrooke Estates."

"How long until the tower is fixed?"

"They estimate a week or so."

"It's the 'or so' that worries me."

"We can get an emergency hotel room through FEMA. But two of the hotels don't have water either, so that makes the waiting list longer. We can stay with Lovey until we get approved."

"I appreciate the offer, but I've got a better idea," Zuri said. "We'll go stay in a Dallas hotel. My daughter needs to relax and must keep her wound clean and her bandage needs to be changed regularly. How is she going to do that with ten people in the house, bottled water, and spotty utilities? While we're there, we can go to the Apple store, and she can get a new phone."

"That's probably for the best. I've ordered a generator, and it should be here late next week. Also Monroe said FEMA will be here Monday and we can get hotel vouchers."

"It's settled. I'll extend the rental car another week. Plus, we can go see a real doctor. I don't trust these country doctors. I'm sure they do the best they can, but I'll feel better if you see someone with more resources."

Two hours later the wheelchair attendant came in. "I can walk," Billie said, but the discharge nurse insisted she be wheeled out. The disinfected hospital air probably had fewer germs, but she relished the breeze and fresh air.

"Can you drive by Lakewood Terrace? I want to see what it looks like," Billie asked Cole. She learned it had been an EF2 tornado with recorded wind gusts of 120 miles. There were mounds of broken furniture, shingles, siding and mangled metal beside the road. Their trailer had come off two of its piers, the skirting was gone, and it was leaning precariously. Trees looked like spooky Disney cartoon characters with branches stripped from their leaves, if they even had branches. The damage was devastating, but everyone was relatively upbeat since there had been no loss of life. A wave of nausea came over Billie and she didn't know if it was the realization of how close she had come to death, from laying in a hospital bed so long or from the pungent odor of sour wet grass, sulfur and wood seeping through the car vent. "I've seen enough."

They checked into an Embassy Suites near southeast Dallas, with adjoining rooms. Billie was enjoying being back in the city, and this was her second time ordering Thai food in three days. Despite a sore thigh and her mother's bossiness, Billie couldn't remember the last time she had laughed out loud or slept so soundly. She and her mother teased Maya about spending so much time on the phone with her latest boyfriend. After days without a phone, she was getting used to not being so connected. Anyone who really mattered knew how to get in touch with her.

The week passed quickly, and Cole had been able to get a room in Calderville. Billie had enjoyed her mother and sister and was sorry they would be leaving. She loved Cole's family—most of them—but missed her own relatives. They pampered her and she almost forgot they were together under stressed circumstances. Surviving the tornado made her realize how precious time was and she vowed to spend more time with them.

Cole drove her back to Calderville, and to their new home at the Super 8, a big step down from the Embassy Suites. Ordinarily she always took the stairs, but her thigh was still sore, so she took what seemed like the slowest elevator in the world to their second-floor room. Calder State's campus had only minimal damage with a few downed trees, so Cole went to work every day. Billie was still on leave and spent most of her day in the hotel room. The highlight of her day was *The Price is Right* and daytime *Jeopardy*. She tried to check email and keep up with Sunrise Bank news, but WIFI was spotty.

Cole was busier than ever and one evening she told him, "I never thought I'd say this, but I miss the trailer. I don't like sharing walls, and elevators." They were supposed to be on a nonsmoking floor, but no one was enforcing it, as Billie discovered the first night when she called the front desk to complain and was told there was nothing they could do. After six days of eating out and trying to store everything in a dorm size refrigerator, they opted to go to their house.

A few houses on their block had blue tarp on the roof, but from the outside, their house looked unscathed by the storm. Inside was another story. The wood flooring was warped, there were big cracks in the vaulted ceiling, water pressure was low, and electricity only worked in half of the house, but it was better than the Super 8.

Boxes were stacked almost to the ceiling and the furniture was pushed to the center of each room. She overdid the moving, unpacking and cleaning the first day, and her body reminded her of the doctor's instructions. She was probably enduring more pain than needed, but after Dylan's experience with prescription painkillers, she was determined to take them only as a last resort.

The sun was shining through the sheet at the window and Billie rolled over and slowly crawled off the air mattress. Their bedroom furniture had been destroyed in the storm and their new furniture was on backorder. The air mattress was slowing down her healing, but at least she had water and a place to lay her head. Many Lakewood Terrace families remained displaced.

Three weeks since the storm, and her doctor had finally cleared her to return to work. Since moving to Calderville, she had been on a whirlwind. The storm had forced her to relax and reflect. But now it was time to return to reality.

Her three weeks off had almost been a hibernation. She began going through her emails, but the list was so long, she decided to wait until Monday and enjoy the last days in her bubble. Unfortunately, a phone call ended that bubble sooner than she planned and the real world came crashing in, when Cole called to tell her Dylan had left rehab again.

CHAPTER 27

Working for the bank may have meant countless meetings and redundant memos, but there was one big benefit—federal holidays. Billie hadn't earned vacation days yet, so she appreciated the breaks. Memorial Day had passed and today she was off for Juneteenth Day, the holiday commemorating the end of slavery in the United States, a day many African Americans considered their real Independence Day. KBLK broadcasts round the clock every day, so she had always worked on Juneteenth Day. On-air personalities broadcast live from locations around Oakland, so Juneteenth was busier than a regular workday. While she missed being in the center of things, she was enjoying being a spectator, with nothing to do but show up.

The Ross County Juneteenth Parade was a community event, and NFL legend Riley Ford was the grand marshal. The parade started at eight thirty in the morning. When the ROTC Corps passed, walking in unison, in their crisp-looking uniforms, Billie thought of Kendra. Her daughter had sent them a large basket of California poppies as a house-warming gift, and Billie was still amazed by her daughter's transformation.

Sororities, fraternities, elected officials, churches, and schools had floats. A white convertible with Hollis Barnes for mayor signs passed by. There was even a float featuring Dr Pepper, which was founded not far from Calderville. But the main attraction was the Calder State marching band, known as the Sizzling Sounds and high-stepping majorettes. She cheered when Cole and the baseball team marched past and he threw her a kiss. The parade route was two and a half miles, in observance of the two and a half years it took for emancipation news to reach Galveston, Texas. The parade ended at the entrance to River Park, where a thick, sweet barbeque aroma permeated the air.

By ten, most people were at the park, and the picnic was in full swing by eleven, with everyone eating their first round of burgers and barbeque. The Nigerian students had a tent and Billie bought jerk grilled eggplant, corn on the cob and fried plantains to take home.

"I see you over there," Reverend Collins said, beckoning for her to come to his table. "Now come over here and get some dessert." The Grove City Revitalization Committee was selling baked goods and Billie bought pound cake for Cole and fried apple pies for herself.

"I don't know if these pies will make it to the house," she said.

"You know where the church is, come back anytime and you can get a refill."

She browsed the vendor tables and bought two Calder State t-shirts. The Alumni Association had a table, and Cole was helping Serena and other officers solicit memberships and donations. FEMA had a table to help people with their claims and the Westside YMCA had a table collecting donations for tornado relief. Several local candidates were passing out information, including Hollis Barnes, a young man many thought had a good chance to be the town's first Black mayor. Even the Ross County Drug Awareness and Prevention Coalition had a table. She briefly looked at the brochures but didn't take one. Dylan had texted a few times in the last couple weeks since leaving New Day. His texts were short, with messages like, *Just checking in*, or *Don't worry, I'm ok*. Of course, she still worried but work and getting the house in order kept her busy.

Someone came up behind her and said, "Hey Ms. Jordan." It was Adrian Butler.

"We're no longer in school. Please call me Billie, although I shouldn't even speak to you after the way you challenged me during the City Council meeting."

"Nothing personal," he said, as he handed a young man a voter registration brochure. "Like I said, I'm sorry about challenging you during the meeting. I get tired of the same old run around."

"Why not work with the system, instead of against it?"

"Have to have a willing partner in order to do that."

"Since I'm on your side, why not work with me?" Billie asked. "How can I help?"

"Come to our next meeting. It's open to the public."

"Do you want me to give the same presentation I gave at the council meeting?"

"That right there is the problem," Adrian said. "You want to come and dictate to us. Unless you're bringing the county checkbook with you, we're not interested in another presentation. Come listen to us for a change. The bank and any other corporate entities always want to swoop in and tell us what to do and how to do it."

"I didn't mean any harm. Maybe if you weren't so combative, you'd get more assistance."

"I know you think you're making a difference, by directing a few dollars to this or that program, but all you're doing is helping them justify the status quo. I have a right to be combative, and if you were more concerned about the people than your job, you would be too," he said and walked away to pass out more brochures.

Billie shrugged her shoulders and browsed more vendor tables. It was already ninety degrees, and she didn't plan to stay much longer. Texas heat was more oppressive than in California. At home, temperatures cooled at night, and you could open windows. This heat was heavy, and it got hot earlier in the day. She headed toward Cole's table to tell him she was leaving, but everyone else seemed to be getting their second wind. The sororities and fraternities were doing impromptu step shows. Billie appreciated the history and significance of Black Greek organizations. She hadn't pledged in college but had several friends in sororities and often featured their social and civic events on KBLK. But now she felt like an outsider. Plus the sight of forty- and fifty-year-old men chanting, stomping, jumping, and grunting wasn't entertaining to her. Especially since she knew Cole would be complaining about his back that evening. They had driven separately, so she went to the alumni table to tell him she was leaving, then headed to the parking lot.

As she walked to her car, Adrian caught up with her, "Hey Ms. Jor...I mean Billie," he said, "I didn't mean to be rude. My sister tells me I need to lighten up. I hope I didn't scare you off, and you'll come to a meeting. Here's my card."

"Don't be surprised to see me there," she said.

The car was hot, and she couldn't wait to get home and cool off. She stopped to get gas, then headed home. As she turned onto Pecan Lane, it looked like someone was on her porch. She started to pass her house, then pull over to look at the security camera app on her phone. But as she got closer, she recognized the visitor. It was Dylan.

Calderville may have been a small town, but Billie and Cole's social calendar was busier than it ever was in California. In Oakland they were busy with their children's sports and school activities. They occasionally attended a play or a jazz concert, but Billie was usually working at those events, so it wasn't really a relaxing night out. They had switched roles, and now Cole had fraternity events, alumni fundraisers, and Calder State programs. Whenever Billie suggested they skip an event, Cole explained protocol. "If we don't support their event, they might not support ours."

"Then you're passing around the same fifty dollars, donating it to each other," Billie said, shaking her head.

She had taken the day off to spend with Dylan. She drove him around town, playing tour guide. They visited a few relatives and went to Walmart. "What do you want for dinner?" she asked. "We're supposed to attend a baseball team banquet, so I hadn't planned to cook anything."

"I'll be okay," Dylan said. "I saw some barbeque in the fridge. I'll eat that. You guys go enjoy yourself."

As Billie and Cole were dressing, she said, "I hate to go out when Dylan just got here. Why don't you go on ahead?"

"We can't babysit him," Cole said. "I promise we won't stay long." These were words she'd heard before, and she knew they had different definitions of "long."

The cafeteria had been transformed into an elegant banquet hall, with a shimmering electric blue and purple draped ceiling, tall lavender floral centerpieces, soft candle lighting, and a purple carpet runner at the room's entrance. A season highlight video looped on screens around the room. Billie and Cole sat at tables up front with coaches, team members and equipment managers. She watched Cole beam with pride as he interacted with the young men. She felt a twinge of regret that after years of practice and competition, Dylan's swimming career was over. His team had gone to the section championships and two of his former teammates were All-Americans. Both goals that Dylan had been working toward.

After the awards and speeches had been given, Billie told

Cole she was ready to leave. "We promised Dylan we wouldn't be long, plus I have water distribution tomorrow," she said.

"Okay honey. Let me speak to a few more parents and we can leave."

Billie understood this was a big deal for the school and looked for a chair. Small groups formed, while a few couples danced. She found a seat at a table near the door and was soon joined by two older couples. "What's a pretty young thing like you doing sitting alone?" the taller man said. "If I were a few years younger I'd twirl you on that dance floor."

"If you were a few years younger, she'd be in diapers," the woman with him said, while holding a chair for him. "Sit your old mannish self down."

Billie smiled as they introduced themselves. Both couples were Calder State alumni, and the flirtatious man was Dr. Kingsley, President emeritus of the board of trustees. He had played in the major leagues a few years before returning to lead the Calder State athletics department. He was complimentary of Cole and loved that more alumni were returning to town. He was a wealth of history, and the conversation wound its way to the upcoming election. "We've got to get our young people more engaged," he said.

"I agree," Billie said. "They need to know their voice matters."

"Everyone gets excited about the presidential election, but state and local elections are more important. We made great strides when Democrats controlled this county. I've been looking for someone to revive the campus College Democrats of America chapter. Would you be interested in being an advisor?"

"I'm not a Democrat," she said.

"Don't tell me you're a Republican."

"I consider myself an independent. College is supposed to teach young people to think for themselves. Giving students a choice between the Democrats and Republicans is no choice at all. There are candidates from the Libertarian Party, the People's Party, and the Green Party they should consider."

"A third-party vote is the same as not voting. Those clowns don't have a snowball's chance in hell of winning."

"What have the Democrats done that's so great?" Billie asked. "Black people remain at the bottom of every statistic from education and health disparities to the wealth gap."

"Things may not be as they should, but they're not like they were. You're evidence of that. I remember when a Black person couldn't go in Sunrise Bank except to mop the floors. My parents couldn't vote and now we have a Black man running for mayor, with a good chance to win."

"I've seen him at a few events. I know everyone is excited about his candidacy. What's his platform?" Billie asked.

"He's a local boy and a Calder State grad."

"That's great, but I'd still like to know his proposals. I moderated candidate forums on my California radio show and it's a mistake to vote for someone just because they're Black. Having a Black person in office doesn't guarantee that person is the best for the job, or they aren't crooked."

"You're new around here, so you don't understand our history. Many people worked hard, worked together and gave up a lot to get us to this point. That Barnes boy will make a great mayor, but he won't get elected if we're not unified, and if our young people don't vote. And as for a third party, that's about as useful as a steering wheel on a mule. All that does is split our vote." Dr. Kingsley's raised voice drew the attention of surrounding attendees.

"Sorry to interrupt, but my wife owes me a dance," Cole said as he led Billie to the dance floor.

"What the hell are you doing?" he asked her. "Do you know who that is?"

"Someone who's still living in the 'we shall overcome' era and doesn't realize..."

"Billie stop," Cole said, and smiled to mask his displeasure. "Dr. Kingsley was the first Black person on the city council and one of the students who integrated the Woolworth's lunch counter. Why are you arguing with him?"

"I wasn't arguing. We were having a discussion, but when he said..."

"You act like your beliefs are fact. People feel as strongly about their convictions as you do. And it's not your job to convert them."

"Then things will never change. It's hard for me to accept backward thinking. It's the reason this world..."

"Have you not heard anything I said?" Cole asked as the record stopped.

"I'm not going to compromise my beliefs to curry favor and go along to get along. Besides, I told you I didn't want to come, then I told you I was ready to go. If you weren't so busy trying to impress your old girlfriend, maybe all of this wouldn't have happened. Did she sweet talk another donation out of you?"

"I should be flattered that you're jealous of Serena, but it's not a good look on you."

"You didn't answer my questions. Did we give any more money?"

"No. Do you have to be such a drag? Can't we have a fun evening without you turning it into a debate?"

"Hanging out with your old girlfriend is not my idea of a fun evening."

"Arguing about politics is not my idea of a fun evening. I don't see how you can be so relentless in your beliefs and ideals."

"And I don't see how you can't."

SECTION IV

Rough Seas

CHAPTER 28

When Billie attended her first Water Works board meeting, she had been a concerned citizen. Now she was an informed citizen. She was still waiting for the three documents she learned about on the Grown Folks Cruise, the water quality report card, department annual review and the financial audit, and had done more research since returning. She had her Texas driver's license and was ready to address the board. However, after speaking with Adrian, they decided it would be more impactful if other community members spoke, since she was viewed as an outsider. "You're right," Billie said. "If the board hears from mothers that rely on bottled water for formula, or elderly residents who can't get to the water distribution centers, maybe they'll be more sensitive to how urgent this is for those on the west side."

"I'm not optimistic," Adrian said, "but we can try."

She thought she knew at least two who would speak and mentioned it the next time she stopped at Lovey's house. Lovey and Amos were on the porch playing gin rummy when she stopped at their house.

"Hey there," Billie said as she got out of her car.

"Hey baby. You should have let me know you were

coming by, and I would have fixed you a plate. Everything I cooked has meat in it."

"No worries," Billie said as she sat on the porch swing. "I'm working with a local group to get something done about the water. Would you be willing to come speak at a Water Works board meeting?"

"Baby, I got better things to do with the time I got left on this earth than to go down there messing with them white folks," Lovey said.

"What about you Amos?"

"Cole said you were a fighter, but you'll have better luck getting a rooster to lay an egg," he said. "That's a lost cause."

"It doesn't have to be," Billie pleaded. "Lovey, you were here during the civil rights movement. You know it takes action to get change."

"I appreciate your gumption," Lovey said, while patting Billie's hand. "Bless your heart."

"How about a chess match?" Amos asked.

"Not today. I've got a few errands to run. I have water for you in my trunk."

"Thank you, but you know I don't worry about this water. Take it over to Grove City. They always need water," Lovey said.

"But your water has contaminants that can be harmful to people your age," Billie said. "I don't have all the reports I've asked for, but I've read enough to know there are big problems."

"I been drinking this water for eighty years and other than a little arthritis, I'm still alive and kicking with no complaints. Plenty stuff to worry about other than water."

Billie met similar resistance with others and was surprised how difficult it was to get folks involved. She thought apathy came from living in a large city, where people believed they were just a number and their input didn't count. But she was finding engagement in a small town just as difficult. Frequent boil notices were a new issue for her, but others had been dealing with it for years. She and Adrian were only able to get a commitment from five people, but they were going forward with what they had.

Billie and Adrian met with their volunteers at Adrian's office. They prepared notecards with key facts and practiced talking points. When they finished, Billie was about to drive off, but realized she left her phone and went back. Adrian let her in with a slice of cake in foil in his hand.

"That looks good. I can smell the lemony flavor."

"Would you like a piece?" he offered.

"No thanks. Somebody prepared that for their man and wouldn't be happy that he's giving it away."

"Not that it matters, but I'm my own man. A friend made this cake."

"If you say so," she said, giving him the side eye. "Most women aren't baking unless they're in a relationship or working on being in a relationship."

"As I said, just a friend. Women are always trying to lock somebody down. I'm taking a relationship break. Life is calmer this way, plus I get a lot of homemade dinners, cakes, and pies," he said with a smirk.

She wondered if maybe she and Cole needed a relationship break, as she recalled him on the phone and barely looking up when she left.

The morning of the meeting, she woke up early, too excited to sleep. However, she was disappointed when she received a text that one of the meeting participants was unable to take off work.

She only worked a half day and was at Mrs. Armstrong's carport at 2:30 PM. Mrs. Armstrong had lived on the west side for seventy years and seemed excited about speaking. When Billie knocked on the door, Mrs. Armstrong peeked through the screen and said, "I won't be able to make it," and closed the door.

Billie was puzzled but drove on to the meeting. As she was grabbing her bag from the back seat, Adrian opened her car door for her. "Today's the day," she announced cheerfully. "I had two cancellations, but you and I can handle their portion."

"We should call it off for today," Adrian said. "The other three cancelled too."

"You mean no one is coming?" Billie asked.

"Just you and me."

"What happened?"

"They received an offer they couldn't refuse."

"A bribe?"

"They don't call it that. But I was told they each received a two-thousand-dollar Visa gift card."

"You've got to be kidding," Billie said, shaking her head. "Well, there must be a way to track down who purchased the cards."

"The person who told me said he already spent the money to fix his truck transmission. Besides, no one's going to admit they received a card," Adrian said.

"This is a scene out of a John Grisham novel."

"Except in our version, no one is coming to blow the whistle on the greedy bad guys."

"I didn't submit my name as a speaker, but I'm going to the meeting anyway," Billie said. "If they're this determined to keep us silent, something must really be going on. I'll just take notes. At least they'll know people are paying attention."

"Help yourself," Adrian said. "I'm going home."

The meeting lasted ninety minutes, with the primary discussion being awarding contracts to paint the main water tower and replace awnings at the public works building damaged during the tornado. A Dallas firm had submitted the lowest bid, but several members wanted to award the bid to a local firm. Billie didn't see how these could be the most critical agenda items and had to restrain herself several times from interrupting the proceedings.

She stopped at Whataburger on her way home. She loved having Dylan with them, but now she had to pay more attention to meal planning. She had planned to prepare grilled salmon with a lemon butter glaze and baked sweet potatoes for dinner, but the change in plans had sapped her motivation. She bought a cranberry apple salad, which she would eat with garlic bread, and ordered a patty melt and fries for Dylan. Cole would probably eat at Lovey's before they went to Bible study.

Maybe Cole is right, she thought. This water business was becoming a thankless mission. Those in power didn't want her to pursue it, and those she was trying to help didn't act like they wanted her help. *Why am I sticking my neck out?* She planned to take a leisurely bath and enjoy a glass of the wine they kept hidden under their bathroom sink.

Paint-stained shoes were in the garage, so she figured Dylan was home. Lovey's neighbor raved about Dylan's work so much that others on their block hired him to do yardwork and odd jobs. They told others and Dylan had to turn away business. Raking leaves, painting and cutting grass were not what Billie had in mind for her son's career path, but for now she was just glad he was clean and staying busy. She heard the shower running when she entered the house. She put Dylan's food in the microwave and decided to catch up on her work emails so the day wouldn't be a total bust. She cleared off the kitchen island, so she could set up her laptop. As she grabbed Dylan's backpack, several items fell out and rolled under the stool. She picked up Dylan's sunglasses, house key, a beat-up wallet, a half-inch Ziploc bag with nine yellow pills, a rolled-up dollar bill—and her Rolex watch. The blood rushed to her head and her heart began racing. She hollered like someone had punched her in the gut, tossed the Ziploc bag across the room and fell to her knees. Her son was using again.

Dylan rushed out of the bathroom with a towel around his waist and asked, "What is it?" Then his gaze went to the pills strewn across the floor. "Mom, I..."

"What? What do you have to say? I cannot believe you would do this to me."

"Let me help you," Dylan said, as he reached for her hand.

"Don't touch me," she shouted, as she struggled to stand. "I've always done whatever I could for you. Even now when others said, Let him fall, let him hit rock bottom, I've been here and you'd steal from me? Getting high means that much?"

"You don't get it. Something takes over, and I can't help it. I've tried," he said, as water dripped and pooled around his bare feet.

"I can't do this with you anymore. Get out," Billie said, as tears rolled down her cheeks.

"I promise not to..."

"We've mortgaged everything to help you. Our credit cards are maxed out, including the ones you stole. Do you know how humiliated I was to have my boss counsel me about financial responsibility? No more. You have twenty-four hours to leave this house."

Billie spent the rest of the evening in her room, and Dylan stayed in his. Cole came in, grinning like he'd won the lottery, "I just got a phone call. Demarcus Jones, the kid from Houston has committed to Calder State," he announced. "Several ranked schools were recruiting him. Chris works with his brother, and we were able to set up an exclusive visit, and he chose us. This is going to transform the program and HBCU baseball."

"That's wonderful for you," Billie said, softly.

"Are you all right?" he asked.

"A little tired."

"Let me make a few phone calls, then I'll help you relax," he said and patted her behind.

Billie lay across the bed, mindlessly changing the channels and heard her husband on the phone. She hadn't heard him this excited about anything in a long time and decided to take a bath and go to bed. *I'll tell him about Dylan tomorrow.*

Billie was awake early the next morning and heard the front door close. She opened the blind and saw Dylan walking down the street. He looked so alone, and it took every ounce of strength not to call him back or drive off and follow him. She watched until she could no longer see him, then went to his room and saw most of the clothes they had bought still hanging in the closet. His backpack was gone, but his phone and her watch were on the bed. Billie made green tea and turned on her computer to get a jumpstart on her day. Month-end reports were due, and she wasn't even half-way complete. The bank was undergoing a restructuring, and her territory had expanded. This was a repeat of what happened at the radio station—more duties, same pay.

Cole's phone started ringing at eight and hadn't stopped. With each call, she heard him excitedly recount the Demarcus Jones story. She tried to focus on her Sunrise tasks, but her mind kept wandering. Dylan didn't know anyone in Texas other than family and she wondered where he had gone. Everyone said this was the way to respond to a loved one's addiction—to let them sink or swim on their own. *Maybe it will get easier as time passes,* she thought.

She couldn't concentrate on work and had absentmindedly watched *The Today Show*, and *The View*.

"I need to talk to you," Billie said, when Cole finally emerged from the bedroom.

"I haven't changed my mind about the DNA test, so I hope that's not what you want to talk about," Cole said.

Billie hadn't changed her mind either, but right now that was not on her priority list.

"Let me get this call," he said and went back into the bedroom.

Billie prepared an early lunch and was sitting at the table picking at her food when Cole came back into the kitchen. "That was Monroe. Dylan's been arrested."

They entered a cinderblock building that blended in with the other well-manicured buildings on the square. Police cars parked outside were the clue that this was the police station. A receptionist took their information, then led them to a windowless room. When she was arrested in Oakland, there were security scanners at every door, armed guards, cameras, and iron bars throughout the building. This almost reminded her of Sheriff Taylor's jail on the *Andy Griffith Show*. They learned Dylan had been arrested for trespassing and possession of a controlled substance. They completed some papers then an officer brought Dylan to the room.

Dylan entered and sat across from them. "Hey," he said scratching his arm. "I guess I screwed up again. You'd all be better off if I was dead."

"This is not the time for a pity party, son. I don't know if we can save you this time," Cole said.

"I'm not worth saving."

"If that's the way you feel, you're never going to get yourself together. I wish I understood you better," Cole said.

"We're going to hire a lawyer and get you out of here," Billie said.

For the next thirty minutes they talked about everything but his drug problem, until an officer opened the door and told them their time was up. "We're changing shifts. You can come back later."

When they got to the car, Billie steadied herself for a few seconds before getting inside. "I shouldn't have let him leave," she said, holding her side.

"What are you talking about?" Cole asked.

"I found pills in his bag yesterday and confronted him. I was so mad. I told him to leave."

"I thought he left for an early painting job. You knew he was using again and didn't say anything?"

"I wanted to tell you, but you seemed so excited about your new baseball player. I was about to tell you when Monroe called you."

"That was almost twenty-four hours ago. How could you keep that from me?"

"I never thought it would turn out like this," Billie said.

"This is a real mess, but in a weird way, it could be for the best. Hopefully he'll wake up and realize this is not a game. It's probably a good thing he was arrested here, rather than somewhere away from us."

"You can't be serious. The Texas legal system isn't known for fairness and compassion to black people. That Barney Fife cop was ready to throw the book at me because I didn't use a signal on an empty street," Billie said. "When we go back, we should be able to bond him out."

"That officer said we can't do anything until Monday."

"I'll bet Monroe can help us," Billie said.

"I think Dylan is where he needs to be. We can't keep rescuing him. If you want Monroe's help, you call him."

"Thanks so much for coming," Adrian said as he walked Billie to her car. Given everything going on with Dylan, she had almost forgotten about the NAACP chapter meeting.

She considered skipping it, but she had missed the last one, plus she figured it would take her mind off Dylan for a few hours.

"Thanks for inviting me," Billie said. "The meeting was very informative. I wish there had been more people here. Although I was surprised to see several white people in attendance."

"We announced that this evening's agenda would be devoted to the water problem. Folks think it's only a west side problem. But what impacts the west side, impacts downtown and the whole county. That's an old strategy to pit powerless people against each other while the real culprit keeps on doing their dirt. Consistency is the key. When there's a water issue, we get a lot of support and publicity and when things are supposedly okay, interest dies down. But decisions and actions taken during the dormant times are what impacts the number and severity of our water issues."

"I've been visiting Calderville for twenty years and never knew it was this bad," Billie said.

"We meet monthly, and I hope you'll come back. I appreciate you coming, especially at a time like this. I know your son is facing some challenges."

"I keep forgetting everyone knows everyone else's business in this town," Billie said, as she pressed the car unlock button.

"I understand how addiction impacts a family. My dad got on crack and became a different person. He lost his job, did some stupid stuff and went to prison. He died there."

"Are you comparing my son to a crackhead?" Billie asked, tilting her head to the side.

"The drug choice varies, but the disease of addiction works the same."

"It's not the same at all," Billie said as she opened her car door. "My son had a debilitating injury and his doctor prescribed painkillers. Please refrain from making assumptions about and speaking on my son, whom you have never met."

"I didn't mean to offend you," Adrian said, stepping back while Billie got in her car, started it and drove off, leaving Adrian waving car exhaust from his face.

CHAPTER 29

"It's been two days, and we haven't seen Dylan. We should get a lawyer," Billie said.

"And pay him with what?" Cole replied. "Monroe said he's been down there several times, and he knows the guards. We'll have to accept that until Monday."

"They can't hold him like that. And heaven help us if we're relying on Monroe. That man is the definition of crooked."

"He's helping us with Dylan. You should be a little more grateful," Cole said.

"I appreciate it, but it feels like making a deal with the devil. He'll eventually come to collect."

"We both want Dylan out. Why are we arguing about this? We've been married almost twenty years. By now being together shouldn't be this hard," Cole said, rubbing his forehead. "I'm tired of fighting about everything."

"And I'm tired of you acting like everything is my fault," Billie said crossing her arms.

"There's a saying that if you have disputes with everyone, maybe it's you and not them."

"There's also a saying that evil triumphs when good men

do nothing. It's like you don't care about anything," Billie said.

"I care, but I'm not going to waste energy on things I can't control. It was okay when you were getting paid for it. But you're not at the radio station anymore. Those activists and marchers you admire are getting paid, either from a so-called foundation or a dubious donation. You should direct your energy toward your own family."

"Well, I'm sorry we didn't achieve world peace yet. Damn, what if Nelson Mandela or Dr. King said I'm not making enough money and quit fighting for change?"

"I never claimed to be Nelson Mandela or any other martyr. We had a good life in California, or so I thought. Now that I'm here, I realize I don't want to fight the power. We seem so different now. Sometimes I think maybe I shouldn't have stayed with you. We thought we were helping Dylan but..."

"You shouldn't have stayed with me?" Billie said with a raised voice. "You were the one who had the affair—remember?"

"I know that was a mistake, but at least that was something I can acknowledge and correct. All this other stuff you're so worked up over is too abstract. You have righteous anger, and I admire your relentlessness. I never participated in any social action stuff on campus until I met you. All I was interested in was playing ball and partying. Protesting and trying to impact change was exciting when I was twenty-two. Your tenacity and passion were sexy and very grown up to me. Now you're just being stubborn and intolerant. It's exhausting. I know one person can make a difference, but at this stage of my life I've accepted that I'm not that one person. I'm forty-two and I want money in the bank, peace, and serenity."

"Do you want serenity or Serena?" Billie asked, then left the room.

CHAPTER 30

Even though it was barely daybreak, Billie was reclining on her patio, nursing a mimosa, and enjoying the damp, musky smell of recent rain. She hadn't slept well. Thunderstorms rolled through during the night, and ever since the tornado, stormy weather put her on edge. Hooting owls, chirping crickets, and croaking frogs had seemed louder than usual, giving her a spooky feeling, reminding her that she was alone in the house. Cole hadn't come home last night; something he had never done. On her relationship show she had heard of all types of bad breakups, from slashed tires to revenge porn posts. She had always advised listeners not to engage in negative behavior. Now she understood how people snapped when their lifestyle, and everything they had worked for was threatened. But she was so shaken, she couldn't cry, plot revenge or be mad. She had stood by her man all the way to Texas, only to be left alone.

The last time she'd had this feeling was on the first Sunday of the football season after the Oakland Raiders moved, the final time. There was a malaise over the whole city that probably seemed silly to outsiders. But for years their Sundays revolved around Raiders' home games. One year they had seats on the fifty-yard line because Maya was dating an Assistant Coach. Locals knew it was a business controlled by billionaires and the world wasn't coming to an end. Yet it still stung, and most residents felt betrayed and jilted. Some local fans still pulled for them after they left, but that seemed like staying in an abusive relationship. He's said he wants to leave. Why pursue someone who doesn't want you?

That was the realization Billie was coming to. Cole didn't want her anymore. Arguments over Chris and even the Water Works board were now intractable issues with no room for compromise. And how could her loving their son and wanting to help him be a reason to leave? Their arguments always ended up in the same place. *You say I'm wrong. The counselor says I'm wrong. I know Dylan's recovery is up to him, but I don't see how knowing someone loves you unconditionally is a bad thing. That could be the thing that helps him through a dark time.*

Even though it was barely dawn on the west coast, Billie called Oakland to hear her mother's reassuring voice. "Billie, I'm going to say something that will probably hurt your feelings, but it's because I love you," her mother said.

"I'm listening," Billie said as she sipped her drink.

"When guests on that Dear Abby show you hosted talked about how much their spouse, boyfriend, or whatever nagged, you told them nagging was a symptom of a bigger problem. That sounds like what's going on with you two."

"We moved here, and Cole transformed into a boring sell-out."

"I thought the same thing when your father started working for the post office. Most people mellow as they age. You and I didn't get that gene. Although there is something to be said for stability and tolerance."

"But Mom..."

"You called me at this ungodly hour, so listen. You're a loving person, honey, but you do everything to an extreme, including love. You wear people out. To tell the truth, I'm surprised Cole lasted this long."

"He's the one hanging out with his ex, spending time with his outside child instead of helping the child he raised, and he gets mad at me for showing care and compassion, since he isn't. Yet all of this is my fault? And all of you want me to give up on Dylan."

"I think you're the one who's given up. You've given up on Dylan's ability to come out of this on his own. The longer you enable him, the longer before he'll take charge of his own recovery. You're the one holding him back."

"How does everything end up being my fault?"

"I warned you that you wouldn't like what I was going to say."

"So, I'm supposed to let my son fall off a cliff? If he had any other disease, you wouldn't tell me to let him work it out."

"Addiction is a disease, but getting clean is a choice. As a mother, it's hard to accept that you can't control your child's choices. You can be mad at me, but I'm telling you the truth."

"I guess you're right. I feel so defeated. My life is crumbling and I'm alone down here in the boonies."

"Hold on for a few more weeks. When you get here, we'll pamper and spoil you and have a good time."

"I don't think I'm coming. I don't want to leave Dylan." Also, coming to her niece's graduation would be another reminder that her son didn't graduate and instead was sitting in a Texas jail.

"We just talked about this. You staying won't change anything. In the long run, this is best for him and for you."

Everyone kept telling Billie that, but it didn't feel like it.

Dylan stayed in the Ross County jail five days. The pills he had were stolen from houses where he'd done yardwork and handyman chores, including Lovey's neighbor. This elevated his charges, so it was taking longer to get him released.

Against Cole's objections, Billed hired an attorney from Dallas and they were due in court at nine o'clock.

She smelled coffee and knew Cole was up. Billie quickly showered and dressed, and they headed to town for Dylan's court appearance. The courtroom reminded her of the scene in *To Kill a Mockingbird*, with a wooden banister and benches and a balcony, where she imagined Black people used to sit. Cole's family filled three rows, and Billie was grateful that they had come. Many residents listened to police scanners, so when anything happened, locals quickly found out. But rather than being embarrassed, Billie was glad Dylan had so much family support.

"All rise," the bailiff stated.

Once the judge sat, he said, "Will the defendant and his attorney please stand?"

Hearing her son referred to as "the defendant" sent chills down Billie's spine. She had heard stories from enough radio callers to know having an attorney was not a luxury. Joellen gave her a few referrals and she found someone willing to come on short notice. She withdrew money from their dwindling savings account despite Cole's objections. She would deal with him later.

"Dylan Jordan, you have been accused of theft of property which is a Class A misdemeanor. How do you plead?"

"Guilty, your honor."

"You are here for a legal matter, but your legal problems are caused by your real problem, opioid abuse," the judge said. "Mr. Jordan, you are a young man and still have a chance to get past this without a record. But you need to get in treatment immediately. You need to be where they will treat your addiction and physical recovery. A regular hospital isn't equipped to do that, and neither is Ross County Rehab Center. There is an excellent facility in Tyler that I've referred others to. But I know you've been to rehab before, and it can be a revolving door. They have a waiting list, but this court can get you in if you're serious about recovery. Are you willing to enter a treatment center?"

Dylan shook his head affirmatively.

"Speak up," the judge commanded.

"Yes sir," Dylan said. "I am serious about my recovery. The previous times I went for my parents. This time it's for me."

"The court can facilitate your placement, but the taxpayers will not pay for it. Do you have means to cover the cost?"

Monroe stood and said, "I'll cover it,"

"Is that acceptable to you?"

"Yes sir," Dylan said.

"After you complete the in-patient portion, you'll be required to perform community service, pay court costs, continue drug therapy, and submit to random drug testing. The individuals that you stole from have agreed not to press charges if you get help, but you must apologize to them. If you are arrested or charged with another crime your diversion will be revoked. I will revisit this case in 120 days. If you meet these rules, I will dismiss your charges."

"You've done so much for us. How can we thank you?" Cole said, as he hugged his big brother.

"No need to thank me. Family is always first. The judge is one of my golfing buddies, we talked a few days ago."

"Boy, you've been given another chance. Don't mess it up," Amos said.

"Hush Amos," Lovey said. "Lecturing didn't keep you out of trouble."

"That's why I can tell him what not to do. This place here ain't no real jail. Believe me, he don't want no parts of prison."

"The stipulations in your diversion program are going to keep you busy," Billie said, as they walked to the parking lot.

"We owe your uncle a great deal of gratitude," Cole said. "Don't let him down,"

"I won't," Dylan said.

"Let's go home and celebrate," Lovey said, putting her arm through Dylan's. "I got up this morning and fixed greens, fried corn, pinto beans, put a roast in the oven, and made peach cobbler."

"I have to stop by the branch first," Billie said.

"Dylan and Cole can ride with us," Amos said.

"I won't be long. Don't eat all the cobbler," Billie said, playfully pinching her son's side.

After a brief stop at the branch, Billie went to Lovey's house. Several cars were in the yard, for the celebration, so she passed the house and turned around to park across the street. As she drove past the house, she noticed people standing on the porch. One of them was Serena. Billie kept driving.

CHAPTER 31

Ross County Water Quality Report Card – EPA Region 6			
Contaminant	*Highest Level Allowed	Maximum Level Noted	Meets Federal Standards
Copper (ppm)	1.3	.5	Yes
Manganese (ppb)	50.0	59.0	No
Mercury (ppb)	2.0	2.3	Yes
Radium (radioactive contaminants)	5.0	2.8	Yes

ppb – parts per billion

ppm – parts per million

* Infants, some elderly, those undergoing chemotherapy for cancer, organ transplant recipients, or people with HIV/AIDS may be more vulnerable to infection from certain contaminants. These people should seek advice about drinking water from a physician or health care provider.

Billie had stayed up late reading the water reports. She'd requested them several weeks earlier, and had gotten the run around because she didn't use the exact terminology. She now knew there were three reports—the report card, the annual review, and the financial audit.

The water quality report card was finally available. It had been posted to their website after the due date, a violation of EPA regulations. Contaminant levels were improved, but that wasn't comforting when she read the fine print, which said levels may be harmful to infant, elderly, and immuno-compromised individuals. The list of ailments covered over half of the town. Also, she learned they had been cited for running water the day before sampling, which flushed water and gave better test results.

The annual review also raised concerns, and she emailed a copy to Adrian. They hadn't spoken since she left him in the parking lot, but she knew he would be interested in the findings. The review was difficult to digest on a computer screen, so she had gone to the branch after hours to use the printer. Even though she'd only read the first pages, she learned the department was criticized for consistently failing to provide timely public notices, inadequate sampling practices and the Water Works director did not hold the proper license.

She was still waiting for the financial audit, but the annual review contained a financial audit summary and mentioned that reserves had illegally been spent to cover deficits, and the report included a list of individuals and companies who had been asked to repay misspent funds.

When she grabbed her wallet, she noticed her phone, which she had turned on silent during her meeting, had several missed calls from Adrian and texts in all caps.

She immediately returned his calls. "What in the world is going on?" she asked.

"I've been trying to reach you all afternoon. Did you read the report you sent me?"

"I started but haven't finished. My understanding is that federal money that was supposed to pay for water infra-structure was misspent."

"Did you see the list of where the money went?"

"I saw it. The names didn't mean anything to me," Billie stated.

"The list includes the former lieutenant governor, and the Bailey brothers."

"Are they country singers?"

"Those guys are hometown heroes," Adrian said. "The Bailey brothers are professional wrestlers. Money also went to Sabine Christian College for their aquatic center."

"I'm familiar with the facility. They were recruiting Dylan, and we spoke to the coach several times. Their aquatic center is state-of-the-art."

"Now we know how they paid for it," Adrian said. "Calder State has to beg for scraps while colleges not even in Ross County get money."

"That's supposed to be a water infrastructure investment. Yet half of the town must boil water every time it rains, not to mention Grove City, which doesn't have water at all. This is indefensible," Billie said. "I can't wait to..."

"Slow down," Adrian said. "This is bigger than Ross County. We need the actual Financial Audit, not a summary. Then we'll have all three pieces of information. Also, we must be intentional on when and how we share this information. We need a plan."

"Helloooo," Billie yelled as she entered the *Calderville Chronicle* building. "Anyone here?"

The old newspaper scent of wood, vanilla, and ink reminded her of her college internship at the *Oakland Tribune*. An obsolete Linotype machine sat in the corner, covered with plastic. Framed front-page posters hung on the walls telling the story of local events from the installation of the first traffic signal in 1936, to catastrophic river flooding in the 1950s and the Woolworth's sit-in in 1963. Hometown heroes such as professional football players Monty Wells and Riley Ford, had been front page news. There was a full front page

extra edition featuring the 1987 Class-A state football champions, with a team picture including Monroe on the front
row. Three typewriters sat on a shelf, collecting dust, as well
as stacks of newspapers. The office resembled a museum
rather than a twenty-first century business.

"Forgive me for keeping you waiting," an older man said
as he emerged from a backroom. "How can I help you?"

"Mr. Gilbert, we spoke on the phone a few weeks ago,
when I was following up on promotional materials you received from Sunrise Bank. But I'm not representing the bank
today. I'd like to discuss a partnership with Calder State's
communications department."

"We had a couple of interns a few years ago. We stopped
during the pandemic and didn't resume. But that's a good
idea. I can't pay them, but I'll do everything else they need
to earn credit."

"They'll appreciate the experience. Can I speak with you
off the record? Did you receive an envelope of information
about Ross County Water Works?"

"I did. So, you sent it?"

"I didn't say I sent it. But that doesn't matter. There's
some damning information in there. Why didn't you print it?"

"Off the record as you say—what proof did I have any of
that was true? And if it is true, it's nothing folks don't know.
Like everywhere else, a few people with money and position
control things around here. Also, the companies and people
implicated are some of the Chronicle's biggest advertisers."

"The Chronicle has a long, proud history. Don't you
owe it to the community to help make things better?" Billie
asked.

"This paper has been in my family for generations, and
I'm trying to hold on, but times are different. The Chronicle
used to be the main local news source, and having a paper
route was a first job for many kids. Those days are gone.

People get news from their phones and computers and don't subscribe to the paper. The paper is basically a tax write-off. Plus, I don't want to be tied up in court."

"If the paper is a tax write-off and losing money, then what difference does it make if your ad revenue drops?"

"Breaking even is a good month and losing money is the norm. But there's a difference between losing money and losing my shirt."

"I know times have changed, but there are papers managing to survive and fulfil their duty of keeping their readers informed."

"The papers you see doing that kind of work usually have a nonprofit structure and are funded by foundations and donors. Some of my biggest advertisers are involved in that information you say you didn't send. I can either expose them and go out of business or live another day."

"Then what's the point of a free press?" Billie asked.

"The so-called free press costs money. I make money from ads and obituaries. The Chronicle includes information about the water problems—not to the extent that you think it should, but you're new around here and that's just the way it is."

Billie thought for sure Mr. Gilbert would jump at the chance to publish a scoop about Water Works. She'd have to come up with another plan.

CHAPTER 32

Billie was so focused on her computer screen, she barely looked up when Lydia spoke to her. "You were here early, so you must be starving. Let's go to lunch."

"It's almost month-end and I need to update my contact logs," Billie said. "I'll work at my desk."

"You're working too hard, and you're making me look bad," Lydia said, with a smile. "Let's go out. My treat."

Billie was so surprised, she looked up from her computer. After numerous attempts to befriend her cubicle mate and barely getting a hello, she'd given up. The bank was so different from KBLK. At the station, they knew each other's families, went to happy hour together, and had even gotten arrested together. But she was hungry for something more than the chickpea salad she'd brought for lunch, so she agreed.

They got into Lydia's pickup truck and went to a dumpy looking building with a full parking lot. "I promise it's better than it looks. Their TexMex is awesome," Lydia said. As they waited for their food, they made small talk before Lydia asked, "We have the same job, and you're always swamped. What's going on?"

"My annual review is coming up and I want to make sure I've met or exceeded all my benchmarks. I've been hearing rumors about restructuring and layoffs. I need to have my work in order. Plus, it keeps my mind off Dylan's situation," Billie said and took a sip of her drink.

"Is that all? You're probably the safest one in the department. It's us old heads they're trying to get rid of. If they offer me a severance package, this time I'm going to take it."

"You mean I'll have to break in a new cubicle mate?" Billie teased.

"They'll just divide my work. They won't hire someone else," Lydia said. "You think you're swamped now. But that's not what I wanted to talk about. I can see you're a hard worker and I wanted to give you a heads up. Some people are suspicious of you and have been asking me strange questions."

"Some people like who? What kind of strange questions?" Billie asked. Her thoughts went to her son. Calderville was a small town, and even though no one had said anything to her, she was sure rumors about his drug use and arrest were rampant. She had decided not to mention it to anyone unless she was asked. And if she was asked, she had her canned non-answer answer ready. Joe Biden had been President, and his son had a drug problem, so Dylan's situation shouldn't affect her employment. *If they try to use that against me, I'll sue them and spread so much bad publicity, they'll be begging me to keep this job*, she thought.

"I'd rather not say who," Lydia said. "But some people think you're taking this job, and your volunteer work a little too seriously, and are getting too big for your britches."

"Why would helping to lessen the city's water woes upset anyone? Besides, I didn't think anyone was even paying attention to me."

"People pay attention when you threaten the status quo, even down to how much you use the copy machine. You need to watch your back."

"You make it sound like the Mafia," Billie said with a chuckle.

"Some of the old guard around here can be just as ruthless. I like you, so be careful."

She likes me, Billie thought. *I sure couldn't tell.* "Since you asked, can I show you something?"

"You don't have a stash of money or drugs in your purse, do you?" Lydia asked. "These places have cameras."

"No, nothing like that." Billie pulled two folded sheets of paper from her purse and handed them to Lydia. "Tell me what you think."

<Riley.Ford> therileyford@gmail.com
To: You
Hey Bill,
I apologize for my late payment and appreciate you renewing my loan. Ramsey told me he had to split my speaker fee payment, otherwise the Water Works system would trigger a second review. He's paying me in thirds, so I will forward the 750K balance to the bank as soon as I receive it.
Thanks again,
Riley

<Bill.Jones> bjones@sunrisebk.com
To: Riley
No problem. We appreciate the opportunity to partner with you and look forward to future business opportunities.
Bill
William (Bill) Jones
East Texas Area President
Sunrise Bank and Trust
254-555-4000 extension 1

<Riley.Ford> therileyford@gmail.com
To: You
Bill,
I do have a concern. Ross County Water Works has been in the news a lot recently and I'm worried my name will be connected and made public. I should probably go make a bunch of speeches to justify the speaker fees. I hope they get this mess fixed soon.
Riley

To: therileyford@gmail.com
Dear Riley,
No need to worry. Your loan is in the name of BEST Limited Liability Company. Since the LLC is not registered in Texas, it would be almost impossible for someone to determine ownership. Your name is not connected in our records. We appreciate helping to bring world class facilities to our area and look forward to great things from the Sabine swim team.
Thanks

"Where did you get this? Never mind. I don't want to know," Lydia said, quickly glancing over her shoulder.

"I usually start my workday by reading email. You told me when I started this job that I could make a career out of reading and researching email messages and to skim and keep moving. My unread list was especially long this morning, so I was rushing through them. It wasn't until the fourth message that I realized I wasn't the intended recipient. But by then I couldn't unsee what I had seen."

"I'm not much of a football fan, but I do know Riley Ford played in the NFL, won a couple Super Bowls, and still holds a few state football records. When he retired he bought several acres outside Ross County and is treated like Jesus Jr. He's always in some TV commercial," Lydia said, as she doused her food with hot sauce. "Wonder why he needs money."

"After I read the emails, I queried BEST LLC and Riley Ford. BEST had a one-million-dollar line of credit that originated two years earlier and the balance is now $750,000. BEST is listed as a real estate investment company with property sales and/or rents as the repayment source."

"I think they switched our drinks. I've got your sweet tea and you have my Dr Pepper," Lydia said, as she beckoned for the waitress. She reread the email then said, "It sounds like Riley Ford is paying the loan with money from the Water Works."

"He funneled the money to Sabine Christian College for a new aquatics center. And get this—his son is on the swim team. Dylan was considering attending there and we were supposed to visit the campus on a recruiting trip. This is a big deal, isn't it?" Billie asked in a hushed tone, then finished her drink.

"It doesn't have to be. You can ignore it, but I know that thought never crossed your mind," Lydia said. "So, what are you going to do?"

Billie sat in her car stunned. She had come to the Dallas office to meet with her supervisor for her annual performance review. Her probation would be over, and she'd get a bump in pay, and a 401K match. She and Lydia planned to meet for a late lunch to celebrate when she returned to Calderville. To avoid traffic, she left early and arrived thirty minutes before her meeting time.

"Ms. Jordan, since you're here, come on in," her supervisor said.

She sat in front of his desk and tapped her foot while waiting for him to start. He pulled a folder out of his drawer then said, "Ms. Jordan, we've reviewed your performance during this probationary period and will not be extending your employment."

"Excuse me?" Billie said, as she leaned forward.

"Due to several infractions, we are letting you go."

"I don't understand," Billie said. "My recommendations have resulted in increased revenues, new customers, and new service opportunities for Sunrise."

"There's no disputing your recommendations have yielded favorable results. For someone without a banking background, you've been very effective. However, there is another issue. During your orientation you reviewed our privacy and confidentiality policies and signed a document acknowledging that you were aware of your obligations. There are different system privileges for different employees. Those policies are safety measures to protect our customers' personal data and money. Employees are prohibited from accessing customer accounts without proper authorization, or for unauthorized purposes."

"I assure you I didn't..."

"All account access is recorded and monitored, and your email account was flagged by IT for access to accounts that were not on your prospect list."

"I developed my own prospect list. That's how I was able to generate those results."

"You should have requested prior approval for any additions to your list. This is something we can't overlook. We're going to have to let you go."

She leaned her head on the steering wheel as tears began to flow. She didn't cry long because the car was hot. She cranked up the air, then headed toward the interstate. As she sat at a red light, she heard a buzzing sound and then swatted at something near her ear. She let the window down, hoping the bug would fly out, then yelled when she realized it was a wasp. She swatted it when it came near her face and jerked to the side. Her car swerved and hit the SUV in the next lane.

Billie's Prius was totaled. The impact threw her against the car door, aggravating her tornado thigh injury, and left her shoulder stiff and tender from the pressure of the deployed airbag. Despite her frantic efforts, the wasp stung her, and she had a dark red swollen knot on her forehead.

"I can't let you out of my sight for a minute," Cole said, when he brought her home from the emergency room.

She leaned on him and shuffled to the front door. When she entered there were two dozen roses on the kitchen counter and an Oakland Raider teddy bear. "Where did you find this?" she asked, picking up the bear.

"My secret. I know things have been rough lately, but you're still my city girl, and hopefully, I'm still your country man."

"Always," she said, reaching for his hand.

"Lovey said to rub honey on the wasp sting. I'll rub other body parts a little later," Cole said with a wink.

Billie finally had time to sip tea and catch up on her reading. Since she had been on a work assignment, she filed on the bank's insurance and could collect worker's compensation benefits. That lessened the financial sting from losing her job. They were waiting on the paperwork to be completed so she could get another car. Cole was driving one of his brother's trucks and left his car for Billie. Most days, she didn't even leave the house.

With long days to fill, she finally had time to review the Water Works board minutes and audit reports she had requested. And with no employer to censure her research, she was ready to make some waves.

CHAPTER 33

"I received an invitation to the Clean Water Coalition Summit in Atlanta next month," Billie said.

"What's that all about?" Cole asked while scrolling through his phone.

"The CWC is one of the largest organizations working for clean water and environmental justice. Someone on the cruise heard the session I moderated and recommended me."

"That sounds like one of those annoying tree-hugger groups. Environmental justice is a distraction. Black folks are worried about real issues like paying bills and not getting shot."

"How can you say that? Nothing is more important than clean water and air. It's not a coincidence that toxic air and poor water are more common in neighborhoods where black folks live. Lovey's house and the whole west side of town are prime examples."

"I'm not saying they aren't important, but you can't get wrapped up in every cause. Besides, we don't need to spend extra money right now. We don't know how long you'll be out of work."

"My hotel and registration are paid for, and I'll get a stipend to use toward my flight. There's a luncheon, banquet and free breakfast, so I should only have to spend money on a taxi."

"If you're going to participate and learn more, I guess there's no harm. If you're going as a speaker or representative of some group, I say no. Remember anything you do or say will be a reflection on me, which means it's a reflection of Calder State."

"I wasn't asking permission," Billie said. "When I said I was invited, I was including you. It's over a weekend so you wouldn't miss any workdays. I thought this would be an ideal getaway for us. We always had a good time in Atlanta. But based on your comments, I see you're not interested."

"You'll be in meetings all day."

"Forget I even mentioned it," Billie said.

"Calder State has a game in Atlanta this fall. Let's schedule a side trip around the game."

"We can do that, but I'm still going to the conference."

Cole muttered something under his breath and left the room.

Billie was sweating as she rushed to her gate. She had driven to the airport and construction slowed her down. She was last to board and as she breathlessly walked down the aisle, she saw Adrian Butler. He was looking at his phone, and she kept walking. Her seat was in the row in front of the restroom, but at least she had the row to herself. She placed her overstuffed bag under the seat next to her and stretched out her legs for her two-hour flight.

Adrian was standing on the jet bridge waiting for his bag as she was getting off the plane. "Hey, there," he said. "Looks like we're both going to be hanging out in Atlanta a few days."

"I'm going to the CWC Summit," Billie said. "I'm really looking forward to it."

"That's where I'm going," he said. "I'm representing the East Texas NAACP district. Would you like to share an Uber to the hotel?"

They were silent during the beginning of the ride but began talking as they sat in traffic. "We keep getting off on the wrong foot, so I apologize again for the remarks I made about your son. I should have been more sensitive."

"Apology accepted. I'm probably overly sensitive and didn't mean to snap at you."

"Then let's start over. My name is Adrian Butler," he said, extending his hand.

They had always been laser-focused on the task at hand during their previous encounters. While inching through traffic, they relaxed and talked about something other than water. She learned he was born and raised in Calderville, had lived in Las Vegas, but moved his family back ten years earlier so he could help his sister take care of their mother after his father, who had been her caregiver, passed. His mother passed a few years ago, but he stayed to be close to his girls. He was divorced, with twin daughters who had just graduated from Calder State and were first year law students at Texas Southern. He had planned to leave town when his girls graduated, but the owner of the medical transport company that he was working for retired and offered to sell him the company. "So, I'm back home. Just my luck," he said. "Vegas finally gets professional ball and I'm not there."

"That's a sore subject," Billie said. "They stole our teams."

"Now you can pull for America's team," Adrian said.

"The Cowboys?" Billie said, while wrinkling her nose.

"Of course. I thought we'd get to the hotel in time to see the kickoff, but it's taking us almost as long to get to the hotel as it took us to fly here."

"Reminds me of home," Billie said.

"Vegas has grown a lot since I first moved there. I don't

miss it. I never understood why anyone would choose to live in a place with wall-to-wall people and traffic."

"And I never understood why people would choose to live in a place without theater, bookstores, or decent coffee."

"Aren't you one of those people choosing to live without theater, bookstores, or decent coffee?"

"Touché. Sometimes I wonder what I was thinking, especially when this unbelievable water situation came up."

"Things happen for a reason. Maybe you came to town, to help with the unbelievable water situation. Sorry I gave you such a hard time. You talk funny, but anybody who's excited about a water conference is okay with me."

"*I* talk funny?" Billie said, giving him the side eye. "Because I know the 't' is not silent in Internet, and that y'all is not a word?"

Adrian tapped the driver on the shoulder, "Excuse me. Is y'all a word?"

"Oh no you don't" the driver said. "I ain't fixin' to git in the middle of yawl's argument."

Billie raised her hands in surrender, and they both laughed.

"I rest my case," Adrian said.

They arrived in time for the Friday evening reception and Billie devoured the hors d'oevures since she missed lunch. All day Saturday and Sunday morning, there were concurrent sessions with experts and activists. They even had a presentation by climate experts that was so scary, Billie didn't understand how anyone could claim climate change was a hoax. She was on a panel with the lady from Flint she'd met on the cruise, a councilman from Jackson, Mississippi, and a representative from Warm Springs Indian Reservation in Oregon, all areas with water quality issues. Billie moderated a panel with former EPA and FEMA employees, and Sierra Club representatives, and filled her notebook with information from other panels. She enjoyed networking with like-minded individuals, and even met former Vice President Al Gore.

Billie and Adrian's return flight was delayed. They hung out in an airport bar and sat together on the return flight. When the flight attendant came through with snacks, Billie was embarrassed that she had fallen asleep on Adrian's shoulder. "Excuse me," she said, smoothing out the side of her hair.

"No problem. Those wild water conference parties can wear you out."

When they landed, Adrian said, "Too bad we didn't coordinate our trip and ride together to the airport. You should come to another meeting. We received valuable information this weekend that needs to be shared. But it would be good for our members to hear from someone other than me sometime. Even though you talk funny."

"When do *yawwwl* meet?" Billie asked. "I wanna make sure I don't *fergit*."

Neither had checked bags, so they parted ways after leaving the terminal. Billie called Cole, but he didn't answer, so she sent a text that she was leaving the airport. There was a computer glitch, and it took forty minutes to exit the parking lot because the payment booths were slow. It was almost ten o'clock, meaning she wouldn't be in bed before midnight, way past her bedtime. But she wasn't sleepy or tired. Who knew a water conference would be so much fun?

CHAPTER 34

Billie had finally gotten the last piece of the puzzle, the financial audit. She may have been employed by a bank, but Maya was the family banker. She had been an accounting major and did Billie's and their mother's taxes.

It had taken weeks to get the audit referenced during the Water Works board meeting she had attended. She had only gotten them last week and read through them, but there was so much jargon, she emailed copies to Maya to decipher.

"Hey girl," Maya had said in a sleepy voice.

"I'm sorry for waking you," Billie said. "I thought wheelers and dealers got up early."

"I get up early, but not before the sun. What's up?"

"I sent you some reports a few days ago, I was hoping you'd had a chance to look at them."

"When you asked me to review a few reports, you left out the detail about it being over one hundred pages. I scanned it, and am now going back through it, but I haven't finished."

"Then tell me what you've learned so far. The meeting is tomorrow," Billie said.

"Let me go to my computer," Maya said. "It's my sister. I'll be back."

"You have overnight company?" Billie asked. "I see you're living it up with Imani away."

"Mind your business please."

"I need to check him out. Send me a picture," Billie said. "How long have you been seeing him? What kind of work does he do? How did you meet? Does he have..."

"Do you want this audit information, or do you want to play twenty questions?"

"Both, but for right now, I'll settle for the audit. It listed material deficiencies, and severe deficiencies, deviations and disclaimers. I had no idea what it all meant."

"You didn't give me much time to look at this, so I hope you're not expecting an elaborate discourse."

"Just hit the high points."

"More like the low points," Maya said. "This federal audit was triggered because the Water Works board had not satisfactorily responded to previous state audits. The main problems are inadequate public notice, lack of a properly licensed operator, failure to make necessary repairs despite receiving state funding to do so, accounts out of balance, inappropriate credit card charges, inadequate segregation of duties, and grant spending in noncompliance with guidelines. The largest recipients were Premier Paper, and BEST LLC. Ross County Rentals was also listed, but they didn't get as much as the other two companies. I'll get more details but that's the bottom line."

"Thanks. This will really help."

"I'll send you my bill," Maya joked. "They say everything's bigger in Texas, sounds like the swindlers are too. You be careful down there."

"I will," Billie replied.

"And don't drink the water," she said before hanging up.

* * *

Billie saw her sister-in-law's text, then looked out the window and saw Joellen's Range Rover in the driveway. She wrapped her housecoat around her waist and went outside. "I am so sorry. I completely forgot we were supposed to go to Dallas today," Billie said. "I won't be joining you."

"I know you're worried about Dylan, but you can't help him if you don't take care of yourself. We'll have brunch then go to the trade market. Sometimes the best prescription is retail therapy, especially if it's wholesale."

"I appreciate you, but I need to stay close to home. Besides, it's not fun shopping with no money," Billie said.

"Then we'll eat, go browse the bookstore, then head back. If anything changes with Dylan we can be back within ninety minutes. You'll feel better if you get away for a few hours."

"I suppose it couldn't hurt," Billie said. "Come inside. It's hot out here already."

Joellen grabbed her Fendi purse and followed Billlie.

"This is a beautiful house. I hadn't been inside since it was finished," Joellen said. "You should have a house-warming party."

"The house doesn't feel very warm right now. I know Monroe told you about me and Cole."

"Don't worry about Cole. You two have been together forever. This is only a bump in the road. Things will work out."

"One bump we could handle. But even before this latest fiasco with Dylan, there was Serena, and now there's my job situation, or should I say lack of a job."

"Didn't you tell me you have a degree in education?"

"I have a master's in education, but my certification expired, and Texas doesn't have reciprocity."

"I can talk to some people at the school board. I'm sure you can sub until you get recertified."

"I'd appreciate that."

"Consider it done," Joellen said.

"Thank you. Sometimes I feel so alone here," Billie said, as her eyes began to water. "It's nice to know, I have at least one friend."

"Don't go getting mushy on me. Let's get going."

"It won't take me long to get ready," Billie said.

"What's all this stuff?" Joellen asked as she sat at the kitchen island.

"Just move it to the side. My desk is on backorder, so the kitchen is still serving as my office," Billie said, while walking to her bedroom. "Since I have time, I'm doing more research on the Water Works. I've got some questions you can follow-up for me."

"Email me your findings. I'll follow-up, but not today," Joellen said, as she turned the stack of papers around so she could read them. "We've got enough serious stuff going on. Today we're going to pamper ourselves and enjoy this beautiful, sunny day."

As promised, Joellen got Billie into the school district. She subbed two weeks before getting an extended assignment in a sixth-grade class at Tenth Avenue Middle School. She was a sub so the central office reconfirmed her assignment every Monday, but Principal Moore assured her she could work as long as she wanted, since they were short staffed.

Education hadn't been her original career plan, but just like at Calder State, she enjoyed working with young people. There were just a few classes she needed to take to be certified to teach in Texas, and her backup plan was to enroll in Calder State in the spring semester using Cole's discount. Her first plan was to find another job anywhere but Texas, but she couldn't make definite plans until Dylan's situation was resolved.

On the Tuesday after Labor Day, they were greeted by a

note at the employee entrance, instructing them to report to the cafeteria. Principal Moore ushered them inside, then went to the front and said, "May I have your attention? I have an announcement, and I wanted to tell you in person instead of sending an email you may or may not read. We're having visitors tomorrow. The NAACP Texas State Conference President, a Channel 6 reporter from Dallas, our state representative, and someone from Attorney Benjamin Crump's law firm are coming to do a story on the district's water problems. They're coming here and to two other west side schools. They've been instructed not to show any student's faces. If they ask you any questions about the water situation, your response is, *We're doing the best we can to help our students succeed given the less-than-ideal circumstances.* That's it. Anything else, refer them to me. We want to show unity, so wear your school t-shirts. When they arrive, we'll sound the announcement chime, so you'll know they're on campus, but class instruction should continue as usual. Any questions? Good," she said, before anyone could ask anything. "If you don't have a shirt, stop by the front office. We have extras."

"The media attention will be good. Maybe things will get fixed." Billie said, as she and Mrs. Samson, the teacher across the hall from her, went to their classroom.

"It's just a distraction. Nothing will change."

"But there are national big shots involved—Ben Crump may file a class action lawsuit," Billie said.

"And who pays the lawsuit? Our taxes. Which gives people another excuse to move away," Mrs. Samson said. "I've already retired. I'm only subbing a few days to pay for a new kitchen and if Principal Moore said not to say anything, that's what I'm going to do."

"So we let it stay like this?" Billie asked. "Think how much instruction time is lost due to bathroom breaks. Test scores would probably improve if the kids had decent bathrooms."

"Not much we can do about it."

"There isn't if we don't say anything."

"Bless your heart," Mrs. Samson said, as she walked away shaking her head.

Billie was part of a four-teacher, sixth-grade team, and their goal was to increase the students' performance on the state test they would take in the spring. Since the scores were mediocre last year, Billie suggested they try a different approach. She invited Lydia to speak about the importance of math in real life, and they played games which reinforced math concepts that would be on the state test. She suggested a field trip to the Chronicle building which would cover units in history and writing, but Principal Moore told her there was no money in the budget for field trips. So, she invited Mr. Gilbert to come speak to her class and he agreed. She was finishing lunch at her desk and looked up when she heard a knock on the door.

"You're early," Billie said, as Mr. Gilbert came in. "Thank you so much for coming."

"No problem. I reckon if I influence them when they're young, I can get my next generation of subscribers. By the way, I have two interns from Calder State and they're doing a great job."

"Glad to hear it. The students will return from their bathroom break in a few minutes. It's supposed to rain this afternoon, so the aide took the students out earlier than their assigned time."

"Outside?" Mr. Gilbert asked.

"Yes. This building has low water pressure, and the students use the portables outside. The locks aren't working on all of the portables so it's taking longer."

"I heard about the portables a while back. I didn't know

they were still using them," Mr. Gilbert said. "That's a sin and a shame."

When her students returned to the classroom, Billie introduced their guest. Mr. Gilbert discussed his family's newspaper and that when he was their age, the last thing he wanted to do was work at a newspaper. But now he was amazed at the history he witnessed and proud that his paper helped keep people informed. The students asked a few questions but weren't as engaged as when Lydia visited, probably because she was talking about money. However, they were respectful, and the next hour passed quickly.

Billie stepped in the hall to thank Mr. Gilbert and heard a commotion, so she quickly went back inside. As she walked in a chair hit the floor. One girl had a handful of another girl's braids, and they had toppled over the desk. As she was trying to pull them apart, students were cheering like they were at a ball game. "What's going on in here?" Mrs. Samson asked as she rushed in. The School Resource Officer also came in and separated the students. Billie led the student into the hall and asked, "So what happened?"

"She said I smelled like a dead skunk, and everybody laughed," Raine said, holding a handful of weave she'd pulled from another girl's head.

"We don't put our hands on others just because they say something we don't like. You should've come to me."

"Yes ma'am."

The aide took Raine to the principal's office. Between the classroom guest and then the fight, Billie knew there was no use trying to teach in the remaining time left of the school day. They had mentally checked out and were ready to go home. They weren't any more ready than she was. After a long thirty minutes of self-directed study time, she dismissed her class and grabbed her purse, planning to walk out right behind them, when a parent came in the room.

"Miss Jordan, I'm Raine's mother."

"She's in the principal's office," Billie said.

"I'd like to speak with you first. I spoke with Raine on the phone. I know she was wrong, but there is another side. She's started having her monthly and she's sensitive about it. I guess I need to have her bathe more than once a week. She has eczema and her skin is extra sensitive. They say our water is okay, but whenever she bathes in it her eczema flares up. I was too tired to boil water yesterday, and I've run out of bottled water. I told her to just wash up really good, so this is mostly my fault."

The conversation with Raine's mother kept playing in Billie's head as she drove home. After pulling into the garage, she grabbed her school T-shirt and went inside. She was so disgusted she pulled out the wine bottle they had been hiding behind the cake mixer in the bottom cabinet and poured herself a drink. Thank goodness it was Friday.

The weekend passed quickly. She spent Saturday preparing lesson plans and visited Dylan on Sunday. She was disappointed that Cole didn't join her, but his schedule was more flexible than hers and he said he'd go during the week. They spent Sunday evening in their pool, including finally having a "dirty swim," sex in the pool. They were at home, but still felt like they were sneaking around. It felt good to be care-free, even if just for a few hours. Billie's good mood carried over until Monday morning and she was humming a Whitney Houston tune when she stopped in the office to pick up keys as she had done for the past four Mondays.

"Ms. Jordan, you aren't on the list we got from central office," the secretary had said.

"Are you sure?" Billie asked. "I understood this assignment would last the entire semester."

"I'll double check with Principal Moore," the secretary said.

After a few minutes, the secretary returned and said, "She'd like you to come in her office."

"Ms. Jordan, I'm glad you stopped in. You weren't reconfirmed to return this week, but I considered you part of the Tenth Avenue Middle family, so I wanted to thank you for all you've done and at least say goodbye."

"I didn't check the district portal this morning. I assumed I was coming here," Billie said. "Did you get a permanent teacher?"

"No."

"And I haven't received a notice that I'm being sent somewhere else. Maybe it was an oversight."

"Sit down a minute," Principal Moore said as she stood and went to close the door.

"Teaching may not be a good fit for you. You have innovative ideas and are great with the kids, but public education is very bureaucratic. The school board has established guidelines which district administration must adhere to, and it has set guidelines that principals must assure are adhered to and that means teachers must adhere to my guidelines. I specifically told everyone what our response during the media visit was to be, and you violated my instructions."

"I answered their questions, and..."

"Ms. Jordan, I would love to have you here, but the decision was out of my hands. You didn't hear this from me," she said in a low voice. "Mrs. Nash over-rode my request."

"Nash—you mean Serena?" Billie asked.

"She's over finance and doesn't usually get involved in personnel, but certain people were unhappy with your interactions during the media visit. I wish you well."

The bell rang as Billie got in her car. She saw a few late students hustling to the door, including Raine and her older sister. Billie called the district office to be sure her exclusion wasn't an oversight. It wasn't. She checked the district website for other openings, but based on what Principal Moore said, it was unlikely she would get another assignment.

She hadn't even known the delegation was still on campus. Her class was headed to lunch, and she noticed the cameraman trying to fill his water bottle from the water fountain. With barely a trickle coming out, Billie told him they didn't drink from those fountains. Next thing she knew, the whole crew was at her classroom door, asking her questions about the water. She answered their questions, then suggested they look inside the portable potties and asked, *"would you want your child using a glorified outhouse two or three times every day?"* That was the quote that was used in the news story.

With a heavy sigh, she drove past the Porta Pottis and headed home. She regretted leaving her students and losing a paycheck, but she didn't regret speaking up.

Since she was home early, she cooked vegetable lasagna and made a salad and chocolate cake.

"Somebody's in a good mood," Cole said when he came in. "We need to hop in the pool more often. I can't remember the last time you came home and cooked on a weekday."

"Looks like I'll be cooking a lot more," Billie said. "My Tenth Avenue assignment was ended."

"I know you were attached to those kids. That goes with teaching. Even at my level, I feel a little sad when the semester ends. But then you get a whole new crop and start all over again."

"I doubt if I get another crop. The principal told me I've been taken off the list."

"What happened?" Cole asked.

"After the press conference last week, I spoke to..."

"Dammit Billie. Why are you on this crusade?"

"You haven't even heard my side," Billie said.

"I've already heard it. You've had issues with the bank, Calder State, and now the school district. Is everyone else the problem? You are the common denominator—so maybe it's not them."

"How everyone can be so nonchalant about this poison water is beyond me. If you had heard my student Raine's story you'd feel the same. What's going on is not right."

"A lot of things aren't right, but plunging my family into financial ruin isn't going to make things better."

"So we should turn a blind eye to the inequities around here? That's why things never change."

"They aren't going to change because you keep getting fired from jobs. You've got to find a more effective way to express your concerns."

"I can do that, or we can just leave. I can't live with such hypocrisy. I've never been fired before. You and I are barely speaking, and they've tried to imprison me and my son," Billie said while pacing. "It's obvious Texas isn't for us. With department head on your resume, I'm sure you can find another faculty position. I can sub until I find something permanent."

"People live here and deal with it and make changes—not the way you would do it, or as fast as we would like, but this is real life. Things don't get resolved by the end of the radio show."

"That may be, but I don't think I can be one of those people," Billie said. "And for the record, little Miss Serena played a big part in me losing the job."

"Why would she do that? Nothing is ever your fault," Cole said, shaking his head.

"Kelly called and said she's working with Love Media and they're hiring. She said it's a lot different from KBLK but if I was interested she can probably get me an interview. I hadn't seriously considered it, but maybe I should."

"Do what you want," Cole said. "You always do."

CHAPTER 35

Dylan was near the end of the first phase of his diversion—in person treatment for forty days. Billie had made the eighty-mile roundtrip each Sunday. As she drove home, her son's words haunted her.

"Looks like I finally got what I wanted when I was a kid," Dylan said.

"What's that?"

"A big brother. Dad introduced us. Chris seems pretty cool."

Billie counted to ten and her calm demeanor belied the surge of anger bubbling beneath the surface. After her visit, she drove directly to Lovey's house. She slammed her car door and stormed to the porch where Cole and his Uncle Amos were sitting.

"Looks like somebody is madder than a wet hen," Amos said, as he raised his beer can. He leaned and whispered to Cole, "Just say you're sorry. It'll be easier that way."

"What's wrong?" Cole asked.

"You introduced Chris to Dylan?"

"It's not a secret. I wanted him to hear it from me. They're brothers and should know each other."

"I'll go inside and let you love birds talk," Amos said.

"You are so self-centered," Billie said, with a foot on the bottom step. "Dylan is fragile right now. He doesn't need something to make him feel insecure. It's like you are replacing him with the son you always wanted."

"That's ridiculous and he's fragile because you baby him."

"Maybe I baby him because you don't. Have you been to see him—without your love child?" she asked with a raised voice.

"Billie, this isn't the time or the place for this conversation," Cole said, looking around.

"The devil stays busy," Lovey said, as she came to the screen door, with a Dr Pepper can. "We haven't been out of church thirty minutes and he's stirring up strife."

"You can blame it on the devil, but I'm only trying to protect my son. I know Cole is your baby and can do no wrong, but I'll be damned if..."

"I don't know what's going on between you two, but this is still the Lord's day," Lovey said sternly, as she grabbed Billie's arm. "My chamomile plants are ready. Come help me pick a few batches."

"I mean no disrespect, but this isn't a good time," Billie said.

"It won't take long. Cole, go make sure I turned off the air conditioner in my bedroom," Lovey said, as she opened the gate fence and beckoned for Billie to follow her. They entered her garden and walked down the path to the back door. They passed rows of carrots, peas, and cabbage.

"Forgive my manners. Would you like a cold drink? A doctor invented it, so it should be okay for your diet."

"No ma'am," Billie replied with a smile.

"Cole says you have a problem with Chris," Lovey said while putting on her straw hat.

"I don't have anything against Chris. I just think Cole

should get a DNA test. You watch daytime TV. There's an entire reality show category centered around false paternity accusations. What I'm asking is not unreasonable."

"You got that right. I know plenty of people right here in town who raised children that they thought was there's but weren't."

"Then you agree with me," Billie said.

"But it's not up to me, or you. Cole doesn't want to hurt Chris by suggesting his mother is a liar, or worse yet, was a loose woman. Don't be too hard on him," Lovey said, as she handed Billie a basket and pointed to the stakes with drooping, ripe, bright red tomatoes. "Those boys bounced around quite a bit before coming to live with me. I should have taken them right away, but I was so depressed at losing my only daughter, it took me a while to get myself together. It was hard losing both their parents. Monroe became obsessed with money because he equated it with stability and didn't want to ask anyone for anything. He sold the Chronicle, cut lawns, and swept at the barber shop on Saturdays. He saved every penny. Cole's way to cope was to be a people-pleaser. He's trying to do what he thinks is the right thing."

"It seems like Cole is trying to please everyone but me," Billie said.

SECTION V

Making Waves

CHAPTER 36

The Calderville Chronicle
News For You Since 1922
Sports Section
The Calder State Vikings football team has had early season success, despite Calderville's continuing water problems. Coach Wagner stated, "Preparing for our games has given the team something to focus on, other than the water crisis. The team has been staying in a hotel, but it's still a hardship. Without reliable water, we have don't have air conditioning or ice. We can't use toilets or take showers. It also hurts our recruiting. I hope city leaders fix this once and for all."

The semester started with record enrollment and high hopes. Cole had upper-level classes and was enjoying teaching at his alma mater. Billie had never seen him so enthusiastic about teaching. But four weeks into the semester, Ross County received two months' worth of rain in two days. The rain caused the reservoir to overflow, resulting in bacteria in the water supply. The mayor issued a boil notice, and west side residents resumed what was now a familiar routine of boiling water, filling jugs, and hoarding bottled water.

Rossbrooke Estates had running water, but even those with water were encouraged to conserve. Billie had just come from the grocery store. When she pulled into the garage, she felt the rumbling bass before she heard it. When she walked inside, five young men from the baseball team greeted her. Pizza boxes were on the counter, plates were in the sink and soda can were strewn across the coffee table. She noticed duffel bags on the floor.

"Hello Mrs. Jordan," one of the players stated. "Thanks for letting us stay with you."

"No problem," Billie said, even though that was news to her.

"With the campus water issues, I thought it would be good for the guys to have access to a real bathroom for a few days," Cole said as he maneuvered a video game controller.

By the fifth day, their guests needed more items from campus. Cole was conducting an online class, so Billie took the young men back to campus. As they entered campus, they passed a group of students marching in front of the administration building. They held signs that read: POLLUTED WATER IS VIOLENCE, NO WATER NO PEACE, and ALL CALDER STATE LIVES MATTER. Billie pulled over and rolled down the passenger window.

"Hey Ms. Billie," Marcus said as he came to the car. "I'm following your advice. If you do what you've always done, you'll get what you've always had. We've started a campus chapter of Young, Gifted, and Green to protest and lobby for clean water. This is our third day out here."

Aisha waved from the sidewalk and said, "Come join us. We pay a lot of money to this school and deserve better facilities. Why should the football team be taken care of, but no one else?"

"She's right," one of the baseball players said. "We went to regionals and they're treating us like we don't even count."

"Guys, you're just here to pick up more clothes. Cole wouldn't want you to—"

"You got any extra signs?" another player asked Aisha while opening the car door.

"Wait guys," Billie said, as they all exited her car.

She took a deep breath, then drove to the faculty lot and parked. *If you can't beat them join them,* she thought, as she went to join the marchers.

"What were you thinking?" Cole asked as soon as Billie walked in the door.

"I told you what happened. I didn't even know they were protesting. The boys wanted to march. I tried to talk them out of it."

"I'll bet you did," Cole said. "You are determined to get me fired. I guess you want both of us to be unemployed. I've already heard from parents of two of the boys. I recruited them and assured their families Calder State would take care of them, not arrest them."

"It was a peaceful protest. Campus police overreacted," Billie said.

"Thank goodness Serena was nearby. She called and told me what was going on."

"Saint Serena to the rescue," Billie said and rolled her eyes. "I'm so tired of hearing about her."

"If it weren't for her, you'd still be sitting in the campus security building," Cole said.

Serena was on campus and saw the protestors. She also saw campus police trying to move the crowd, which was getting louder and larger. She called Dr. Kingsley, and he came to the courtyard. He promised to meet with a few students to hear their concerns and to aggressively pressure the state for increased funding so they could build their own water supply, like some other state campuses. "This will take time, and you may not personally benefit from the improved infrastructure, but take comfort in knowing you have made a difference for future students. No one is more frustrated than I am, but I promise transparency and inclusion." When he finished speaking, Marcus and Dr. Kingsley shook hands. The students cheered and agreed to suspend the marches.

"Why are you upset? The students executed their strategy, got a specific action plan and learned an important lesson. They can make a difference."

"And I'm learning that you'll never change," Cole said.

"There was a time when you said you never wanted me to change," Billie said softly.

"Then maybe I'm the one who's changed," Cole said. "We aren't going to get better are we?"

"I don't know how to be what you want anymore and still be me."

"And I can't tell you if you don't know. I'll stay at Lovey's a few days," Cole said, then grabbed his keys and left.

CHAPTER 37

Kendra was in town, her first visit to Texas since they moved. Billie and Cole had picked her up together and told her they were breaking up. She took it in stride, and Cole and Billie managed to be civil during her stay. Since Billie wasn't working, they visited Dylan every day and filled up on Lovey's home cooking. Billie had been a Walmart-snob, but now went at least once a week and during their two-hour shopping trip, she showed Kendra around like she owned the store. Saturday morning, they had brunch at Lovey's, then were on their way to see Dylan. As they were riding on the highway, Billie answered a call from Reverend Collins.

"Miss Billie, I'm going to make an announcement during tomorrow's service, and I'd like you to be there. I promise not to preach too long," he said with a chuckle.

"I'm taking my daughter to the airport tomorrow. Can we get together Monday?"

"What time is her flight? I can swing by tomorrow before morning service, or even this evening. It won't take long."

"We're going to see Dylan right now and I'm not sure

what time we'll return," Billie said. "I promise to call you on Monday."

"Reverend Collins asked me to come to church tomorrow," Billie said after she hung up. "But I think we deserve to sleep in. I'll visit him Monday." She had even put it in her calendar to be sure to call him first thing Monday morning.

"I'd be glad to meet him," Kendra said. "He sounds like a hoot."

"Maybe we can visit him tomorrow on our way to the airport," Billie said.

After visiting with Dylan, they stopped at the west side Dairy Queen before heading to the house. As they were walking to the car, they heard a loud *boom*.

"What was that?" Billie asked. "Is someone doing fireworks?"

"That didn't sound like fireworks," Kendra said, licking her chocolate-swirl cone.

They heard sirens and saw police cars driving by. "I don't know what happened, but it doesn't look good," Billie said.

As they walked back to the car, Billie asked the security guard "What's going on?"

"Fire over in Grove City."

Billie rushed to her car and headed toward Grove City. The closer she got, she could see gray smoke in the sky and the sharp smell of burning plastic seeped through the car vent. About three blocks from the church, the street was blocked. She got out of her car and saw Adrian helping redirect traffic. "What happened?" she asked him.

"Fire at Bethel. We lost Reverend Collins."

After taking Kendra to the airport, Billie drove to the Collins' home and there were several cars parked outside.

She had heard so much about their family from Will and Shaun, she felt as if she knew everyone and expressed her condolences and introduced herself at the same time. After paying her respects, she noticed Adrian and a few others in the backyard and went to join them. Adrian pulled her to the side and filled her in on the details. Reverend Collins had gone to the church on Saturday, as he always did to make sure everything was in place for Sunday service. He was the pastor, lawn care person, and repairman. Late that evening, Mrs. Green across the street said she saw smoke coming from the church and called 911. More neighbors streamed outside. Pastor's car was in the lot, so they knew he was inside, but the building became engulfed in flames so quickly, no one could go inside. The county fire department came, but they quickly emptied the water tank on their engine. Since there was no water service, all they could do was spray a fire retardant on the church.

"I spoke with him yesterday morning. We were supposed to get together tomorrow. I can't believe he's gone," Billie said. "Such a cruel way to die, especially for someone who battled for water. How could this happen?"

"I think the question is not 'how,' but 'who?'" Adrian said.

"You don't think this was an accident?"

"Do you?"

CHAPTER 38

"I'm proud of you," Cole said as Billie dressed for the funeral. "It's my hometown, but you're the one who's really become a part of this community. Once I left, I didn't keep up with anything other than Lovey and Calder State."

"I thought I would be spending long evenings reading and drinking sweet tea in a quaint, sleepy little town. But this place has more drama than the *Young and the Restless*."

"I didn't know Reverend Collins, but I've heard he was a man of integrity who helped a lot of people. Are you sure you don't want me to go with you?" Cole asked.

"No. I may stay afterward and help serve the food. I'll be fine."

Monday morning after the fire had died down and cooled off, firefighters went through the ravaged church remains and found Reverend Collins' charred body two feet from the door. Shaun and Will identified his body by the gold tooth, and they refused to let Mrs. Collins see the body.

The official cause of the fire was listed as Class C—electrical, but Adrian's words still nagged at her. She wasn't someone who saw a conspiracy behind every corner, but Reverend Collins' death did make things easier for Monroe and everyone else on that audit list.

Since the church building was destroyed, the service was held at West Side Missionary Baptist Church. The sanctuary was bigger than Bethel's and it was still standing room only. It was an emotional two-hour service, and Billie was thankful they didn't need her help when it was over.

She greeted family members after service, lingering especially long with Shaun and marveling at Jenna who was crawling and pulling up on anything or anyone she could find.

"This still seems surreal," Adrian said, as they stood outside the church.

"I feel so bad because he wanted to see me, but I put him off because I was hanging out with my daughter. That reminds me, his daughter handed me an envelope," Billie said, as she pulled the envelope from her purse, and opened it. "It's cell phone records."

She handed the pages to Adrian as she scanned through them. "The last two calls are circled," Billie said. She input the number in her phone and Monroe's contact information came up. She showed the phone to Adrian.

"What would those two be conversing about?" Adrian asked.

"I don't know, but I'm going to find out," Billie declared.

"I don't appreciate you summoning me like I'm your bitch," Monroe said when Billie answered the door. "What do you want? I don't have a lot of time."

"The last calls on Reverend Collins' phone were to and from you. What did you talk about?"

"Are you still trying to play Nancy Drew? The man is dead, let it go."

"You didn't answer my question."

"And I don't intend to. My phone calls are none of your business."

"I'm thinking he probably said something to you about the kickbacks you've been getting and…"

"We bid for those contracts, and everything is in order. I hope you're not planning to make this Grove City thing some kind of *cause célèbres*. I'm sorry for his family but nothing has changed. He wasted all that time and energy marching and protesting—for what? All he did was stir up a few people, but nothing has changed. They even had to take up a collection for his funeral."

"He was trying to make a difference, not get rich."

"Money is the difference maker. And if folks are making deals under the table, it doesn't bother me as long as I get my cut. The more I have, the more I can help. It's called doing well while doing good. A broke nigga' can't do nothing for nobody."

"You don't care about anything but money. You're that house negro Malcolm X warned about," Billie said.

"Money buys security, influence, and a seat at the table. That righteous talk works until you need something. Then you're looking for money, a favor, or both, like everybody else. I didn't see you complaining when I gave you money for your down payment or when you were begging me to get your strung-out son out of jail," Monroe said as he jangled the keys in his pocket. "You claim to be such a student of black history, then you should know it was people like A.G. Gaston, Jesse Turner, and Mollie Moon who kept the civil rights movement afloat. And like you're doing, so-called activists called them 'uncle toms' and sellouts. So if you want to call me a sellout, that's fine. I'm in good company."

"It's amazing how two people raised in the same household can be so different."

"You think my brother doesn't care about money? But I

guess at this point it doesn't really matter what you think about Cole. He's finally found someone who's passionate about him and not saving trees."

"Go to hell."

"You called me. I'm leaving, but hear this—if you're suggesting, even hinting that I had anything to do with that old man dying, I will have you in court and take everything you own."

"Thanks to your brother, that won't be much. But there is something I want you to have," Billie said, as she handed him two sheets of paper. "That's the investigation list from the Water Works audit."

"What are you doing with it and why are you showing it to me?" Monroe asked.

"I'm not from around here, but they tell me Riley Ford is a big deal. Why would his company be on a Water Works report?"

"I don't know what you're talking about."

"I'll bet you do. They're all bank customers and BEST LLC is just a front for Ford to funnel money through. Your company is on that list too. The dollar amount isn't as large as some on the list but having your company included makes your dealings suspect. Also your wife had a conflict of interest and you've been getting more money than you disclosed. Ross County Rentals is just like you, full of shit. I'll bet that's what Reverend Collins told you, although he would've said it much nicer."

"I guess I haven't made myself clear. You need to mind your nappy-headed business. If you had been doing your job instead of snooping around my accounts, you might still have a job at the bank. And if any of this insanity you've concocted is mentioned again, I'll sue you and that bank for defamation and invasion of privacy."

"This is all public information. No one cared enough to connect the dots."

"Is Dylan's situation public information too?" Monroe asked. "And aren't you looking for a job? Employers may think twice about hiring someone whose son is a thief."

"He's not a thief," Billie stated. "I knew you were low-down, but didn't think you were low-down enough to use my son, your nephew, as leverage."

"I wouldn't want to compromise your principles by using my influence or not being transparent. You do understand."

"I understand perfectly," Billie said, then closed the door.

CHAPTER 39

Billie scanned the menu, even though she knew what she wanted. She was meeting her sister-in-law for lunch, although she wasn't sure Joellen would show.

"Sorry I'm late," Joellen said as she scooted into the booth. "I had to stop by Lovey's, and you know there's no such thing as a short conversation with her."

"I'm sure Monroe told you about our run-in last week. I'm surprised you didn't cancel today," Billie said.

"Monroe doesn't pick my friends. Besides, I want to follow-up on a few things you two discussed."

"If you're here to talk about Water Works, save your breath," Billie said. "Let's order to-go and get out of here."

"I'm not asking you to ignore your findings. Shady stuff has been going on at the Water Works for years, but as long as certain people got what they wanted, the powers that be looked the other way."

"I'm surprised to hear you say that, since you're a board member."

"What better way to get information than from the inside? There's more mess going on than Carter has pills. There is a lot more I can tell you."

"Sounds like you and I are on the same side, but I guess

having Monroe involved puts you in a difficult predicament."

"It's not a problem. We all want the same thing, for Calderville to prosper and grow—including the west side. But there's no reason my family can't prosper and grow too. Monroe is taking advantage of opportunities people who look like us don't usually get."

"That sounds like justification for fraud. Double-dealing isn't more tolerable just because it's Black people."

"We want the same thing. My brother has represented the west side on the city council but can be more effective as mayor. He's won the primary, and should win in November, but we don't need any last-minute hiccups. We need the rumors about Reverend Collins to die down. Just hold on to your information until after the election. Then we'll expose everything you've found, plus more. My brother will get credit for cleaning up Water Works, and with a new administration, the state will release millions for improvements. Hollis already has contractors lined up."

"Contractors or do you mean kickbacks?"

"My family has been prominent in this county for a long time. Nothing happens without somebody making money from it. That's the way the world works. But that doesn't mean we can't get things done."

"Sounds like Calderville will be swapping one set of crooked leaders for another. I can't wait to leave this place."

"There are people who believe in my brother and have him in mind for a state office. Calderville mayor is the starting point for what some believe will be a great political career. You claim you want change. This is how it's done."

"If he's looking for a long career, then why not start it off right? I believe Hollis has good intentions, but I don't want to contribute to a cover-up. Let me think about this."

"Let me show you something that will help you make

your decision," Joellen said as she handed her phone to Billie. "Scroll up."

Billie tapped the screen to make the image larger, but she recognized the face right away. It was a picture of Dylan and a student she recognized, but didn't know his name, sharing a needle.

"Dylan has been tested several times and has gone over and above everything required in the diversion program. I don't believe these are real. People can do anything with AI these days."

"The judge may take more convincing than just your word. You mentioned an interview in California. Something like this could hinder your move."

Billie grabbed her purse and said, "This is blackmail. All along I thought Monroe was the snake."

CHAPTER 40

As the plane circled out over the Pacific for its final descent, Billie gazed in reverence at the familiar coastline, and the bluish-teal water made her smile. She texted her sister to let her know the plane had landed. She had worked hard to fit in, but Ross County just wasn't for her. This is where she belonged. Her family, memories and network were here. Her mood had been lighter these past few days, once she made the decision to return. Housing was expensive, but Zuri had always rented, and if her mother moved with her, she could afford to buy, probably not in Maxwell Park, but maybe she'd try a condo or townhouse.

She applied for jobs online, and Kelly had gotten her an interview with Love Media. She had already had two virtual interviews. They wanted her to host a weekday show, like her KBLK show, and now she was coming for an in-person meeting to work out the details. They were starting a mature urban satellite channel, called Grown Folks' Radio, and wanted her to be one of the on-air personalities. Ordinarily she would have been offended to be called "mature," a nice way to say old, and "urban," a code word for Black. But she was too anxious to get out of Texas to be worried about labels and stereotyping. Dylan's diversion would be over, and they could reboot in a familiar place. Maya was throwing Imani a going away party and Billie was able to schedule her meeting to coincide with the party. With only a carry on, she went directly to the BART station, and an hour later, she was at her mother's door.

"I'm so happy to see you," her mother said. "I ordered Thai food. Maya is coming over after she shows a house, but we don't have to wait for her to eat."

Billie devoured the soup, rice, and spring rolls like someone who hadn't eaten in days.

"Someone is coming over," Zuri said while clearing the table. "My fiancé." Before Billie could comment, Zuri told Billie about the man she'd met online, had been dating almost a year, and planned to marry.

"Why haven't I heard anything about him and what do you know about him?"

"I figured this relationship would be like the other disasters, so I didn't say anything. He lives in Los Angeles. He's retired from the post office and has three adult children. His wife died four years ago and he's a super sweet guy. We've been visiting back and forth but want to make our relationship permanent. I'm moving to LA."

"You can't move. Me and the kids may be moving back. Love Media made me an offer and we're meeting again tomorrow. They even said I don't have to broadcast from California."

"I can't arrange my life around you girls, and you can't arrange yours around your children. Besides, I thought Kendra was reenlisting."

"I'm hoping to talk her out of it, and that she'll go to college."

"Let her decide," Zuri said.

"You're the one who protested against the military industrial complex."

"These days it's not only the military involved in defense.

Large segments of the economy are interconnected, so you can't avoid it. The good part is, she'll meet men with a trade and benefits. Girls outnumber young men in college now, and the ones who are there are burdened with student debt."

"Seems like an extreme way to find a man, but that's beside the point. I'm still not sold on this dating thing. It's probably a scam. You can't trust those dating apps. They groom you for several months before asking for money. Dating someone is one thing. Getting married is another, and getting married and leaving town is even more risky."

"I thought you'd be pleased that I'm finally settling down. For a young person, you're so cautious. Sometimes you have to take a risk," Zuri said.

"At twenty-one, not sixty-one, Mother."

"I've kissed a lot of frogs to find this prince. Maya has checked everything except his DNA. He's not wanted or a serial killer. If we lived in the same town, dating would be easier. We've done long distance and now we want to be together. I don't have a house or job, so it's easier for me to move than for him. He asked me a while ago, but I told him he'd have to put a ring on it. He did, so I'm moving. Please be happy for me. I know this sounds silly, but I want a wedding, a real one, with bridesmaids, tons of flowers, and a reception."

"But Mom, how can . . ."

"We'll talk more later, okay? I've got a book club meeting this evening. You can come if you like."

Billie went to the living room and laid back on the couch, trying to absorb the news she'd received. She dozed off and was awakened when Maya came in the door.

"Hey there. I hope there's some food left."

"I had planned to get seconds later, but Mom's news has my stomach in knots," Billie said. "Why didn't you tell me?"

"I figured she could tell you herself. She's really happy."

"You've met this guy and he's legit?"

"So far. So good. I ran all the background checks I could find. Not even a parking ticket. I think it's good for her not to be alone."

"I suppose, but isn't she a little old for all this?" Billie said. "A big wedding won't be cheap."

"As long as I don't have to pay for it, I don't care," Maya said. "I think it's kind of cute. If she can find love at her age, that means there's hope for the rest of us."

"I think I've used up my 'true love' quota," Billie said, wistfully.

"Nonsense. I'll straighten you and my brother-in-law out when I come for homecoming in a few weeks. I've never been to a HBCU game. It sounds like a really good time. Plus, I want to see the palace you and Cole built."

"You might have to settle for pictures. Hopefully, it will be sold by then."

"Why would you do that?" Maya asked. "I thought they said you could work from anywhere."

"I can, but Calderville is not on my 'anywhere' list."

"Starting over is always a financial setback. Maybe you should reconsider," Maya said.

"Everyone said I should try something new. Been there. Done that. Now I'm ready to get back to civilization. I've got a sister with the hook-up. Surely you can find me a deal somewhere."

"The market here is even crazier than when you left last year, plus interest rates have increased."

"Then clean out your extra bedroom. I'm leaving Texas as soon as I can."

After Billie's interview, the rest of her trip was for fun. She, Maya, and her mom went to their favorite restaurants, went on a jazz dinner cruise, and stayed up much past Billie's bedtime.

Billie spent Saturday morning in the hair salon. Aisha may not have been a professional, but Billie had been spoiled having her come to her house to do her hair. It was almost noon when she left the salon, and she seriously considered cutting her hair. *This is precious time I could spend doing something else,* she thought.

She changed clothes then she and her mother headed to Imani's celebration. "Your father beat us here," Zuri said as they parked in her sister's driveway. "Whenever we went somewhere, we were always the first ones to arrive. Reuben believed in being on time. I'll give him that."

"I assume that's his car," Billie said, as they parked behind the midnight blue Expedition with the 'Navy Grandpa' bumper sticker.

"Aunt Billie, I'm so glad you're here. I wasn't sure if you'd be able to make it from Texas," Imani said, while giving her aunt a big hug.

"I wouldn't miss this," Billie replied, as she handed her niece a gift bag. "Here's a little something to help you at USC." She'd given her a book of Maya Angelou poems and a check. The check wasn't as large as she would've liked, but she knew Imani would still be pleased.

"Billie, you look well. Texas agrees with you."

"Hello Reuben," she replied.

"And Zuri, you don't age. It's good to see you."

"Thank you," she replied, as he kissed her cheek. "You don't look so bad yourself."

Billie couldn't remember the last time her parents had been in the same space. She hadn't expected fireworks, but she hadn't expected syrupy greetings and flirting either.

"Can you believe them?" Billie had whispered when she had a moment alone with Maya in the kitchen.

"Whatever happened between them, they've made peace with it. Mom has someone in her life and Dad and his wife have been together for years. They've both moved on, and you should too," Maya said, as she added lemons and glasses to a tray and pushed it toward her sister. "Take this to the patio."

Maybe they were this cordial because they hadn't been married long. *I can't imagine being that chummy with Cole,* she thought as she took the tray outside.

Billie had forgotten how nice it was to sit outside without being attacked by swarming insects and killer ants. After being in Calderville, with wall-to-wall blue skies, quiet nights and a faint earthy smell, she noticed that the yards were smaller, the neighbors were closer, the streets were noisier, and tall houses blocked more of the sun. Whenever Cole had complained about having close neighbors, she had dismissed him, but now she understood. Her sister's house was beautiful with a professionally landscaped yard, decorative pavers and arched, curved windows. But the neighbors in these fancy neighborhoods were only a few feet away. It was almost like being in Lakewood Terrace.

After leaving her sister's, she met Kelly for cocktails at Gelila's Place. They caught up on each other's lives, and Kelly filled her in on Love Media office politics. "As long as I can get out of Texas, I'll be happy being the coffee girl." She got home late to find her mother sitting in the kitchen drinking tea.

"Is everything okay?"

"It is now," Zuri said. "I know you're grown, but I couldn't sleep until I knew you were in the house safely."

Billie kissed her mother's cheek, then said, "I guess we never stop worrying about our babies." She and her mother spent the next two hours talking and she didn't go to bed until after midnight. By the time she headed back to Texas, she was exhausted, but excited and optimistic about moving back home.

CHAPTER 41

Dylan fulfilled his community service by serving as a lifeguard at the community center. He was obligated to do one hundred hours before the end of his diversion and had completed them within three weeks. He did such a good job and there was such a need, the Parks and Recreation Department asked him to return next season.

Today they were returning to court to report on the status of his diversion. It was a formality because the judge already had the paperwork about Dylan's inpatient treatment, community service, and restitution.

"When we get out of here, I'm treating for lunch," Dylan said.

"Okay, Mr. Big Spender, you should probably save your money," Billie said.

"This is the least I can do. I know it's not much, but I want to show you both how much I appreciate all you've done for me. Let's go to Broadway Diner. They have the best chicken fried steak. I could eat it every day," he said, while scratching his arm.

"I'll need a hearty meal to sustain me during our driving lesson," Cole said, pretending to fan himself.

"Ha. Ha," Dylan said. "The sun was in my eyes, and I

didn't see that kid on the bike. Next time I'll be sure to wear sunglasses." Cole had been taking Dylan practice driving, so he could take his road test when his diversion ended.

Billie's stomach growled and she scooted her chair to mask the sound. They had been prompt for their nine o'clock court time for what they thought would be a quick proceeding, so she had skipped breakfast. But it was now almost noon. Finally, the judge called Dylan to the bench.

"You have met all diversion program requirements and the charges in the case of Ross County v. Dylan Jordan are dismissed." Dylan turned around and gave his parents the thumbs up sign.

"However, something has come up since your last court appearance. There's a warrant for your arrest in California. You are being charged with violation of the Mann Act and statutory rape of Amy Flanery. Based on the charges, you will be extradited to California."

"What in the hell?" Cole shouted. "The Mann Act—is that even still a law?"

Billie sat confused and bewildered. The judge's gavel brought her back to reality, as he ordered Dylan and his attorney into his chambers. Billie, Cole and Monroe followed them, but the bailiff stopped them.

"Please let them come," Dylan said.

The judge nodded his head and closed the door behind them. "I just learned of this a few hours ago. The young lady died last month, and based on information from their investigation, the district attorney has filed charges."

"What type of investigation?" Billie asked. "Dylan hasn't been in California for months."

"The charges don't have anything to do with her dying. They go back several months. I wanted to make sure I understood everything before I made the pronouncement, which is why you've been here so long. Mr. Jordan, do you understand the charges against you?"

"I can't believe she's dead," Dylan said.

"I'm sorry about her dying," Cole said. "But we don't have the luxury of being sentimental. This is serious."

"It's like she's reaching from the grave to take you down with her," Billie said.

"It's not her. It's her parents," Dylan said. "They said I got her strung out, but she was using when I met her."

"Do we have their contact information? I'd like to talk to them," Billie said.

"That's what you're not going to do. We need a lawyer," Cole said, while scrolling through his phone.

"What do we do now?" Cole asked the judge.

"We've contacted the Alameda County District Attorney to see how they want to handle this. We're obligated to hold you for ninety days. If they don't pick you up within those ninety days, we can let you go."

"You're going to hold him in jail? What happened to innocent until proven guilty?" Billie asked.

"You can waive extradition, and voluntarily surrender to the authorities in California. But I may be able to work out another option. We can try to release him on bond. We will require Mr. Jordan to check in with the court weekly, wear an ankle monitor, and not leave the county."

"I suppose you want him to wear a striped jumpsuit too," Billie said.

"The other option is for us to talk to Amy's parents. Prosecuting Dylan won't bring her back, and I'm sure that's not what Amy would want," Billie said.

"Absolutely not," Cole said. "We're going to let our lawyer handle this."

"I agree," the judge said. "Her parents have no say-so in this matter, and I don't advise you to speak with any potential witnesses."

"We need legal advice. What do you suggest?" Cole asked Dylan's lawyer.

"First suggestion—hire an attorney licensed to practice in California. Unfortunately, I can't help you."

Billie let out a heavy sigh, she was anxious to return to California, but not under these circumstances.

CHAPTER 42

The doorbell startled Billie since she never had company. She looked at the camera on her phone and saw that it was Joellen. "What do you want?" she said through the speaker.

"I'd like to talk to you," Joellen said.

"If you've come to talk about your blackmail, do what you want. I'm sure you know what's going on with Dylan, and I don't have time for your garbage."

"I have a proposition for you," Joellen said. "Can I come in? I know someone in California who can help you."

Billie took a deep breath, then let her sister-in-law in and led her to the folding chairs in the living room. The furniture had finally come, but Billie hadn't removed the plastic wrap, since she was hoping to move soon.

"I love this color," Joellen said. "Where did you order it from?"

Billie gave her a blank stare and didn't answer.

"Okay, here's the deal," Joellen said as she leaned forward. "I don't practice, but I do have a law degree and know people. I can get someone in the Bay Area to take your case. The Mann Act is always a stretch and is used to prosecute a criminal enterprise. If it's used to prosecute one person, historically there have been racial overtones. That won't be hard to prove here, especially since Amy had a history of running away. But that still costs money. You and Cole have contacts, but its best to get someone who specializes."

"You can recommend someone?" Billie asked.

"Yes. And they'll do it pro bono. I'll be tied up this weekend with homecoming, but I can set up a conference call for Monday."

"And what do you want in return?" Billie asked, crossing her arms. "I know you're not doing this for the love of your nephew."

"You do something for me. I do something for you. We both want justice. We just go about it different ways."

"I know this is a busy weekend for you, but we need to act quickly. The DA has moved up your son's extradition date to two weeks," Joellen's friend, Attorney Lane said.

"Thank goodness for smart phones. What did we do before we had this technology?" Joellen asked as she adjusted the camera for their FaceTime call.

"Dylan, did you look at the questions I sent?" Attorney Lane asked.

"Yes sir."

"Great, then this shouldn't take long, and you all can get to your homecoming festivities."

"How old were you when you met Ms. Flanery?"

"Seventeen."

"How old did she say she was?"

"I don't remember us talking about it. I think Amy said she was seventeen too."

"In your statement, you said she rented a car and drove to Phoenix. How did she rent a car at seventeen?"

"I didn't ask, although she did have a couple of fake IDs."

"And you mentioned she charged the car. What about other expenses?"

"She paid for everything," Dylan said.

"We'll request credit card history to prove that she financed your travel across state line and had fake IDs. This should be easy to prove," Attorney Lane said. "What about text messages between the two of you—I'd like your cell phone records. This will show that she pursued you. I'll ask for hers, too. There's a high probability she arranged some drug deals. This could end up backfiring. Sounds like Ms. Flanery was the one instigating criminal acts. We're going to sue her family, ask for a settlement, and for them to pay attorney's fees."

"Sir, I know you have a job to do, but I don't want to smear Amy's name," Dylan said.

"You're kidding, right?" Joellen said. "I hope this doesn't sound heartless, but the girl is dead. Nothing she can do with her name now."

"Son, let her parents worry about her name. We're doing what's best for you," Cole said.

"You always told me to treat others the way I would want to be treated. Amy was a real friend, and I wouldn't feel right turning against her."

"Please let me speak with Dylan alone," Attorney Lane said.

They left Dylan in Joellen's office and went to the kitchen. "He'll change his mind once we talk to him," Cole said.

"I'm not going to go against his wishes. The attorney will have to come up with a different strategy," Billie said.

"Your son doesn't mind doing drugs and stealing from old people, but draws the line at saying bad things about a dead junkie? What a warped sense of integrity. I guess the apple doesn't fall too far from the tree," Joellen said, shaking her head.

"We'll talk to him," Cole said, drumming his fingers on the kitchen counter.

"You're the one always saying let Dylan stand on his own and make his own decisions. Well, this is a decision he's made," Billie said. "If Lane can't work with that, we'll find someone else."

"Dammit Billie, now you want to encourage his independence," Cole said.

"If Dylan won't cooperate, and you won't intervene, don't forget my original proposal," Joellen said, as she grabbed a bottle of water from the refrigerator. "I still have pictures."

"What pictures?" Cole asked.

Section VI

Uncharted Waters

CHAPTER 43

"I'm going to the restroom and to get barbeque nachos before the line gets long," Maya said. "Do you want something?"

"You can't leave now," Billie said. "You'll miss the best part of the game."

Fifty seconds remained in the second quarter. The score was tied, and the vibe was electric. Tailgaters were making their way inside and seats were filling up. But they weren't coming inside because of the score. They were coming to hear the bands, what many considered the main attraction. HBCU marching bands have dazzled audiences from presidential inaugurations to Super Bowls, and tonight promised to be no different.

Dr. Kingsley made welcoming remarks. Next the homecoming court was presented. Then the athletic director spoke, and encouraged everyone to cheer their award-winning baseball team. As the team came on the field, Billie saw Cole. It was the first she'd seen of him since their meeting with Attorney Lane, and a tear rolled down her cheek. Maya grabbed her hand and said, "Don't worry. Things between you will work out." Billie appreciated her sister's optimism, but at this point, their marriage was over and all they shared was a determination to save their son.

With the preliminaries over, it was time for the main event and cheering for the bands was as loud as if not louder than for the football team. The Sizzling Sounds performed an Earth Wind and Fire medley, and their precision moves had everyone on their feet. Billie cheered along with the crowd, but she was preoccupied with Dylan's case. Attorney Lane and Dylan weren't connecting, and she planned to ask Maya to recommend someone.

Other than not wearing shorts, so his ankle monitor wouldn't show, Dylan seemed unconcerned about his looming legal troubles. She had spotted him and his new "friend" sitting together a few rows away earlier, but now both seats were empty. He claimed she wasn't his girlfriend, but she was the first girl he'd introduced to the family. Billie had gotten the rundown on his new "friend" and learned she was from Beaumont, Texas, attending Calder State on a track scholarship, had a 3.7 GPA, and was an engineering major. Between his new "friend" and studying for his GED, she was seeing less of him. But she figured that was a good thing. For months he seemed lost, but now he was more at ease and focusing on his future. They just needed to get past this latest roadblock.

The sun was setting and there was a faint breeze. Calder State had a comfortable lead with three minutes to go, and Billie suggested they leave. "This is my last night, and I haven't gotten in that gorgeous pool all weekend. Let's go skinny dipping. Isn't that a southern thing?" Maya said, as they walked to the parking lot.

"You watch too many movies. Besides, these giant Texas mosquitos will eat us alive."

"This weekend has been so much fun. I'm going to need

a day to recuperate when I get home. It's nice to see people of all ages, together without incident, having a good time. I'm already marking my calendar for next year."

"Well, you'll have to find a hotel," Billie said. "I won't be here. I accepted Love Media's offer."

"Didn't you say you can work from anywhere? You've got a beautiful house and a town full of good-looking men. Straight, single, Black men our age are scarce at home, and half of them want white women. I know Cole is acting like he's lost his mind, but it's probably just a midlife crisis. Besides, there's more fish in the sea."

"Actually, there aren't. Did you know at the current rate the oceans will be fishless by 2050?"

"And you're going to stay manless if you don't quit..."

"I could care less about getting a man. But if I were interested, he wouldn't have to be Black. And, who said I must have a man our age? I'll be a cougar."

"Girl, that's worse. They can screw like the Energizer bunny, but they're immature, usually broke, and usually have baby-mama drama."

"Sounds like you've had experience," Billie said with a raised eyebrow.

"Sounds like you need to mind your own business. Just remember what I'm telling you."

"A man is not on my to do list. My priority is trying to put our lives back together. Kendra is still trying to talk me into coming to Chicago. But my two-day snow experience last spring was enough for me. I'm not interested in living in a cold climate."

"Plus, who knows how long Kendra will be stationed there? Real estate in the Chicago area isn't cheap and taxes are high," Maya said.

"I really want to come home. The best thing you can do for me is to find me somewhere to live so I can leave this wretched place."

"What part of town do you want to live in?" Maya asked.

"I'm not choosey. I wish I could get back into Maxwell Park, but I probably can't afford it. Surprise me."

"I'm telling you, this is the perfect setup right here," Maya said, as her sister pulled into the garage. "I really love this house."

"Then hopefully it will sell quickly. Besides, once all the water kickbacks and funny money business comes out, there will be a line of folks trying to run me out of town. Better to leave on my own," Billie said, as she quickly texted Dylan since he'd left the game early.

"You told me about all of that," Maya said. "You may not like Monroe, but he is family. If it's fraud, as you say, he could be charged with a crime. How do you think Cole will feel knowing you helped implicate his brother?"

"Right now, I don't care how Cole feels. That's been the problem, worrying about how everyone else feels, except me."

"But how does this impact you? I know what they did was shady, and they cheated a lot of people, but does that directly impact you? You weren't even living here."

"You sound like you're on their side. Why would you want me to sweep this under the rug? Especially when you know he wouldn't do the same for me."

"He helped you get your house, and paid for Dylan's rehab."

"Why are you pleading his case?"

Maya took a deep breath, then said, "Because he's Imani's father."

Billie blinked several times and stared at her sister, trying to comprehend what Maya had just said.

"We messed around back in the day. It was a whirlwind romance. He sent me money, took me to fancy restaurants, and flew me to concerts. We had an intoxicating seven months. I was even considering transferring to Calder State. It seemed so romantic, two sisters, dating two brothers."

"Except I didn't even know you were dating."

"He said he didn't want my family to get mad, since he was so much older than me. Of course, I later found out he wanted to keep quiet because he had a fiancé. I was young. What can I say?" Maya said and shrugged her shoulders.

"Does he know about Imani?"

"He may suspect. I told him I was pregnant. He said it wasn't his and sent me five hundred dollars for an abortion, which obviously, I didn't get. I never called him again."

"I am speechless," Billie said.

"He's the definition of slimeball, but that doesn't mean I want to see him go to prison or lose his livelihood."

"Looks like Dylan is here and left the patio light on," Billie said, as they entered the house. "Were you ever planning to tell Imani?

"Let's go for that swim," Maya said as she pulled her shirt over her head.

"You didn't answer my question."

"Then you should take the hint."

"You go ahead," Billie said. "I'm going to see what Dylan is up to. I've told him so many times to turn lights off when he leaves a room." She went in his room to close the blinds and was alarmed to see his ankle monitor and a screwdriver on the floor. As she went to pick them up she heard her sister.

"Billie! Come here!" Maya shrieked.

Billie rushed to the kitchen as Maya was sliding the patio doors open. "There's something in the water!"

Billie rushed to her sister's side, then shouted. "Oh my God. It's Dylan."

★   ★   ★

Sitting across from Cole at Dylan's hospital bedside gave Billie flashbacks. Dylan had been in an incubator three weeks after he was born. Kendra stayed with Zuri while Billie and Cole spent as much time as they could at the hospital. Once they brought him home, for years, he was in and out of the hospital with asthma. As time passed, his attacks become less frequent and less severe, and he hadn't had an attack since middle school. How ironic that the thing that helped him—swimming—was the thing that now had him in the hospital.

The doctors asked how long he had been in the pool, so Billie watched the security camera. It had been like watching a silent horror movie.

Dylan had been sitting in the pool chair with his head-phones on. He pulled a mirrored plate, a rolled dollar bill, and a razor blade from his backpack. Billie knew her son used drugs; she was past the denial stage. But to see him using knocked the wind out of her. The process took less than three minutes. He snorted then neatly put the paraphernalia in the backpack. He stepped into the pool and climbed onto the lounge chair. His phone beeped and he went to the edge to retrieve it. As he was putting it back near his backpack, he dropped it in the water and when he reached to get it, the pool chair flipped over and hit his head. The accident was even more devastating when Billie realized it was her text Dylan was answering.

His body went down slowly, in an awkward position. Water in the spot he went down began turning purple, and then there was nothing. No movement or noise for seven minutes. Seconds later Maya could be heard screaming then Billie appeared on camera. Maya and Billie jumped in the pool and found Dylan near the bottom. They pulled him to the top and placed him on his back. Maya began chest compressions, while Billie called 911. The dispatcher asked several questions, *"Was he conscious? Was he bleeding?"* and instructed them on what to do until the ambulance arrived.

The first time Billie watched the video she screamed when Dylan fell in the water, even though she knew he would be rescued. What they didn't know was how being underwater that long would impact him. The doctors said since he was a swimmer, he had above average lung capacity, which increased his chances of survival. Doctors said the possibilities ranged from no lingering effects to brain damage. He spent two days in intensive care, unresponsive and on a ventilator. He had started breathing on his own and had been moved to a step-down unit, but his body was also going through withdrawal, so they were keeping him sedated.

The only silver lining was that the extradition process was on hold, giving Billie more time to figure a way out of this mess. Maya didn't know an attorney who could take Dylan's case right away, and Attorney Lane seemed to be working for Joellen and Cole, not Dylan.

Billie knew what she had to do.

CHAPTER 44

Billie called her sister to let her know she was in town, then sat in the rental car parking lot a few minutes trying to figure out the navigation system. She was headed to Moraga, a town northeast of Oakland. She'd never spent much time there but today; her future was in Moraga. After inputting the address, she was ready to go. Her return flight was this evening, and she had no time to waste. She practiced her speech as she drove.

Thank you for agreeing to meet with me. Sometimes the lawyers get so caught up in the case they forget we are the clients. When I learned that my attorney contacted you, I immediately booked a flight We are not interested in damages, a countersuit, or payment for attorney fees. I will not presume to understand how it feels to lose a child. I do understand that you loved Amy and still love her and want justice. But charging my son will not bring justice, it will only add another victim to the scourge of opioid abuse. Prosecuting my son will not bring her back. We both know in their own twisted way, they cared about each other, and punishing Dylan is not what she would want.

Amy's parents told the DA they didn't want to drag their daughter's name through the mud and would not assist with the case. The charges were dropped.

CHAPTER 45

Billie was amazed how much lighter her head felt and how much time she saved since she cut off her locs. With the stress of the last few months, she had neglected her hair, and the roots looked raggedy. Even worse—there were several gray streaks. She believed in the natural look, but wasn't ready for gray hair, so she had gotten Aisha to cut and color it. Billie stared approvingly at her new curly style, and lighter auburn color, before stepping in the shower. The primary bathroom was huge, and she loved having a separate tub and shower with a rainfall showerhead. The phone rang twice while she was in the shower. When the caller didn't leave a voicemail, she figured it was a telemarketer and stayed in the shower a little longer since her next place probably wouldn't have a shower this fancy. When she stepped out, she saw two missed calls from Adrian and called him back.

"I've been calling you," he said as soon as she answered. "I just sent you a text. Did you see it?"

"See what?"

"There's going to be a press conference by the state Water Commission and Ross County Water Works in fifteen minutes. Did you contact them?"

"Maybe I did and maybe I didn't."

"I thought we agreed to do this together," Adrian said.

"You've got deep roots here and more to lose than I do. Although, I'm not saying I contacted anyone."

"You are one hard-headed woman. I'll call you when it goes off."

Billie turned on the television. *The Price is Right* was on for a few minutes, then she saw a breaking news announcement scroll across the bottom of the screen.

The Attorney General has begun an investigation of discrepancies, misspent funds and other irregularities in Ross County Water Works, involving NFL Hall of Famer Riley Ford, the former lieutenant governor as well as others. We will share details as they become available.

CHAPTER 46

Dylan's goldenrods were in full bloom and along with the newly laid sod, the yard looked like a candidate for lawn of the month. Despite lavender candles throughout the house, Billie couldn't mask the ammonia and manure smell sneaking underneath the door and through the windowsills. The smell was supposed to wear off in about a week. She felt a twinge of guilt, knowing the fertilizer chemicals were contributing to the CO_2 in the air. Her initial plan was to seed the yard and let it grow naturally, but they didn't have weeks to wait for grass to grow. The realtor said they would get more views, and the house would sell at a higher price if the yard was already landscaped. Since they wanted to sell quickly, Billie agreed to laying sod.

The house was going on the market in a week, and Billie was finishing getting it ready. Since they'd only been there a few months, this task was easier than preparing their Oakland house had been. Boxes were stacked throughout the living and dining room. Boxes that had never been opened were in the garage. She needed to continue packing but had agreed to meet Lydia for lunch.

"I've never seen you in jeans," Billie said, when she walked into the Calder Cantina.

"I'm loving retirement. Now I see how rich folks feel, getting paid for doing nothing." When their department was downsized, Lydia had taken a buyout offer.

After they talked about Billie's plans, and gossiped about the bank, Billie said, "I want to ask you something. Did you send that information I shared with you to the media?"

"In the words of my grandmother, sometimes it's best to stick to your own knitting."

"I guess that's another one of those Texas sayings," Billie said with a smile.

"I'm going to miss your clueless behind," Lydia said.

"And you didn't answer my question."

"Is everyone in California as nosy as you?"

"You'll have to visit and find out."

After her two-hour lunch with Lydia, Billie returned to the house to continue packing. Cole had accepted a position at Rice University and had already moved to Houston. Billie was staying in the house until it sold. She could work from anywhere, and had considered going to Missouri, to be near Dylan's rehab center. But she was learning that she couldn't plan her life around Dylan. The best way she could support his recovery was to let him learn to stand on his own. Her first choice was to return to Oakland, but the equity from the house sale would not get her in a decent house, plus her credit was still messed up. When she looked at apartments, rent was as much as a mortgage, and rather than fork over first and last month's rent, plus a security deposit, she figured she'd be better off using that money for a down payment. Maya was on the lookout for a deal but warned it would probably be a fixer upper. Kendra was still trying to convince Billie to come to Chicago. A few people were encouraging her to stay in Texas. Since she could work from anywhere, she was keeping her options open.

At six o'clock, she put the tape and scissors away, fixed a quick snack, then got ready for her meeting. She changed into a sundress and grabbed a sweater. Even though it was ninety degrees, she knew air conditioning inside would be freezing. She blew out all the candles and left.

Twelve minutes later she was pulling into the parking lot. For all the drama in Calderville, she did like the short driving times. *How much of my life has been spent in traffic?* she thought.

She went to the refreshment table and was about to turn her phone on silent and saw a new text. *Enjoyed dinner last night. Looking forward to the next time. P.S. You can't get good TexMex tacos in CA.* She quickly replied to Adrian with two smiley emojis, then found a seat in the circle, with a Dr Pepper in her lap. The Nar-Anon meeting was about to start.

EPILOGUE

Six months later.

The Calderville Chronicle
News For You Since 1922
EXTRA! EXTRA!
Calderville Chronicle Wins Pulitzer Prize for
Local Reporting
The prize was granted for stories exposing a multi-million-dollar embezzlement at Ross County Water Works. State and federal funds meant for water infrastructure improvements were diverted to benefit board members' family and friends, including NFL Hall of Famer Riley Ford. Banking officials are also implicated. Senior Editor Gilbert stated when he saw school children standing in line in the rain to use portable restrooms, he knew something had to be done. Indictments are expected.

The Chronicle's staff and supporters were gathered at the Calderville Cantina to celebrate the award. Mr. Gilbert had invited Billie and insisted she sit at his table. Before cutting the cake, he asked for everyone's attention and asked Billie to stand. "None of this would have happened without this remarkable, tenacious, and maybe a little stubborn woman. She refused to look the other way and is a reminder that one person can make a difference."

"I don't know what to say," Billie said, while everyone clapped. "Y'all have been so kind."

Mr. Gilbert raised his glass of sweet tea in a toast and said, "We owe her a big thank you and we're proud she now calls our little town home."

Adrian nudged her side and whispered, "I'll give you my big thank you later. Break time is over."

AUTHOR'S NOTE

Something in the Water includes aspects of two consequential issues, water quality and opioid abuse. The U.S. Department of Health and Human Services has declared prescription and nonprescription opioid misuse a public health crisis, and identified treatment, education, and harm reduction the most effective ways to combat what is now called opioid use disorder. This is a change from the response to the 1980's crack cocaine explosion, when drug use was viewed as a moral fault and the primary approach was the legal system and incarceration.[1] This new approach seems to be working. After peaking in 2022, overdose deaths are declining.[2]

If you have a "Dylan" in your life, resources include Nar-Anon, a program for family and friends of addicts (phone - (800) 477-6291, website - www.nar-anon.org), and the Substance Abuse and Mental Health Services Administration, a 24-hour national helpline (800) 662-HELP (4357) for treatment referrals. https://findtreatment.gov.

The Jordans relocated, partially to help Dylan's recovery, only to run into another crisis—water. In 2013, to save money, the Flint, Michigan, city council voted to switch their water supply from Detroit to the Flint River. Almost immediately, residents complained of rashes, hair loss, foul smells and discolored water, but were assured the water was safe for consumption.[3] General Motors plant officials said high chlorine (used to disinfect water) levels could corrode car parts and returned to Detroit water in 2014. The water was switched back to the Detroit system in 2015. I was disgusted with this callous treatment, but as the news cycle moved on, I moved on. However, two incidents here in Memphis made this issue real to me.

The path of a proposed pipeline to transport crude oil from Texas and Oklahoma to Gulf Coast refineries for export passed through majority black neighborhoods in southwest Memphis. Company officials stated this location was the "path of least resistance." Memphis' primary water source is an underground aquifer and the pipeline would've made our drinking water vulnerable to an oil leak or spill. Local groups fought the pipeline and protests drew national attention. In 2021, the project was cancelled.[4] Unfortunately, the victory was short-lived. The Tennessee state legislature passed a bill allowing them to preempt local government authority over oil and gas projects.

Then, after an ice storm, my neighborhood endured nine days without running water. After two days, I went to a hotel. But what about those who couldn't afford a hotel, especially since area hotels doubled and tripled their rates (thank goodness for my hotel points).

Water issues may not be in the news every day, but millions are dealing with its consequences daily. For instance, Jackson, the Mississippi state capital, has had instances of low water pressure and sewage in the streets for decades. The governor declared a state of emergency in 2022 when flooding and failure of a water treatment plant, which was already running on its backup, left 150,000 residents without running water for weeks during the peak of summer.[5] In August 2024, the Kansas Department of Health and Environment issued a Do Not Drink order for a portion of Saline County. This neighborhood has endured years of dirty, smelly water and residents were notified the water was unsafe and shouldn't even be boiled.[6] Yikes!

Lead poses serious health risks, especially to children. Lead pipes were banned in 1986 but remain in millions of older homes and schools. The National Resources Defense Council describes it as drinking through a "lead straw."

Chicago and Cleveland have the highest number of service lines containing lead and Florida has the most of any state.[7]

Tap water is regulated primarily by the Safe Drinking Water Act (SDWA), which is enforced by the Environmental Protection Agency (EPA), state and local agencies. However some medical organizations claim federal standards are insufficient.[8] They indicate children, pregnant women and people with compromised immune systems may be more vulnerable to certain contaminants and advise them to consult their physician about tap water safety.

Water quality problems are caused by lead pipes, aging infrastructure- which leads to leaks, inadequate wastewater treatment, illegal dumping, and chemical runoff from pesticides and fertilizer. Extreme temperatures caused by climate change also adversely impact water quality. People of color and older communities are disproportionately impacted.[9]

A writer in Jackson, Mississippi, won the *2023 Pulitzer Prize for Local Reporting*, for her series about misspent federal funds intended for low-income individuals.[10] Her articles weren't water related, but many were outraged to learn the state funded a former professional athlete's pet projects while school children used outdoor toilets and residents lacked running water.

Even worse, consider Sand Branch, Texas, a small unincorporated area approximately fifteen miles southeast of downtown Dallas, that has no water. Founded as a freedman's town after the Civil War, it has never had water pipes or a sewage system and their wells are contaminated.[11] In 2020, a local pastor who was a vocal advocate for Sand Branch residents died in a mysterious fire. Hmm...

To learn the status of your community's water, visit the EPA website https://www.epa.gov/ccr or https://mytapwater. org/. Learn how your elected officials are voting on these issues and get involved with organizations in your area working to ensure clean water. Also, check with your public water system to determine if your home has lead service lines.

Something in the Water fictionalizes these issues and events as background for a story about the Jordan family. Hopefully in addition to being entertained, you also gained awareness of these two public health issues. In the words of James Baldwin, "not everything that is faced can be changed, but nothing can be changed until it is faced."

END NOTES

[1] *Whiteout - How Racial Capitalism Changed the Color of Opioids in America* by Helena Hansen, Jules Netherland and David Herzberg discusses drug policy and race. University of California Press 2023.

[2] McPhillips, Deidre, *US Overdoses Have Fallen Sharply In Recent Months, a Hopeful Shift in Trends,* CNN Health, September 19, 2024.

[3] De La Torre, Miguel, *Gonna Trouble The Water Ecojustice, Water, and Environmental Racism*, Pilgrim Press 2021, page 119.

[4] *https://www.southernenvironment.org/news/victory-for-southwest-memphis-byhalia-pipeline-is-done*, July 2, 2021, Southern Environmental Law Center.

[5] Kohli, Anisha, *What Life Is Like for Jackson, Miss., Residents Living Without Clean Water,* TIME, September 3, 2022.

[6] Kite, Allison, *Dirty Water Inconsistent Billing Plague Neighborhood Near Salina,* Kansas Reflector, May 8, 2024.

[7] Baron, Valerie, *New EPA Data Point to Which States and Cities Have the Most Lead Pipes*, nrdc.org, May 30, 2024.

[8] Lau, Jay, *Improving drinking water quality in the U.S.*, November 20, 2024, Harvard T.H. Chan School of Public Health.

[9] Natural Resources Defense Council, *Watered Down Justice*, September 2019.

[10]Mississippi Today, *Anna Wolfe and Mississippi Today win Pulitzer Prize for "The Backchannel" investigation*, May 8, 2023.

[11]Gray, Allen R., *The drama, tragedy, and neglect of a Godforsaken Sandbranch*, North Dallas Gazette, July 6, 2022.

Discussion Questions

1. Billie and Cole had different approaches to handling their son's addiction (compassion vs. tough love). Who do you think acted most appropriately and why?

2. How do you feel about Monroe's philosophy that money is the ultimate equalizer?

3. Billie and Cole worked through Cole's infidelity, and it is rarely mentioned. If someone is unfaithful one time, should you take them back? Explain your answer.

4. Serena and Maya both withheld information about their children's paternity. Can you describe instances when this might ever be justified?

5. Historically Black Colleges and Universities (HBCU) were founded during a time when laws prohibited African Americans from attending most colleges and universities. Since that is no longer the case, do you believe HBCUs still have a role to play or is this reverse discrimination?

6. Was Billie justified in asking for a DNA test? Is it a deal-breaker?

7. How would you have handled Serena?

8. Billie had never worked in an environment where she "code-switched," defined as the practice by someone in an underrepresented group (consciously or unconsciously) adjusting their language, behavior, or appear-

ance to fit into the dominant culture. Is that a smart career strategy or is it unauthentic and phony? Explain your answer.

9. What do you think happens to the characters after the novel concludes?

10. Have you personally been impacted by climate change? If so, how?